"Set sail with your cargo of strumpets for some other lonely colony, where that manner of vice is tolerated. You, and they, are not welcome in Nova Scotia!"

The dazed look fled Jocelyn Finch's attractive features. An indignant glare took its place.

Unfortunately, it did nothing to detract from her beauty.

Sir Robert wished it had.

"How dare you?" Mrs. Finch wrenched the glove off her impossibly delicate fingers.

She surged up on the tips of her toes and struck him across the cheek with the glove. For such a small scrap of soft kid leather, it stung like the very devil.

"I demand satisfaction for that vile insult, sir!" she cried. "How dare you sully the reputation of me and my charges with your disgusting accusations?"

Then she struck him dumb by asking, "And, pray, when did the state of holy matrimony become a *vice* in Nova Scotia?"

* * *

Harlequin® H [illegible] 06

Praise for bestselling author DEBORAH HALE's latest books

Highland Rogue

"This is an updated classic with timeless characters and well-developed humor."

—*Romantic Times BOOKclub*

The Wizard's Ward

"In her first crossover foray into fantasy, romance writer Hale nicely blends the two genres in an upbeat, feel-good story."

—*Publishers Weekly*

Beauty and the Baron

"Deborah Hale delights with midnight ball, stargazing and a wonderful cast of characters."

—*Romantic Times BOOKclub*

Border Bride

"Excellent characterization and a nicely detailed Welsh setting give this medieval an intriguing flavor readers will find hard to resist."

—*Booklist*

Whitefeather's Woman

"This book is yet another success for Deborah Hale. It aims for the heart and doesn't miss."

—*The Old Book Barn Gazette*

The Bride Ship

DEBORAH HALE

TORONTO • NEW YORK • LONDON
AMSTERDAM • PARIS • SYDNEY • HAMBURG
STOCKHOLM • ATHENS • TOKYO • MILAN • MADRID
PRAGUE • WARSAW • BUDAPEST • AUCKLAND

ISBN 0-373-29387-9

THE BRIDE SHIP

This edition published by arrangement with Harlequin Books S.A.

www.eHarlequin.com

Printed in U.S.A.

Available from Harlequin® Historical and
DEBORAH HALE

My Lord Protector #452
A Gentleman of Substance #488
The Bonny Bride #503
The Elusive Bride #539
The Wedding Wager #563
Whitefeather's Woman #581
Carpetbagger's Wife #595
The Love Match #599
"Cupid Goes to Gretna"
Border Bride #619
Lady Lyte's Little Secret #639
Beauty and the Baron #655
The Last Champion #703
Highland Rogue #724
The Bride Ship #787

Other works include:

LUNA™ Books

The Wizard's Ward
The Destined Queen

Please address questions and book requests to:
Harlequin Reader Service
U.S.: 3010 Walden Ave., P.O. Box 1325, Buffalo, NY 14269
Canadian: P.O. Box 609, Fort Erie, Ont. L2A 5X3

This book is dedicated with love and admiration
to two special young men, Brendan and Jamie Hale,
who make the duties of motherhood a true pleasure.
You are my heroes!

Chapter One

Halifax, Nova Scotia
May 1818

An urgent knock on the door of his study distracted Sir Robert Kerr in the midst of drafting his quarterly report to the Colonial Office.

"Come in, Duckworth." The governor's pensive squint furrowed into a scowl at the sight of his aide. "Did I not leave instructions…?"

"That you were not to be disturbed, Your Excellency?" Young Duckworth finished Sir Robert's sentence, as he had a rather annoying habit of doing in moments of crisis.

But this was an ordinary day, of no dire import. At least none of which the governor was aware. Yet his secretary's boyish face looked flushed and his voice sounded breathless. "So you did, sir, excepting in case of general calamity."

One corner of the governor's lips arched in a wry smile as he laid down his pen. His reference to "general calamity" had been meant in jest—something he had never been very good at conveying.

When he rose from his chair, Sir Robert's neck gave a twinge. He reached back to knead the tense muscles. How many hours had he been hunched over his desk composing that blasted report? Perhaps it would do him good to get up and move about.

"Tell me, what general calamity has beset our fair colony today?" He strode out to the entry hall on the heels of his aide. "Is the brewery on fire? Are we being invaded by some foreign fleet? Has the bishop fallen into the harbor?"

"None of those, Your Excellency." Once again, Duckworth missed the governor's attempt at levity. He shoved Sir Robert's hat into his hands. "I think you had better come and see for yourself, sir."

With that suggestion, Duckworth turned and fled out the front door of Government House, leaving Sir Robert with little choice but to follow if he wished to appease his curiosity. Grumbling under his breath, the governor jammed on his old-fashioned tricorne. What had put Duckworth in such a stew? And why was he being so confounded mysterious about it?

The pair of sentries who stood guard over the front entrance of Government House were talking together in hushed, urgent tones when he stepped outside. The instant they spotted him marching down the steps, both soldiers snapped to attention.

"One of you stay here. The other come with me." Sir Robert beckoned the larger of the two men. "I may have need of you."

"Aye, sir!" the sentries replied in chorus, jumping to obey his orders.

Sir Robert discerned a flicker of eagerness on the face of his escort, and a shadow of disappointment on that of the man ordered to stay behind. In either of their places, his reaction would have been quite the opposite. His former career in the army had taught him to be wary of surprises.

As he marched north along Hollis Street, his old foot

wound from the Battle of Corona gave a twinge as it often did in damp weather. He ignored it, reaching up to anchor his hat against the bracing spring wind. He could not afford to slow his pace or he might lose sight of Duckworth, who had just rounded the corner onto Salter Street, which sloped down toward Power's Wharf. What manner of trouble had washed up with the morning tide?

It seemed Sir Robert was not the only citizen of Halifax curious to find out. Almost as many spectators had thronged onto the wharf as had turned out the year before last to welcome his arrival in the colony.

"Make way!" With belligerent energy, the sentry he'd brought from Government House endeavored to clear a path through the crowd. Either the young solider enjoyed ordering civilians about, or he was eager to get a good view of the proceedings, himself. "Make way for His Excellency, Governor Kerr!"

Bracing himself to meet whatever lay ahead, Sir Robert marched down the quay. He turned his gaze toward Halifax Harbor and beheld…absolutely nothing out of the ordinary.

A small ship had tied up at the wharf, its sails furled, gently rocking on the waves. Sir Robert could make out the name *Hestia* painted on the prow. The Hestia was sailing under British colors, he noted with a mixture of relief and surprise. That meant it was not a pirate ship, nor did it belong to some foreign fleet.

Why, it looked like any one of hundreds of vessels that arrived here in the course of the year bearing cargo or passengers. What had drawn so many good citizens of Halifax down to Power's Wharf to watch an ordinary ship unload?

A small flutter of white caught the governor's eye. Someone standing on the ship's deck was waving a handkerchief. Sir Robert surveyed the deck more closely. Crowded along the port railing, staring toward the crowded wharf, were a large number of young women. The bright colors of their hats and wraps made a festive contrast to the sober browns and grays of the ship's hull.

"What in blazes…?" he muttered under his breath.

The wind…or something else…crammed those words back into his mouth.

A woman began to make her way down the gangplank. One of the crewmen offered to assist her, but she shook off his arm and continued on her own, in spite of the precarious sway of the ship. The wind whipped her skirts in a buttery yellow ripple, exposing a pair of shapely ankles.

She walked with the dainty grace of a dancer. Yet her movements also suggested the brisk, determined stride of a general inspecting troops. The paradox unsettled Sir Robert, as did everything else about the situation.

Once she reached the wharf, the woman swept a gaze over the crowd and smiled. At that moment, an obstinate ray of sunshine thrust its way between the fast-scudding clouds to sparkle on the churning water of Halifax Harbor and on the smiling woman in the yellow dress.

The milling, muttering crowd fell silent.

"How charming!" said the woman, echoing the very words that had formed in Sir Robert's mind about her. "You have arranged a welcoming committee to greet us!"

Before anyone could disabuse her of that notion, she continued, "Of course, you must be vastly relieved to see us at last. I hope you have not suffered any anxiety of our being lost at sea. I must confess, there were moments during our voyage when I feared we might be."

Sir Robert considered pinching himself. The past half hour had the baffling quality of a dream. Perhaps he'd fallen asleep at his desk while drafting his report and imagined all of this.

As he stared at the woman before him and listened to her bewitching voice, he could not help regretting the necessity to wake up and get back to work. Surely it would not hurt to spend a few moments more in a dream that had turned so pleasant.

He stepped forward to get a better look at the woman. "I fear there must be some mistake, madam."

He bowed over her hand, surprised to discover how low he had to bend. From a distance, her regal bearing had made the lady appear taller. As he leaned toward her, Sir Robert realized how small and delicate a creature she was. It kindled a queer, soft ache in his chest that extended out to his arms. He vaguely recognized the sensation as an urge to protect her, a ridiculous compulsion, since he knew nothing about her—not even her name.

"What manner of mistake?" the lady asked. "We were expected, were we not?" She fixed him with her gaze.

Sir Robert's cravat tightened around his throat and a wave of dizziness almost made him stagger. What in blazes had come over him?

Never in his life could he recall taking any special notice of the color of a woman's eyes. Now he could not help but take notice. Hers were a light, lively brown with glints of gold and silver that put him in mind of a speckled trout. Beneath her present look of puzzlement, they seemed to dance with merriment or mischief. Or, perhaps, an answering flicker of the curious fascination that had taken hold of him?

But that was foolishness. He had never been the sort of fellow women looked at in that way. The few ladies who crossed his path seldom bothered to look at all. That was how Sir Robert had always preferred to keep matters—until he'd stared into the eyes of…

"I must confess, madam, I have no idea who you are or

what has brought you to my colony." He wanted to find out, though. Her identity in particular. Hard as he tried to maintain his accustomed indifference to such matters, his mind fairly itched with curiosity.

A look of dismay tightened her delicate features and quenched some of the sparkle in her eyes. Sir Robert found himself wanting very much to spare her any distress.

"Something must have happened to the letter." She glanced back at the ship. "I suppose we *should* have waited for an answer before setting out, but the time was growing late. Besides, I felt certain the gentlemen of Nova Scotia would extend us a warm welcome. And you *have*—far beyond my expectations."

Those words rekindled her luminous smile, which sent a rush of warmth through Sir Robert.

"I am Mrs. Finch." She performed an elegant curtsy. "Mrs. Jocelyn Finch."

The discovery that she was married flooded Sir Robert's belly with a cold heaviness, as though it were the hold of a ship smashed by a stray cannonball and rapidly taking on water.

Mrs. Finch raised her voice to carry over the muted murmur of the crowd. "It is my pleasure to bring the men of your fine colony a shipload of charming ladies to assuage their loneliness."

The murmuring around them gained force and volume, like a breaker gathering itself to dash against the rocks.

For a moment the governor stood mute, too stunned by Mrs. Finch's brazen declaration to reply. If she had upended a chamber pot over his head, Sir Robert could not have felt more sullied or humiliated.

Ever since assuming his position in the colony, he had waged a strenuous campaign against the evil of prostitution, so rampant in garrison towns like Halifax. His efforts had met with scant support. Everyone from the admiral to the Colonial Office back in London seemed to look on the contemptible trade as an unfortunate but necessary support for the soldiers and sailors on duty in the colonies. Rather like the armorers or the quartermaster corps. Even the bishop was tepid in his condemnation of the Barrack Street brothels.

Sir Robert could not share their casual endorsement of a trade that fostered disease, disorder and degradation. If that qualified him as the "stiff-rumped prude" some of his enemies called him behind his back, he made no apology for it. Until now, he had managed to ignore the slights and subtle challenges to his authority mounted by those who opposed him. But he could not ignore this brazen invasion by a shipload of harlots, flouncing into the city under his very nose!

Had the comely Mrs. Finch been meant as a bribe to secure his compliance? The degree to which she tempted him to abandon his scruples outraged Sir Robert.

"Madam." He fairly trembled with the effort to contain his indignation. "The men of *my* colony would be better off to suffer a little loneliness than the ills they are likely to incur by consorting with your *ladies*."

It gave him a rush of bitter satisfaction to watch her dainty jaw fall slack. No doubt the little vixen had believed him quite smitten with her charms. Instead, she had given him more reason than ever to keep his distance from the fair sex.

"I suggest you get back aboard your vessel." Sir Robert stabbed his forefinger toward the ship and spoke in a ringing tone of righteous authority. "Then set sail with your cargo of strumpets for some other lonely colony, where that manner of vice is tolerated. You, and they, are not welcome in Nova Scotia!"

The dazed look fled Jocelyn Finch's attractive features. An indignant glare took its place. Unfortunately, it did nothing to detract from her beauty.

Sir Robert wished it had.

"How dare you?" Mrs. Finch wrenched the glove off her impossibly delicate fingers.

Before Sir Robert could anticipate what she meant to do, she surged up on the tips of her toes and struck him across the cheek with the glove. For such a small scrap of soft kid leather, it stung like the very devil.

"I demand satisfaction for that vile insult, sir!" she cried. "How dare you sully the reputation of me and my charges with your disgusting accusations? How dare you order us away from this colony?"

Before Sir Robert could rally his composure sufficiently to answer, she fired off a final question that struck him dumb again. "And, pray, when did the estate of holy matrimony become a *vice* in Nova Scotia?"

Her words rocked Sir Robert back on his heels with far greater force than the blow from her tiny glove had done. "Matrimony?"

Mrs. Finch gave a nod of grim, defiant triumph.

"Ma-tri-mony." She spoke the word again, her tongue and lush lips lingering over each syllable with provocative enjoyment. "Perhaps you have heard of it? A man and woman living together in the state of *holy wedlock*, having vowed their mutual lifelong devotion?"

Oh, he knew about matrimony. Had he not studied to avoid it ever since he'd grown old enough to contract such an alliance? Marriage distracted a man from his duty while saddling him with further responsibilities. Sir Robert told himself he did not envy Mister Finch his singular distraction of a wife.

Jocelyn savored the bewildered air of the odious man before her. To think her first glimpse of him had made her question whether her heart *had* truly died upon the battlefield with her darling Ned! The man's dark good looks and air of distinction had drawn her to him immediately. The modest gallantry of his initial addresses had quickened something inside her that had long lain fallow.

That very favorable first impression had only made his subsequent behavior all the more vexing. She'd been buoyant with pride to proclaim her mission in the colony, foolishly hoping her announcement might provoke a smile from him.

Instead, he'd stared at her as if she were a bit of filth he was anxious to scrape off the bottom of his immaculate boots. No man had looked at her with such contempt since the day her father had cut her off without a farthing for marrying against his wishes.

Then, in front of half the male population of the town, he had denounced her as a bawd-mistress! Recalling the strenuous efforts she had made to protect Vita Sykes's virtue during their voyage, Jocelyn might have laughed of that preposterous accusation. If she had not been boiling with indignant fury, instead!

Her glove came off almost before she knew what she was doing. If she'd had a male escort with any gumption, he would have called her slanderer out for such an insult. Since she had vowed to make her own way in the world, without the assistance or hinderance of any man, she would have to defend her own honor—and, more importantly, that of her charges.

Just then, she could have cheerfully put a bullet through...

Who *was* this man, anyway? It seemed indecent, somehow, that he should inflame her emotions to such a pitch in so short a time, without bothering to introduce himself.

While he stood there, momentarily stunned by her counterattack, Jocelyn seized the opportunity to press her advantage. "Furthermore, what gives *you* the right to declare our ship is not welcome in Nova Scotia?"

Before he could answer, an anxious-looking young man detached himself from the crowd on the quay.

"Begging your pardon, ma'am." He bowed to her. "This gentleman is His Excellency, Governor Sir Robert Kerr. He *does* have the authority to order your ship out of Halifax Harbor if he chooses."

The governor? Jocelyn stared at Sir Robert Kerr in horror. She had just challenged the governor of Nova Scotia to a duel. Could her mission to the colony possibly have gotten off to a worse start?

Chapter Two

Sir Robert's *dream* was rapidly turning into a nightmare!

He had publicly slandered Mrs. Finch and all the young women in her charge with the worst insult a man could make regarding a lady's honor. She had responded by slapping his face and challenging him to a duel in front of half the town. The ugly gossip would set tongues wagging all over Halifax before the town clock up the hill struck another hour!

Would there be *any* other topic of conversation over local tea tables that afternoon? Sir Robert could picture his opponents consuming such morsels of damaging tattle as though they were rich little cakes iced with gleeful malice.

Worst of all, while the crowd gawked and snickered behind his back, and Mrs. Finch regarded him with a mixture of dismay and disdain, he froze in a way he had never done in the heat of battle.

Had he been a fool to take up this post? The Duke of Wellington's personal recommendation had touched and flattered him. He wanted to acquit himself well to justify the duke's faith in him. And to confound certain Whitehall factions who carped at the number of "Wellington's Waterloo Warriors" being given plum colonial appointments.

But he was a military man, not a diplomat.

Fortunately, young Duckworth rallied to his support. "It would seem explanations are in order, Mrs. Finch, but this is hardly the proper time or place for them. Is it, Your Excellency?"

That was all the prompting Sir Robert needed. "No, indeed," he snapped. "This is not a matter to be debated on a public wharf."

He turned to the sentry he'd brought from Government House. "Disperse this crowd at once. Surely *some* of them have duties they ought to be attending."

How Sir Robert wished he'd issued that order the moment he had arrived!

Under cover of the soldier's enthusiastic bellows for everyone to move along and their buzz of annoyance at being deprived of an amusing spectacle, Sir Robert addressed himself to Mrs. Finch. "I think you had better come along with me to Government House, madam, where we may review your situation in private."

His invitation came out sounding like an order, which he was far more accustomed to issuing.

Mrs. Finch turned back toward the ship. "May I bring the girls along? After the rigors of our voyage, they are anxious to get dry land under their feet again, poor dears."

Sir Robert could not afford to let their plight arouse his sympathy. "I'm afraid that will not be possible."

If he let them disembark before he'd decided how to deal with the situation, what was there to stop them from melting off into the town and getting up to unthinkable mischief? "Until this matter is settled, the young ladies and your crew must be confined aboard."

"Confined?" Jocelyn Finch spun to face him again, her fine

dark brows drawn together in an indignant frown. "As if they were a pack of criminals? I have never heard of such a contemptible lack of hospitality!"

"May I remind you, madam," Sir Robert warned her in a tone he had often used with subordinates who questioned his orders, "you are *not* guests in this colony. You have arrived unannounced and uninvited. I have only your word as to your business in coming."

Perhaps her mission was not as despicable as he'd mistakenly assumed. That did not mean he approved of it.

When the lady began to sputter and looked tempted to use her glove on him again, he made a valiant effort to moderate his tone. "In the interest of *their* well-being, as well as the peace and order of this community, I must insist."

Anxious to escape her outraged glare, he turned to the young soldier who had done an efficient job clearing the wharf. "Well done, Corporal. Now, I want to you to stand guard over this ship. Until you receive further orders from me, make certain no one gets on or off. Do you understand?"

The corporal snapped a crisp salute. "Aye, sir!"

Fortified by the soldier's respect, Sir Robert confronted his contemptuous visitor once again.

"Government House is this way." He nodded toward Salter Street and took several brisk strides in that direction before he realized Mrs. Finch was not following him.

What now?

He look back to find her still standing where he'd left her, with Duckworth hovering anxiously nearby. "Are you coming?"

"Walk, you mean?" She glanced around at the ironstone warehouses that lined the docks.

"It is no distance." He beckoned her with an impatient wave of his hand. "We could be there and back ten times before a carriage could be fetched."

Duckworth nodded. "Government House is only a block up the hill, ma'am."

The lady paid him no heed except to stare up the steep slope of Salter Street.

"Have you no intention of offering me your arm, at least?" She addressed the governor in a tone chillier than a North Atlantic winter. "Or do I not merit so small a courtesy?"

Few things put Robert Kerr out of temper worse than a suggestion he had done less than his duty.

Trudging back to where she stood, he muttered, "This is *not* a social call! Besides, I did not suppose you would accept if I had offered."

He thrust out his arm at a stiff, awkward angle to demonstrate he took no pleasure in the civility she had demanded from him. And perhaps to convince himself, as well.

"Your Excellency?" Duckworth scurried along beside them. "Shall I inform the kitchen staff you will have a guest for tea?"

Over Mrs. Finch's head, the governor fixed his aide with a severe look. He preferred to take a modest tray in his study, continuing to read reports and sign papers between sips of tea and bites of biscuit. Now he would be obliged to offer the vexing woman his hospitality.

"Madam, would you care to discuss your situation over tea?" He tried to ignore the warm pressure of her hand on his arm.

For a moment, her frosty manner thawed. "Proper food? Oh, I should be most grateful! When our ship was blown off course by the storm, some of our supplies were lost. We have been on very tight rations the past fortnight."

Before the governor could think what to reply, his aide piped up, "I'll go on ahead then, sir, and alert Miz Ada."

Off Duckworth dashed, leaving Sir Robert all on his own to deal with a devilishly awkward situation. He was not much accustomed to conversing with women and went out of his way to avoid it whenever possible. Now he had little choice.

Before he could marshal some manner of civil remark, Mrs. Finch spoke—or rather gasped. "I beg…your pardon, sir. But would you…kindly…*slow down!*"

A swift sidelong glance confirmed the lady was hard-pressed to match his brisk parade-ground march up the hill. Her face had flushed to a high color. And her bosom, of which he had a far clearer view than he would have liked, heaved in a most unsettling manner. What if the creature swooned into his arms or some such nonsense?

To his horror, the governor's body roused at the prospect of another man's wife in his arms. That was enough to curb his stride. Where was *Mr. Finch,* anyway?

"Your husband?" he asked. "Is he back on the ship? I have no objection to him accompanying us." Perhaps, between them, he and Finch could settle all this, man to man.

Trust him to choose the worst possible thing to say, then blurt it out in the most bald, offensive manner possible. Judging by the look that came over Mrs. Finch's face, Sir Robert had no doubt that was exactly what he'd done.

By now, Jocelyn had been a widow longer than she'd been a wife. Time and necessity had taught her to speak of her late husband without excessive distress. Why should the governor's abrupt remark make her eyes sting and her lip quiver?

Perhaps it was his offhand presumption that Ned must be alive. Or perhaps it was the foolish rush of attraction she'd experienced upon first meeting Sir Robert Kerr that had made her feel disloyal to her late husband's memory. Though she doubted he meant to distress her, Jocelyn refused to give him the satisfaction of knowing he had.

"My husband has been dead nearly three years, sir." She

congratulated herself on getting the words out without her voice breaking.

The muscles of his arm tensed in response to her words and he checked his rapid pace further still as they turned onto a wide avenue that ran parallel to the harbor. "Waterloo? We lost too many good men that day."

Jocelyn sensed he was speaking from intimate knowledge rather than in general terms. "Ned was killed on the previous day at…"

"The crossroads." Sir Robert heaved a sigh that betrayed grief with an edge of bitterness. "You have my most sincere condolences, Mrs. Finch."

So her husband's commanding officer had written when informing her of Ned's death. That and her widow's pittance might buy her a cup of chocolate.

The governor meant well, Jocelyn told herself. She should try to cultivate his sympathy by every possible means. But she could not subdue the hostility he had roused with his offensive assumptions about her mission to the colony.

"This way." He led her off the street onto a broad driveway that sloped gently up toward a large, elegant stone mansion.

In Jocelyn's opinion, the pair of wooden sentry boxes on either side of the fine double staircase rather spoiled the classic lines of the house. Still, it looked like the sort of place where one could expect to be served a bountiful and toothsome tea.

The courteous young man from the wharf threw open the front door as the governor ushered Jocelyn up the stairs. "It has all been arranged, Sir Robert. Tea will be served in the drawing room, shortly."

The poor fellow still sounded winded from his run, though Jocelyn had to admit the distance from here to the wharf would not have merited the fuss and delay of summoning a carriage.

"Thank you, Duckworth." The governor handed his hat to the young man. "Your assistance this afternoon has been invaluable, as ever."

He gestured toward a doorway on the left-hand side of hall. "Through here, if you please, madam. You will find the drawing room just beyond the receiving room."

Jocelyn glanced around as she walked through a light, handsomely proportioned room that housed a pair of blue satin sofas, several small mahogany tables and over two dozen chairs without looking in the least crowded. Did His Excellency expect her to be overwhelmed by such grand surroundings.

If only he knew! Compared to some of the great houses in which she'd lived or visited, Government House was quite modest and restrained. The drawing room proved even more stately, with its fine Brussels carpet, elegant hanging luster and rich claret-colored draperies. Still it was nothing to awe the daughter of a marquess.

Jocelyn sank down gratefully onto one of several brocade-upholstered armchairs clustered around a tea table. Reminding herself of all she had at stake, she summoned every ounce of charm she could muster to assail Governor Kerr.

"What an elegant residence you have here, sir! It looks very modern. Were you responsible for having it built?"

"Me?" The governor clearly considered her question ridiculous if not downright offensive. "No. For that you must thank Sir John Wentworth and his wife. I should have been content with more modest lodgings. Indeed, I would have preferred them. This is a residence for the type of governor who would rather entertain than work."

What an impossibly dour fellow! He had not taken a seat, but stood before one of the tall windows that flanked the white marble hearth, his hands behind his back. Jocelyn could scarcely resist the temptation to tease him out of his severity.

"Surely entertaining *is* part of the work of a governor." She forced herself to smile, determined to be agreeable in spite of him. "Official receptions, levees, that sort of thing."

He made no reply, but she thought her words sent a shudder through him.

A young footman entered, just then, bearing a well-laden tray, which he set down upon the tea table. The governor thanked him but made no move to take a seat. Even after the footman had departed, Sir Robert continued to stand beside the hearth, looking tense and ill at ease. Jocelyn considered inviting him to sit down, but it was hardly her place.

"Shall I pour?" she offered at last, desperate to commence their discussion. The sooner she cleared up this dreadful misunderstanding the sooner she could fetch the poor girls off that wretched ship.

"If you would be so kind." Sir Robert gave a curt nod but still made no move to sit.

Jocelyn perched one delicate cup upon its saucer and poured a generous measure of steaming amber tea into it. How pleasant it felt to handle fine china and silver again.

She lifted the sugar tongs. "How many lumps, sir?"

It took some effort to keep from grinning. If she'd had a cudgel in hand back at the wharf, she might have given him a lump or two—though not the sweet kind!

"No, thank you," said Sir Robert, but he edged closer to the tea table.

"Cream?" Jocelyn lifted the little pitcher. What a luxury it would be to taste cream in her tea again!

With a decisive shake of his head, the governor perched on the farthest chair away from her and reached for his cup. "I prefer my tea plain."

"Indeed?" Jocelyn poured a cup for herself, then added three good-sized lumps of sugar, followed by a generous dollop of smooth, thick cream. "I like mine as sweet and rich as I can get it, especially after the recent deprivations of our voyage."

The governor made some vaguely disapproving noise, deep in his throat…or perhaps he only meant to clear it.

He reached toward the tray and lifted the silver cover off a dish. Jocelyn's mouth watered in anticipation.

"Bread and butter, Mrs. Finch?"

Bread and butter? Was this the best hospitality Nova Scotia could provide? It took every scrap of restraint Jocelyn could summon to keep from dumping the contents of the dish over her host's head.

Perhaps he sensed her disappointment. "I seldom have guests to tea, especially on such short notice. This frugal fare suits me well enough."

What he said was true, Jocelyn acknowledged with a pang of shame for her ingratitude. All the same, she would so love to have been offered her favorite walnut tea cake or the redcurrant tart for which the kitchens of Breckland Manor were noted.

Sir Robert uncovered the other dish. "Perhaps you would prefer a muffin, instead?"

He pointed to a pair of small china crocks nestled in one corner of the tea tray. "They're very good spread with apple butter or blueberry jam."

"Blueberries?"

The governor nodded. "They grow in some profusion hereabouts on low bushes. They're more purple than blue, as a matter of fact, especially after they've been cooked."

He passed her a napkin. "The things stain like the very devil, but they have a most agreeable flavor."

There was something rather touching about the governor's clumsy, earnest attempts at hospitality. Jocelyn's antagonism began to soften. After the weevily biscuits and thin, rancid stew she'd been forced to eat for the past two weeks, fresh-baked bread with newly churned butter should taste very good indeed.

Taking a thick slice from the plate, she closed her eyes, the better to savor it. Oh, the crisp crust! Mmm, the sweet, wholesome flavor of the butter, so generously spread! Ah, the soft texture of the bread itself!

Suddenly aware of a strained silence, she opened her eyes to find the governor staring at her with a look of mild horror. Oh dear, had she been making all those sounds of enjoyment—the kind she'd sometimes made in bed with her husband?

A fiery blush prickled up her neck to blaze in her cheeks. At the same time, she battled an urge to laugh.

"Please excuse my manners, sir." Despite her most strenuous efforts to contain it, a chuckle burst out of her. "The bread is *very* good."

To stifle any further unseemly levity, Jocelyn took a large bite of muffin. Too large, she realized as her cheeks bulged.

Of course, the governor would choose that moment, when her mouth was so full she could scarcely chew, let alone speak, to say, "Then let us turn to the matter at hand, shall we?"

Jocelyn could only nod and pray she would not choke.

The governor fortified himself with a sip of tea. "Our conversation on the wharf left me rather…confused. You mentioned a letter that was meant to precede you. I received no such message. Perhaps you would be so good as to explain your purpose in coming to Halifax and who sent you?"

Jocelyn worried down her mouthful of muffin and seized upon his last question to answer first. "I have been sent by Mrs. Dorothea Beamish. Perhaps you have heard of her?"

Recognition flickered in the governor's cool, blue eyes.

Her vast wealth and forceful personality had made Mrs. Beamish widely known.

"I have a second letter of introduction from her," Jocelyn hastened to add. "Alas, in all the confusion, I left it behind on the ship. I would be happy to retrieve it and present it to you at your earliest convenience."

Despite the mention of her sponsor, Sir Robert did not look anxious for a second interview. "And what business has Mrs. Beamish in sending a boatload of young women to my colony?"

Had he not heard a word she'd said down on the wharf? Or had he been too busy jumping to his own offensive conclusions to listen?

The words of her former governess ran through Jocelyn's head. *"Remember, my dear, you'll catch more flies with sugar than with vinegar."* That was all very well, but Sir Robert Kerr did not appear partial to sweets!

"You may have heard of the projects Mrs. Beamish has undertaken to prevent young women who find themselves without friends or resources from sinking into lives of vice?"

The governor nodded. "Commendable work." More to himself than to Jocelyn, he muttered, "I could use someone like her in this blighted town."

At last, a scrap of encouragement! Jocelyn seized upon it as eagerly as she had consumed the food. "I am heartened to hear you are in sympathy with our aims, Your Excellency! Mrs. Beamish has established a number of useful institutions for such unfortunate young women back in England. Alas, the need is beginning to outstrip even her resources."

Jocelyn warmed to a subject dear to her heart. "You may not realize, sir, that the late war robbed many of our country's young women of the men who would have wed and provided for them."

The governor's brow furrowed as he sipped his tea. Clearly he had *not* given any thought to the plight of his country's women, and the price they continued to pay for Napoleon's defeat.

"It occurred to Mrs. Beamish that while there is a shortage of eligible men in Britain, there is an equal shortage of eligible women in the colonies. To that end, she has sponsored a bride ship to Nova Scotia. It is my responsibility to chaperone these young women and find suitable husbands for them before I return to London in the fall. If the project is successful, I may bring more brides to the colony next spring, and the scheme might be expanded to other British territories abroad."

She stopped to catch her breath, and to encourage some response from the governor, who had been listening to her with grave, silent concentration.

He did not speak right away when she gave him the opportunity. Instead, he drained the last of his tea, then set the empty cup back upon the tray, his features creased in a thoughtful frown. His hesitation troubled Jocelyn. Surely, despite the inauspicious start to their acquaintance, he must see the mutual benefits of this venture?

At last the governor broke his silence. "So it is your intention to spend the summer wedding these young women off to the men of my colony?"

"Indeed it is, sir. To provide the bachelors of Nova Scotia with companions and helpmates, while offering my charges an opportunity to make good and useful lives for themselves." What fool could fail to endorse such a worthwhile enterprise?

The governor mulled her words for a few moments longer, then rose abruptly and strode back toward the marble mantelpiece.

He was rather like that fine hearth, Jocelyn decided. Handsome in appearance, but hard and cold to the touch. While a cheerful blaze might be kindled within it, she doubted any such fire ever had, or would, warm the empty depths of *his* heart.

For that reason, it came as a distressing disappointment but no great surprise when he announced, "Your idea *sounds* all very well, madam. In practice, I fear it would prove otherwise. This colony is not some frivolous marriage market. The men here have important work to do that requires their full concentration. You saw the idle mob that gathered at Power's Wharf this afternoon. Halifax has no need of such distracting spectacles."

"That was not *our* fault!" Jocelyn surged to her feet and threw her napkin down on the tea tray. "Perhaps if more men in your colony had wives and families to occupy their interest, they would not need to seek diversion gawking at incoming ships."

The governor's stance grew even more rigid and his frown deepened. "You do not know these people, madam. You do not know this colony. Nor are its peace and welfare your responsibility. They are mine."

"How can loving wives possibly be a threat to the peace and welfare of your settlers, sir?" Jocelyn longed to seize the breast of his coat and shake some sense into the man. "Have *you* a wife?"

The instant the words left her mouth, she wished she could recall them. What if, like her, Sir Robert had been brutally bereaved—his heart chilled and hardened by grief?

Her swift impulse of sympathy had no chance to take root.

"Never," declared the governor. "I have never desired such a distraction from my duties, nor the weight of additional responsibility that a family entails. The bachelors of Nova Scotia would do well to follow my example. I will see to it that your ship is reprovisioned so you may return to England or sail on to another colony where you might be more welcome."

Jocelyn could scarcely abide the prospect of another *hour* confined aboard ship, let alone days or weeks. She could not return to England and face Mrs. Beamish with her mission unfulfilled. And what manner of welcome were they likely to receive in another colony, having been turned away from the shores of Nova Scotia?

"You cannot do this to me!" she cried. No man since her father had provoked her to such a rage.

"Not only *can* I, madam. For the good of this colony, I must." He headed out of the room, calling for his aide.

Jocelyn nearly overturned the tea table in her haste to catch him.

"Have you forgotten?" She clutched the sleeve of his coat. "I challenged you to a duel. Are you such a coward that you would bundle me out of town before I can defend my honor?"

He stared down at her with undisguised aversion. "Madam, I have no intention of fighting a duel with anyone, least of all a woman. I made a mistake—a perfectly natural one under the circumstances, I believe. But I am willing to apologize for it in public. I will put a notice to that effect in the *Halifax Gazette* if you wish."

He turned to his aide, who had just arrived. "Remind me of that, will you, Duckworth? But, first, I would like you to escort Mrs. Finch back to her ship."

The governor detached her hand from his sleeve, then executed a curt bow. "I wish you a safe journey, madam."

Before Jocelyn could protest further, he strode from the drawing room.

With a strangled shriek, she lunged for the tea tray and scooped up the blueberry jam pot, determined to hurl it at the governor's pristine marble hearth…for lack of a more deserving target.

Mr. Duckworth stepped in front of her. "Please don't, ma'am. It'll make the most frightful mess."

That was what she wanted. To leave His Excellency with a vivid purple stain to remember her by!

His aide's plea stayed her hand. After all, the governor himself would not be obliged to clean up the mess.

She held the jam pot out to Mr. Duckworth. "I pity you with all my heart, sir, having to work for such a tyrant."

The young man relieved her of the crock before he replied, "There is no man in the colony I'd rather serve, ma'am."

Poor young fool, Jocelyn thought as she permitted him to escort her out of Government House and down toward the wharf. Every step of the way, she struggled to invent an excuse that would prevent her from getting back on that ship. Once aboard, she was certain Governor Kerr would never permit her to set foot off it again. How could she hope to plead her case if she could not communicate with anyone in town?

As they caught sight of the wharf, Mr. Duckworth sighed. "Not another crowd gathered? I hope we shan't need to call out the militia to disperse these people."

The nearer they drew, the more evident it became that these curious onlookers were different from the first group. For they were mostly women.

A number stood around the wharf in small clusters, talking together and pointing toward the ship. A few appeared to be chatting with the young soldier Governor Kerr had left on guard. From their garish dress and forward manner, Jocelyn took them to be the kind of women Sir Robert had accused her of bringing to his colony. Perhaps they had got word of the governor's slander and hoped to catch a glimpse their rivals.

Jocelyn could not recall seeing so many women of ill repute together at one time in London…at least not the parts of London she frequented. If Halifax had this great a problem with flesh-peddling, perhaps the governor had some small justification for jumping to the wrong conclusion about her bride ship. But that did *not* give him grounds for turning them away once he'd discovered their true purpose!

Just then, a woman's voice called from an open carriage parked nearby. "Oh, Mr. Duckling, a word, if you please?"

Muttering "Duck-*worth,* damn it!" under his breath, the governor's aide approached the carriage.

It crossed Jocelyn's mind to run off while his attention was diverted. Perhaps she could find a clergyman, or some other worthy citizen willing to plead her case with the governor. After an instant's consideration, she discarded the idea. How could she hope to find someone to help her, when she did not know a single soul in town, nor how to locate them if she did?

She hung back a bit as Mr. Duckworth approached the carriage. "Why, Mrs. Carmont, what a pleasant surprise. May I be of service, ma'am?"

"Indeed you may," replied the occupant of the carriage, whose voice sounded strangely familiar to Jocelyn. "With a bit of reliable information, if you'd be so kind. It is in very short supply presently. The most preposterous rumors have been circulating about town. Is it true that Barnabas Power imported a shipload of women to cater to the officers of the garrison?"

Duckworth shook his head at the wild story. "A ship did arrive, ma'am, carrying a number of young ladies. But it is my understanding their business in the colony is entirely honorable. Nor have I heard of any connection with Mr. Power except that they have docked at his wharf."

He turned toward Jocelyn and beckoned. "Here is a lady who can tell you better than I. May I present Mrs. Jocelyn Finch. Mrs. Finch, may I present Mrs. Carmont, the wife of our—"

Before he could finish, the woman cried, "Jocelyn? Lady Jocelyn DeLacey? My dear, it is I, Sally Hastings—Mrs. Carmont since my marriage. What a delightful surprise to find you here in Halifax, of all places on earth!"

"Sally, of course! How good to see you!" Back in England, Jocelyn had hated chance encounters with her old acquaintances. But here and now, she had never been more grateful for the sight of a familiar face.

Sally Carmont threw open the carriage door. "Do come dine with me this evening! We have so much to catch up with one another."

As Jocelyn moved to accept the invitation, the governor's aide became quite agitated. "But, His Excellency entrusted me with seeing Mrs. Finch back to her ship!"

"Think nothing more of it, Mr. Duckling." Sally Carmont waved him on his way. "I promise you, I shall deliver her personally once we've dined. I can get my husband to provide us an armed escort, if necessary."

Clearly Sally was someone of consequence in Halifax, for Duckworth appeared torn between the governor's orders and the lady's wishes.

"Please?" Jocelyn appealed to him, hoping she might tip the balance in her favor. "It would mean a great deal to me to spend an evening with an old friend. I give you my word, I will be back aboard ship before midnight. His Excellency need never know a thing about it."

"The governor's instructions were very specific, ma'am."

"Please?"

On the young man's face, she could see the struggle between a kind desire to oblige her and the tyrannical dictates of duty to his master. "I don't suppose a small detour would hurt."

"Not a particle!" Jocelyn pressed a swift kiss on his cheek. "Thank you, thank you!"

"If there's any fuss with Governor Kerr," said Sally, "I shall take full responsibility."

Before Mr. Duckworth could change his mind, Jocelyn bounded into the carriage and Sally ordered her coachman to take them home…wherever that might be.

As the carriage headed in the opposite direction from the governor's mansion, Sally peered at Jocelyn in the waning light of early evening. "You look marvelous, my dear! Tell me, what brings you to Halifax?"

The tiniest, most delicate bud of hope had begun to sprout inside Jocelyn. If her old friend was a person of consequence in the community, perhaps she could help. Didn't Mrs. Beamish always say that when two women put their heads together they were more than a match for any number of men?

She did not have *any number* of men to sway. Only one.

But a very stubborn one.

Chapter Three

Bloody stubborn woman!

Sir Robert bolted his breakfast, irritated to be running behind schedule on account of Jocelyn Finch. The little minx had invaded his dreams, challenging him to duel. Not upon a field of honor, but on the dance floor, in the drawing room... and in the bedchamber!

He could have sworn he'd felt her body beneath him, soft and willing. Her unbound hair had whispered against his cheek. Her scent had filled his nostrils. And when she'd made those sweet little sounds of pleasure and yearning, it had been more than he could bear.

The rest of the night, he'd tossed and turned, half-afraid to go back to sleep in case he should have more such dreams—half desperately wishing he could recapture those tantalizing sensations. At last he had fallen into a barren, dreamless slumber so deep he had not heard the bells of nearby Saint Peter's chiming seven.

As a consequence, he'd risen late to tackle the work on which he'd already fallen behind. The sooner he got that infernal woman and her bride ship out of his colony, the better off he'd be!

Perhaps he ought to go down to Power's Wharf and make certain the *Hestia* weighed anchor the moment it had been re-provisioned? To his horror, Sir Robert found himself anxious to catch a final glimpse of Jocelyn Finch.

Just then, Duckworth entered through the side door from the service hall, looking almost as agitated as he had the previous day when he'd summoned Sir Robert to Power's Wharf. The governor tried not to scowl as he glanced up from his porridge. After all, his young aide had acquitted himself well in this sorry business. Rather better than his master, if truth be told.

"What is it, Duckworth? I'll be done in a moment."

"His Grace the Bishop to see you, Your Excellency."

"The Bishop?" Sir Robert glanced toward the pedestal clock that stood beside the door to the service hall. "At this hour?"

"Yes, sir."

"We did not have an appointment scheduled, did we?"

"Ah...no, sir. I don't believe so."

One more interruption to put him further behind in his work. Sir Robert sighed. No help for it, he supposed, if the spiritual lord of the colony wished to speak with him.

"Show his Grace into my study, Duckworth, and offer him some refreshment. Tell him I shall be along directly."

Once his secretary had gone, Sir Robert hurried through the rest of his porridge, though he had scant appetite for it. His habit of not wasting food was too deeply ingrained to be abandoned, even on account of a call from the bishop.

Once he'd cleaned the bowl, he washed his porridge down with a strong brew of West Indies coffee. Then he strode off to his study.

"Your Grace." He bowed to the bishop, a tall, austere man with a long, aristocratic face. "To what do I owe the honor of this unexpected visit...at this hour?"

"Too early for you, am I, Governor?" The bishop resumed his seat as Sir Robert settled behind the desk. "I'd heard you were a notorious early riser. I wanted to catch you before your day was half-done."

Sir Robert gritted his teeth. "I am running a trifle late this morning, as it happens. What can I do for you?"

The bishop fixed him with the sort of solemn look to which his patrician features were so well suited. "I've come to talk to you about this bride-ship business, and urge you to give the matter your prayerful consideration."

Sir Robert barely stifled a groan.

The bishop's private sermon on the virtues of matrimony lasted the better part of an hour. Sir Robert scarcely had a chance to get a word in. Not that it mattered, for his protests seemed to fall on deaf ears.

He had finally bid the bishop farewell, promising nothing more than to seek divine guidance in the matter, when Duckworth announced three members of the Privy Council were waiting in the reception room to speak with him.

"Will you see them separately, sir, or together?"

"Together, I suppose." The quicker to get it over with. At this rate, Mrs. Finch and her troublesome charges would cost him another day's work. "I can't think how the bishop came to know so much about the whole business. He was one of the few men I did *not* see milling about Power's Wharf, yesterday."

"You know how gossip travels in a town this size, sir." Poor Duckworth looked as if the whole business were his fault.

"Don't fret," Sir Robert tried to reassure him. "We'll let them all have their squawk, then we'll send Mrs. Finch's bride ship packing and get back to work."

"Indeed, sir." Duckworth did not appear very hopeful as he hurried off to the reception room to fetch the council members.

By the time they left his office, Sir Robert was in need of a strong drink, though it was not yet noon. The gentlemen, all leading citizens of the colony, had made their views on the bride ship fully known. Since two of the three were magistrates, Sir Robert had to admit, they put forward a number of convincing arguments. They might have swayed him if he had been in the frame of mind to be convinced...which he was not.

The whole tempest this business had stirred up, and the time it had stolen from more important matters, convinced him more firmly than ever that Halifax would be well rid of Mrs. Finch and her fool ship!

"Your Excellency," ventured Duckworth with an anxious apologetic air, "Mr. Barnabas Power begs the courtesy of a short interview."

No doubt Duckworth had rephrased Power's request in more mannerly terms. To Sir Robert's knowledge, the former privateer, now rumored to be the richest man in British North America, never *begged* anything of anyone.

"Oh, very well." He threw up his hands in temporary defeat. "Might as well waste the *whole* day. Show Mr. Power in."

Unlike the bishop and the privy councillors, Barnabas Power wasted no time or excessive civility in coming to the point of his call. "Don't be an ass, Kerr. What's the harm in welcoming these women to the colony?"

"Surely I don't need to tell you, sir." The bishop and the privy councillors were all married men, but Barnabas Power, though a good ten years the governor's senior, remained a bachelor with no sign of altering his marital state. "Would you have risen so far and so fast in the world with the cumbrance of a wife and family?"

The merchant considered Sir Robert's words, which was more than the bishop had done. But then he shook his head. "That's different. I'm not some simple farmer or lumberman scratching out a living. Mark me, they'll scratch a lot harder and better when they've got families to feed and help them out with the chores."

That made a kind of sense, much as Sir Robert hated to admit it.

"I don't need to tell you," Mr. Power continued without waiting for a reply from the governor, "business has gone from bad to worse in the colony since the good times of the war. This may be just the nudge it needs to pick up again. Ladies buying dress goods, folks purchasing wedding gifts."

"I shall certainly give your advice in the matter my most careful consideration, Mr. Power." Consider it, then discard it. Sir Robert was not about to be bullied into changing his mind, now. Otherwise Power and his merchant cronies would run roughshod over him for the rest of his tenure in office.

"You do that, Kerr. A canny captain knows when to trim his sails to suit the wind. And just between us, I have nothing against marriage. Now that I've made my pile, I've got my eye out for the right sort of wife. I don't know but that pretty Mrs. Finch might suit me. Have you heard her father's the Marquess of Breckland?"

It was difficult to say which of those revelations unsettled the governor worse—that Jocelyn Finch was the daughter of a nobleman, or that Barnabas Power had his eye on the lady.

The merchant gave a derisive chuckle. "To think you as good as called her a whore out on my wharf yesterday! When is that duel between you to take place, by the way? I'd like to make a wager on the outcome."

His tone left no doubt which combatant he intended to back.

"I'm sorry to disappoint you, Power. There will be no duel. I have assured Mrs. Finch I will have a full apology for my mistake printed in the *Gazette.* Good day to you, sir."

Mr. Power ignored this pointed invitation to be on his way. "You'd do well to look for a wife, yourself, Kerr. The right sort of woman could be an asset to a man in your position."

"I appreciate your interest in my welfare." Sir Robert sauntered toward the door, hoping Power would take the hint and go. "I shall give your advice my—"

"Careful consideration." The merchant finished his sentence in a mocking tone. "You know, Kerr, there comes a time when a man's got to quit *considering,* and act."

Without any bow or other civility of leave-taking, he departed.

Sir Robert returned to his desk, clenching and unclenching his fists. He could not recall when he'd spent such a disagreeable morning. All over some trifle when there were many crucial matters that required his attention.

"Who's next, Duckworth?" he growled when he noticed his aide skulking outside the door.

"No one else, sir."

"Thank heaven for small mercies!" Sir Robert sank onto his chair then picked up his pen and unstopped his inkwell.

Duckworth cleared his throat. "There is one small matter I'd like to broach with you, if I may, sir."

"Very well." Sir Robert looked up from his papers. "But make it quick, like a good fellow. I can't afford to fall further behind."

"Yes, sir. Thank you, sir. You see it's about—"

Whatever it was about, Sir Robert did not learn, for Colonel William Carmont marched in past Duckworth and tossed a copy of the *Halifax Gazette* onto the governor's desk. "Have you seen this?"

Will Carmont was the one man in the colony Sir Robert did not expect or desire to stand on ceremony. They had served together under General Wellington in the Peninsular War, becoming firm friends in spite of their differences in temperament.

"Seen what?" Sir Robert picked up the newspaper and opened it. "What has Mr. Wye got a bee in his bonnet about now?"

Considering how the morning had gone so far, he wasn't sure he wanted to know.

"You can guess, can't you?" Will pushed a few documents aside to perch on the corner of the governor's desk, while Duckworth withdrew from the room. "It's the same thing everyone in town is talking about."

Sir Robert read a few lines of the editorial—an overwrought diatribe about some fancied Colonial Office conspiracy to keep the citizens of Nova Scotia in bondage to the motherland, by neglecting to foster their long-term interests. He could make nothing of it until he spotted the name "Mrs. Jocelyn Finch, née Lady Jocelyn DeLacey" halfway down the page.

"Of all the ridiculous…!" He threw down the paper. "I tell you, Will, this town would be a good deal better off if people were less preoccupied with such trivialities!"

The colonel shook his head. "To a man who's sick to death of his own cooking and his own company, this isn't trivial. And in case you haven't noticed, the colony's full of men like that."

"Don't start in on me, too, Will. I've heard nothing all morning but what sound spiritual, social and business sense it makes to turn these young women loose upon Nova Scotia."

"You won't hear a word from me on any of those subjects."

"That's relief."

"No, indeed." Will picked up the newspaper. "I have come to warn you of the trouble that may befall if you *don't* reconsider. Dorothea Beamish is a woman of considerable influence. When all this gets back to her, she could make things damned sticky for you with the Colonial Office."

Sir Robert cursed under his breath. "I hadn't thought of that."

The colonel treated him to a look of exasperated pity. "I don't believe you're thinking with a very level head about this whole business. And that's not like you at all. You seem to have taken some daft prejudice against it, based on an unfavorable first impression. A *false* first impression, let me remind you. If you just give Mrs. Finch a chance, you'll soon find what a charming, capable woman she is. She hasn't had an easy time of it these past few years. You of all people should be able to sympathize with her situation."

Sir Robert sat back and folded his arms across his chest. "How do you come to know so much about the lady's qualities and situation, pray?"

Will looked a trifle surprised by the question. "You haven't heard?"

Sir Robert did not like the sound of that. "Perhaps you had better tell me."

And perhaps *he* had better face the distasteful possibility that he might be wrong.

"This is a much tastier breakfast than we've enjoyed in a good while." At a table in the ship's crowded galley, Jocelyn savored the modest luxury of a fresh egg. "I don't mind that we've had to wait until past noon to get it."

Lily Winslow concentrated on her eager consumption of plump, crisp sausages. "I heard the men who brought these provisions say they were compliments of His Excellency, the governor, from his very own farm. Imagine, the governor of the colony taking such an interest in our welfare! He must be a very kind man."

Sir Robert Kerr—kind? The good reports Colonel Carmont had given her of the man last night over dinner could not keep a bitter chuckle from rising in Jocelyn's throat.

"If he's taking such an interest in our welfare," said Hetty Jenkins, "why don't he let us off this stinking boat before we all go barmy?"

Several more of Jocelyn's charges took up the question.

"Why won't they let us disembark?"

"When can we go ashore, Mrs. Finch?"

"Yes, Mrs. Finch—when?"

Jocelyn glanced around the dimly lit galley at their anxious faces. She did not have the heart to tell them upon how slender a thread their hopes hung. "Now, my dears, we must exercise a little patience. I fear the ship carrying our letter of introduction must have been lost at sea. So our arrival in Halifax was quite unexpected."

From what little she had seen of the town, last evening on the way to the Carmonts', Halifax had not appeared very large. Finding suitable accommodations for so numerous a party might prove difficult. Against her will, she felt a glimmer of sympathy for Governor Kerr.

"But they are happy to see us, aren't they?" asked Lily, the orphan daughter of a country parson. Her calm manner during the rigors of the voyage had won Jocelyn's respect and trust. "Such a great crowd came out yesterday to bid us welcome."

"Yes, indeed," replied Jocelyn, referring to the size of the crowd, not the sentiments that had motivated it.

She sensed that curiosity, not goodwill, had drawn most of yesterday's onlookers. If only she and her charges were given a fair chance, she believed they could win a sincere welcome from the colonists. Certainly the gentlemen to whom Sally Carmont had introduced her last night seemed well disposed toward her mission. But would their support prove strong enough to sway their stubborn governor?

The ship had not been ordered out of port—yet. Jocelyn seized upon that as a hopeful sign. "I'm certain everything will be arranged soon, and we will be at liberty to disembark."

She prayed so, at least. These fresh provisions from the governor's farm were a great boon, to be sure. But the strain of forty women crowded together for weeks on end was beginning to take its toll on everyone's temper. After returning from her lovely dinner with the Carmonts, Jocelyn had been called to settle no less than a dozen quarrels among her charges.

"The first thing I mean to do when I get ashore," said Louisa Newton, a pale girl who had suffered from violent seasickness for much of the voyage, "is kneel down and kiss dry land!"

Some of the others laughed and nodded their agreement.

"I shan't waste my kisses on the ground," announced Vita Sykes, a saucy little minx who had caused Jocelyn no end of trouble since they'd set sail. "I mean to kiss the first man I see. There were a few fine-looking ones on the dock yesterday. That governor fellow you went off with wasn't half-bad, Mrs. Finch. Is he married?"

The bold question brought a stinging blush to Jocelyn's cheeks.

Before she could find her voice to answer, Hetty Jenkins cried, "A fine governor's wife you'd make, Vita, with no more morals than a cat. I saw you, last night, pawing at that soldier who was guarding the gangway!"

"You've got sharp eyes, carrothead!" Vita grabbed a large fistful of Hetty's bright red hair. "How'd you like them scratched out, eh?"

Hetty's fist flew but missed Vita to box one of the other girls on the ear. By the time Jocelyn threw herself into the fray it had escalated to a full-scale brawl.

"Enough!" she cried. "Stop this at once!"

She squealed when grasping fingers found her hair and pulled.

"If this does not stop…" Sharp fingernails scored her cheek. "I shall send everyone involved straight back to England!"

Her threat calmed the mayhem a little, but she wasn't sure they could all hear her above the racket.

"Mrs. Finch!" The first mate's resonant bellow accomplished what she had been unable to, freezing the galley in a silent, violent tableau.

Into the stunned hush, he announced, "Visitors to see you up on deck, ma'am."

Visitors? "Tell them I'll be along, directly," Jocelyn answered in a tone of false brightness.

Once the crewman was out of earshot, she ordered Vita and Hetty confined to their cabins.

"As for the rest of you," she announced in a harsh whisper, "I did not want to tell you this, but not everyone is anxious to welcome us to the colony. If word of this kind of behavior gets out I fear we will be sent packing!"

She glared at every young woman brave enough to meet her eyes. "Now remember what is at stake and conduct yourselves accordingly."

She swept out of the galley amid a subdued chorus of "Yes, Mrs. Finch."

As Jocelyn hurried up the steep stairs to the main deck, fear and hope warred within her. Had she been summoned to witness their departure from Halifax...or for some eleventh-hour reprieve? Hope gained the upper hand when she found Colonel and Mrs. Carmont waiting for her, along with Governor Kerr.

Sally's smile twisted into a grimace when she caught sight of Jocelyn. "My dear! Whatever happened? Are you all right?"

For an instant, Jocelyn puzzled what her friend meant. Then, a gust of salty sea air made her cheek sting.

The fight! Her summons to the deck had driven it from her mind entirely. With one hand she reached up in a futile effort to tidy her hair. The other flew to her face to cover the scratches. Dear heaven, she must look like the worst type of woman Governor Kerr had accused her of being!

She braced herself to confront his disdainful stare. Instead, his stern countenance had softened in a look of concern. That unsettled her further.

"I'm fine, truly! I just had a little tumble below deck."

The moment the words left her lips, she wished she'd swallowed them. For *tumble* had another meaning…

Was it just her fancy, or did the governor's firm mouth twitch from a suppressed grin?

When he spoke, however, he sounded serious as ever. "Ships can be tricky places to keep one's footing. You must take care, Mrs. Finch."

His feigned concern for her well-being goaded Jocelyn. "May I remind Your Excellency that I would prefer to be ashore where I would not have to be so careful of my footing. What brings you here, sir? Have you come to see us off in person? Bid us a safe voyage?"

If that were the case, there could be no advantage to holding her tongue. She'd give Governor Kerr a piece of her mind before he evicted her from his colony.

The governor shook his head. "As a matter of fact, I have come on a rather different errand."

"Pray, what might that be?" Though she warned herself to keep her hopes in check, Jocelyn could not suppress them altogether.

"Upon reflection," said the governor, "I see I may have acted rather hastily yesterday."

Yes! Yes!

When he hesitated, she prompted him. "And…?"

The smile of triumph froze on her lips when he replied, "I have decided to accept your challenge to a duel, after all."

Chapter Four

No doubt it said terrible things about his character, but Sir Robert could not help relishing the look of dismay on Mrs. Finch's pretty face when he accepted her challenge. It eased his sense of defeat…a little. The woman had outmaneuvered him, damn it! No soldier could be expected to bear that with good grace. Least of all when he felt a sneaking sense of admiration for his adversary's resourcefulness.

"A-accept?" For an instant she looked ready to swoon.

Together with her tousled hair and the scratch on her face, it roused that absurd protective urge he'd felt the first moment he set eyes on her. Had recent events not demonstrated the lady was more than capable of looking after herself?

Before he could reach out to her, Mrs. Finch composed herself. A steely light flashed in her eyes. "Very well, sir. Choose your weapon. Pistols? Swords?"

Mrs. Carmont rushed to her friend's side. "Surely, you cannot mean it, Sir Robert? A gentleman engaging a lady in armed combat violates every code of civilized behavior!"

As he contemplated the ladies facing him arm in arm, one the picture of violent antagonism, the other of righteous indignation, Sir Robert fought to keep a straight face. "Quite so, Mrs. Carmont. I wish to offer combat of a different nature. One in which my size, strength and experience will not give me too great an advantage over a female opponent."

"Indeed?" Mrs. Finch hid her relief quite well. "What manner of combat do you propose then?"

"Chess. Are you familiar with the game, ma'am? If not, perhaps we could make it draughts instead."

"It has been some years, but I used to play chess rather well. When and where do you propose to hold the match?" The set of her mouth warned Sir Robert she would be ready for him.

"Two hours hence at Government House, if you are willing," he replied. "I believe it is in both our interests to settle this matter without further delay."

"I agree." She looked surprised to find herself addressing those words to him. "But I am curious, sir. Yesterday you told me you intended to have an apology printed in the newspaper."

Sir Robert nodded. "It has already been drafted and dispatched to the editor, whom I believe you have met."

"Er…yes. Mrs. Carmont was kind enough to introduce us." She seemed to clutch her friend's arm a little tighter while Sally Carmont's expression dared him make fuss over what she'd done. "But if you have issued an apology, my honor is satisfied. Why is this chess match necessary?"

"Because, madam, you have persuaded a number of influential citizens that your bride-ship scheme would benefit the colony. I still believe that certain drawbacks outweigh any possible advantages. But I am willing to give you the opportunity to *win* my cooperation."

"You mean if I best you at chess, we can stay?" Her eager smile made Jocelyn Finch look even more beautiful, if that were possible.

The governor replied with a curt nod. "*If* you win our match, I shall make arrangements for you and your…young ladies to remain in Nova Scotia. If I win, you must set sail tomorrow morning without any further protest or effort to circumvent my authority. Agreed?"

At least the little minx had the decency to look faintly ashamed when he mentioned circumventing his authority. She did not allow her conscience to trouble her long, however.

"It is." She offered him her hand to seal their bargain.

As he wrapped his fingers around hers, Sir Robert felt a bewildering compulsion to raise them to his lips. Stifling the foolish inclination, he took a firm hold and shook her hand instead. "I shall await you at Government House."

Before Mrs. Finch could reply, her friend spoke up. "I will fetch her there in my carriage, Your Excellency."

Was the woman implying some reproach that he'd made Mrs. Finch walk the trifling distance from the wharf to his residence? Clearly these ladies were determined to put him in the wrong, whatever he did.

He gritted his teeth. "That would be most obliging of you, Mrs. Carmont. Now if you will excuse me."

Sir Robert turned to the colonel, who had been watching the whole exchange with an amused grin that vexed him no end. "Will you accompany me, Carmont, or do you reckon the ladies require an armed escort as far as Hollis Street?"

His friend chuckled. "Any fool daft enough to molest these two deserves the trouncing he'd get. *You,* on the other hand, might require protection from the bachelors of Nova Scotia when they hear you intend to send all these lovely ladies packing to some other fortunate colony."

"*Et tu,* Carmont?" Sir Robert growled.

He knew the futility of trying to wage a battle without a

single ally. But it galled him to surrender without a fight. He vowed to give his pretty, conniving adversary a fight she would not soon forget!

What had made her accept his offer? Jocelyn could not wrest her attention away from the governor and Colonel Carmont as they disembarked and strode from the wharf. She had not played chess in years, while he looked like just the sort of cool, calculating fellow who would excel at the game.

But she sensed this was the only chance the governor would give her. For the sake of her charges, she must seize it—no matter how great a disadvantage she would suffer. Besides, the governor had roused her antagonism such that she could not resist his challenge. She half wished she could confront him on a more violent field of honor—with pistols, or duelling swords…or hand-to-hand combat.

Quite ridiculous, given the way he towered over her! Yet some furious part of her longed to strike him a physical blow. Another part yearned to shake his haughty self-control. A very tiny, traitorous part wondered how it might feel to be pinned beneath him.

"My word!" Sally Carmont's tinkling laugh roused Jocelyn from her wanton fancy. "You do have the most singular effect on our honorable governor, my dear."

Jocelyn made a wry face. "What? Is Sir Robert usually more demonstrative in his manner?"

"Demonstrative?" Sally burst into such a gale of laughter she could scarcely catch her breath. "Quite the contrary, I assure you! Will swears he is the best of men, but I have always found him unbearably severe. I vow, he spoke more and with greater feeling these past few minutes than I have heard him speak in the past month altogether."

"I refuse to take either the credit or the blame for Sir Robert's recent behavior," Jocelyn insisted. "It is the situation that has provoked him, though I cannot fathom his prejudice against my mission."

For all she denied ruffling the governor's composure, it intrigued her to think she might possess that power. And it restored a little of her self-respect, which was shaken by the suspicion Governor Kerr might hold some of that same power over her.

"Do not slight yourself, my dear," said Sally. "I believe you have more effect upon Sir Robert than either of you is willing to admit. Now fetch your hat and let us be off. We have less than two hours to prepare for this duel of yours."

"Of course, how clever to think of it!" Jocelyn started off toward the galleyway. "You and I can play a few practice matches at your house before I have to face Sir Robert."

"Chess?" Sally's mouth puckered as though she had bitten something sour. "Don't be silly! We must fix your hair. And I have a new gown I believe will suit you very well."

"What does my appearance matter? I mean to beat the governor at his own game, not make a conquest of him."

Sally Carmont wagged her forefinger. "Why should any woman want to beat a man at *his* game when she may so easily vanquish him at *hers?*"

"I have no idea what you mean." Jocelyn headed toward the hold.

Sally called after her. "No matter whose game a woman plays, appearance and charm are two potent weapons she cannot afford to neglect if she means to win."

On other men, perhaps. But Governor Kerr? Jocelyn had never met a man less likely to be swayed by feminine charm. This had the bothersome effect of making her want to compel his admiration, however reluctant.

When she reached the lower deck, Jocelyn found her charges much subdued.

"Please, ma'am," said Lily, after one of the other girls nudged her, "has anything been decided? Will we be allowed to stay in Nova Scotia?"

"Perhaps." Jocelyn did not want to raise false hopes only to dash them later. "I am going to Government House, now, for more...*talks* with Governor Kerr about our situation."

The girls looked relieved and hopeful, clearly trusting in her powers of persuasion. Jocelyn wished she could be as sanguine of her chances as they. The bravado with which she'd accepted Sir Robert's challenge was ebbing rapidly.

Perhaps sensing her uncertainty, Lily asked, "Is there anything we can do to help, Mrs. Finch?"

"You can all maintain your best behavior during my absence." Jocelyn surveyed the group, meeting the eyes of one or two girls capable of causing trouble. "Those of you so inclined might pray for my success."

"Pray?" cried Louisa. "Is it as bad as that? Whenever folks fall ill and the doctor says to pray, you know it's hopeless!"

Pulling out her handkerchief, she began to sob into it, joined in her lamentations by several other girls. A few more sensible among the group rolled their eyes at this display.

"It is not hopeless!" Jocelyn grabbed her hat and jammed it on her head, skewering it in place with a decorative but dangerous looking pin. "Now stop this blubbering at once!"

That only made the tearful ones weep harder. Jocelyn chided herself for not keeping her impatience in check. "Perhaps a turn around the deck in the fresh air might do you all good. I promise to do my very best for you."

Clasping Lily's hand, she muttered, "Try to keep them calm until I get back."

With that, she fled to the deck as if something frightful were nipping at her heels. In truth, something was. The haunting specter of defeat and the daunting prospect of crossing the ocean so soon again in charge of forty young women in their present overwrought state. Before Jocelyn would let that happen, she would battle Governor Kerr with a sword or pistol!

Sir Robert could scarcely have felt more keyed up if he'd been going to fight a real duel. For the fifth time in as many minutes, he checked at the clock to the left of the drawing-room door. It did not surprise him that Mrs. Finch was late. In his experience, women cared far less about punctuality than men.

He might have strode over to the window to watch for Mrs. Carmont's carriage but a cluster of men crowded in front of it, talking together. These were the same council members who had called on him this morning to express their support for Mrs. Finch and her bride ship. Sir Robert had invited them to witness the chess match to satisfy them that he was giving the woman a chance.

He hoped they would notice her tardiness, a small foretaste of the disturbances she and her shipload of marriageable women were likely to unleash upon the colony. To his annoyance, none of them seemed to mark the time. Neither did Will Carmont, who lounged in an armchair beside the hearth perusing the *Gazette.* No doubt he was too well acquainted with his wife's dilatory habits to look for her an instant before she arrived.

All heads turned when Duckworth threw open the morning-room door to admit a young footman bearing tea. When they saw it was not the ladies after all, the gentlemen returned to their conversation and the colonel to his newspaper.

"Any sign of Mrs. Finch *yet,* Duckworth?" The governor made no effort to conceal his impatience.

"Not yet, sir. But the bish—"

Before Duckworth could get the rest out, Barnabas Power

stalked in followed by the bishop. "What's all this nonsense, deciding matters of colonial policy over a chessboard? What will be next? Cutting cards for land patents? Throwing dice for government appointments?"

Would that be so much worse than the present system of influence and patronage? Sir Robert wondered. For once he exercised enough tact to bite his tongue.

When he began to stammer his reasons, Power cut him short with another gruff question. "Why was I not invited to watch?"

"M-my apologies, sir." Suddenly this whole idea seemed as frivolous a waste of time as he had condemned Mrs. Finch's mission for being. "I assumed you would be occupied with more important matters."

Power reached into his trouser pocket and jingled some silver. "I'm never too busy to make a little easy money." He called out to the youngest of the council members. "Say, Brenton, would you care to lay a small wager on the outcome of the governor's duel with Mrs. Finch?"

"With pleasure, sir!" Lewis Brenton beckoned him toward the window. "I was just discussing that very subject with Mr. Chapman and Mr. Sadler when you arrived."

Grumbling under his breath, Sir Robert stalked to the middle of the room, where a small card table had been set up and his chessboard placed upon it. He made a few practice moves, nudging forward king's and queen's pawns. Will Carmont returned to his newspaper once again, while Duckworth fetched tea for the governor's guests.

Finally, a full half hour after they were expected, a footman announced Mrs. Carmont and Mrs. Finch. Sir Robert quickly shifted all the chess pieces back to their original positions then strode forward to greet the ladies.

He bowed then gestured toward Barnabas Power and the

others. "I believe you are already acquainted with the gentlemen, Mrs. Finch."

This time she betrayed no embarrassment at being reminded of how she had gone behind his back. Instead, she acknowledged her allies with an elegant curtsy. "I have had that honor."

The men, none a day below thirty, grinned at her like a gaggle of calf-eyed schoolboys. Though Sir Robert had an almost irresistible urge to box their ears, he could not dispute the effect Mrs. Finch had upon them.

She looked quite a different woman from the one who'd emerged from the *Hestia*'s hold earlier that afternoon. Her hair had been dressed in a different style—a very becoming one with wispy curls framing her face. A pale green gown showed her slender figure to advantage and made her look the embodiment of springtime, which was so keenly anticipated in the colony.

Lewis Brenton made no effort to conceal his admiration as he swept her a very deep bow. "The honor is ours, Lady Jocelyn."

His words flustered her in a way the gentlemen's stares had not. A flush mantled her cheeks and though the corners of her lips still curved upward, all the sparkle went out of her smile. "If you would be so kind, sir, I prefer to be addressed as 'Mrs. Finch,' in honor of my late husband."

Sir Robert was familiar enough with forms of address to know that the daughter of a marquess could continue to be called "Lady" even after she had married beneath her. He wondered what lay behind Jocelyn Finch's insistence on dispensing with her title. For the first time since learning of her lofty connections, it occurred to him to wonder what a noblewoman was doing chaperoning a shipload of emigrant girls.

Her remark seemed to dumbfound the rest of the party for

a moment. Sir Robert rushed to fill the awkward lull with the first words that came to mind. "Of course we shall call you by whatever name you wish, Mrs. Finch."

It was not a witty remark but, like him, blunt and to the point. Still, it served well enough. The tension in the room relaxed and in Mrs. Finch's eyes he detected a flicker of gratitude.

It prompted him to continue. "Since these gentlemen have expressed some interest in our…disagreement, I thought they might care to observe its resolution."

He wanted them all on hand to see him win, fair and square, and to bear witness that Mrs. Finch had willingly accepted his terms.

Barnabas Power seemed more interested in eyeing the lady as if she were a prize mare on which he planned to bid. "We've come to cheer you on, ma'am."

She rewarded him and the others with a glowing smile that made Sir Robert smart with resentment. "How very kind of you, when you all must have so much more important business to occupy your time. I am flattered by your attention."

They were equally flattered by her, the governor had no doubt of it. Did they not see the skill with which she was playing them? If the lady was half as proficient at chess, she might give him more of a challenge than he'd bargained for.

"Your point is well taken, Mrs. Finch. We are all busy people and this matter has already occupied more of our time than it merits." Sir Robert gestured toward the chessboard. "Shall we begin without further ado?"

She cast him a venomous glance. Then, with the graceful but determined gait, she approached the chess table and took the chair at the "white" end of the board. "I hope you will not begrudge me the small advantage of first move, Your Excellency."

It was clear she considered him anything but *excellent.*

"Indeed not." He sank onto the chair opposite her, pleased to be playing his accustomed black. "I would insist upon it."

"Enjoy your game." Mrs. Carmont pulled off her gloves. "I could do with a cup of tea. May I pour for anyone else?"

While the spectators swarmed to the tea table to refill their cups, Mrs. Finch picked up the white king's pawn and advanced it two squares. Sir Robert nodded his approval of this sound opening. He countered by moving his king's pawn forward to block hers.

She surprised him by slipping her queen out on the diagonal. After a moment's consideration, he moved out his queen's knight. Mrs. Finch stared at the board with grim concentration then picked up her bishop and shifted it several spaces forward.

Teacups in hand, Sir Robert's guests clustered around the table, watching the match. The bishop greeted Mrs. Finch's move with a murmur of approval. No doubt he could see how her aggressive play threatened a checkmate.

Or would have against a novice opponent. Sir Robert nudged his knight pawn forward to endanger her queen. While she studied the board, her brow furrowed and her pretty mouth compressed in a tight line, he got up and helped himself to tea. When he turned his attention back to the board, he found she had moved her queen to bishop three, still threatening the mate. He advanced his knight to a square defended by his queen. Mrs. Finch's little sortie had failed. He would put her on the defensive now.

She stared at the board for so long Sir Robert wondered if she ever meant to move. He beckoned his aide and whispered, "Go to my office and fetch me some papers, like a good fellow."

Duckworth hurried away, returning with the requested documents before Mrs. Finch reached for her knight. After a little dithering, she placed it upon the king-two square.

Then she turned to Mrs. Carmont. "I could do with a cup of tea, if you please, Sally. Plenty of cream and sugar."

She had barely spoken before Sir Robert pushed his bishop forward. That done, he picked up one of his papers and began to read. If the woman was going to take an eternity making up her mind over every move, he could use the time to catch up on some of his work. Work she had interrupted and distracted him from.

The rest of the party seemed impatient with her slow play, too. After watching the opening moves of the game with interest, they withdrew in small groups to various parts of the room, talking quietly together.

Mrs. Finch paid them no heed, except to look a trifle relieved to be free of their scrutiny. She sipped the tea Mrs. Carmont had poured for her while examining the chessboard with a puzzled look. Perhaps she was wondering if his bishop posed any threat to her, never guessing he had simply moved the piece to get it out of the way.

Sir Robert read over the land grant petition in his hand. It seemed to be in order. The petitioner was a Scot recently mustered out from one of the Highland regiments that had served with distinction at Waterloo. He was thirty-two years of age and unmarried. That information reminded Sir Robert of what Mr. Power had said that morning about men being more productive citizens when they had families to support. He could not help wondering if one of the young ladies from the bride ship might make a suitable wife for a new settler like this one.

The soft but insistent sound of Mrs. Finch clearing her throat drew his attention back to the chessboard. "I have made my move, sir. It is now your turn."

"Of course." He glanced at the board and saw she had brought her queen's knight forward.

Sir Robert quickly replied with his queen's pawn. Then he returned to his work, instructing Duckworth to check that the requested land did not encroach upon Crown forest reserves before issuing the grant. The next petition had come from a widower with three young children. A new wife would be a necessity for that poor fellow, not a distraction.

"Is there some difficulty, Sir Robert?" asked Mrs. Finch in a tone of genuine concern.

"No, indeed." He looked up from the paper. "Is it my turn again?"

She nodded.

Sir Robert scanned the board, then moved his bishop to threaten her queen. Enough conservative play, waiting for her to make a mistake he could exploit. He wanted the matter settled and Mrs. Finch gone before he was bothered by any more second thoughts.

Only after he had made his move did Sir Robert recognize the weakness of his position. He hoped Mrs. Finch would be too intimidated by his threat to her queen to see it. By now he should have realized she was not the kind of woman to be easily intimidated in any situation. He tried to keep his face impassive when she ignored the threat, reaching for her knight instead.

Ivory clicked softly against ebony as she took his knight with hers. "Check."

Jocelyn tried to keep any note of premature triumph from her voice as she removed Sir Robert's knight from the board, the first capture of the match.

There were likely hundreds of ways he could beat her yet. Especially now that she had put him on his guard. He might be a more experienced player than she, but he would have to spare the match more than a crumb of his attention if he hoped to win.

Still it boosted her confidence to have made that first capture. Unless she was mistaken, there might be better yet to come. What would her father think if he could see how she was making use of the skills he had taught her?

She recalled those long-ago years as if seeing them through a window of golden glass. How she had reveled in the attention the marquess had lavished upon her, then! Mistaking it for love when he had only been cultivating her as an asset of potential value in his quest for dynastic power. At least Governor Kerr was forthright in his dislike of her.

Jocelyn watched with mute satisfaction as he scrutinized his position more closely before capturing her knight with his queen. His scowl told her he knew what she would do next and she did not disappoint him. Her queen took his undefended bishop. From now on, if she could simply trade him piece for piece until the end of the game, she would win. But she had learned not to underestimate Sir Robert Kerr. A pity he had not learned the same about her.

The flurry of captures brought their spectators back to hover around the table whispering to one another. Sir Robert castled kingside. Jocelyn advanced her queen's pawn. After a moment's deliberation, he moved his queen's rook to defend his king on the other side. As soon as he let go of the piece, a flicker of his brow told Jocelyn he had seen his mistake but hoped she would not.

When she brought her bishop forward, he cursed under his breath. The man recognized trouble when he landed in it—she would give him that. What a shame he also imagined trouble where none existed.

A series of captures was inevitable now. All he could do was minimize the damage. His queen took her bishop. Her queen took his. Their audience broke into a spatter of applause.

Jocelyn willed her hand not to tremble as she lifted the teacup to her lips. The match was now hers to lose, but she could not hope to maintain the advantage of Sir Robert's inattention. From now on he would be watching very closely indeed to exploit any mistake she might make. Somehow the tantalizing prospect of victory unsettled her more than the fear of defeat.

They continued to play, the governor taking his time and studying the board carefully before each move. That gave Jocelyn time to plan, as well, anticipating what his next move might be and how she could best counter it. Several strategic moves gave way to another flurry of captures that robbed the governor of a knight and three pawns in exchange for Jocelyn's bishop and two pawns.

She sensed the moment he knew he was beaten. His moves picked up tempo once again and seemed calculated to bring the game to a swift end. He did not concede defeat, but fought on, allowing her to savor the triumph of a complete victory.

In the end, her queen alone placed him in checkmate, his king boxed into a corner.

"Bravo!" Sally squealed.

The gentlemen applauded Jocelyn's win, some with more vigor than others. She understood why a few moments later when they exchanged small sums of money.

The governor rose and extended his hand over the chessboard. "Well played, Mrs. Finch. I hope you will allow me the opportunity to redeem myself in a rematch during your stay in Halifax."

As they shook hands, Jocelyn lowered her voice for his ears alone while the others were discussing their wagers. "I shall be honored to play you again, sir, if that is your wish. But the outcome of this match does not impugn your skill. We both know you allowed me to win."

He made no effort to release her hand. "For the sake of my

pride, I wish I could claim that were so, but I assure you it is not. In my arrogance, I yielded you an advantage, but you had the skill and resource to capitalize upon it. You are a formidable opponent, ma'am."

Over the years Jocelyn had received many of the usual compliments gentlemen lavished upon ladies. Tributes to her beauty, her charm, her accomplishment, even her wit. Why then did Sir Robert's bald, grudging scrap of praise set her insides aflutter? Or was it the warmth of his hand as he clung to hers, only now letting it go?

She was done with such feelings, Jocelyn insisted to herself. And she resented the governor for provoking them, though she knew it had never been his intention.

"You have only begun to see my formidable nature, sir. I mean to prove you wrong about the bride ship—that it will be an unmixed blessing to your colony."

"I hope you will succeed, ma'am." He did not look by any means convinced that she would. "For the sake of the colony, I sincerely hope so."

Chapter Five

The waters of the harbor were calm and mild fog wrapped around the *Hestia* when Colonel and Mrs. Carmont dropped Jocelyn off at the wharf late that afternoon.

"How can I begin to thank you for all your help?" She squeezed Sally's hand. "If not for you, I would be headed back to England in disgrace."

"It was a pleasure," Sally assured her. "And most diverting to watch you get the best of Governor Kerr."

"Now, Sally," her husband protested, "I've told you before, you must not be so hard on the poor man. He may be a bit too sober for your taste, but he is an excellent fellow who has done a great deal of good for the colony."

"For the settlers, perhaps." Sally's pert tone told Jocelyn she enjoyed teasing her husband. "But Halifax society has been unbearably dull since he took office. I feel certain that is about to change for the better."

"You, my dear wife, live entirely for pleasure," Will Carmont scolded fondly.

Sally chuckled. "That is better than living for misery, don't you think?"

"You have me there!" The colonel patted his wife's hand.

The good-natured domestic banter between the Carmonts brought a pang of longing to Jocelyn's heart. It reminded her so much of the way she and Ned had carried on in the early days of their marriage.

"Why don't you come and have a celebratory dinner at our house?" asked Sally.

"Thank you for the offer, but I had better not." Jocelyn endeavored to sound brisk and cheerful as she nodded toward the ship, swathed in a ghostly mist. "I must waste no time telling my girls the news. They have likely been at sixes and sevens ever since I left."

Her guess proved true. Before she could get a word out, half a dozen girls had tattled to her about the behavior of the others. Louisa looked as though she had not stopped crying the whole time Jocelyn had been away. And poor Lily looked ready to tear her hair out.

"Please, Mrs. Finch," she begged as soon as she could get a word in, "what's to become of us? Has it been decided yet? May we stay in Nova Scotia or will we have to leave?"

Grasping Lily's hand, Jocelyn cried, "We can stay!"

A sweet thrill of success bubbled within her, even more potent than when she had placed Sir Robert's king in checkmate.

Her news provoked a torrent of questions.

"How did you convince the governor?"

"Where are we to stay?"

"Can we get off the ship now?"

That question almost caused a stampede toward the galleyway.

Jocelyn had to shout to make herself heard over the din. "Not tonight, I'm afraid!"

A deafening chorus of wails and groans filled the hold.

"Hush now!" Jocelyn covered her ears to drown out the din.

"One more night aboard ship will not kill us. It is certainly better than several more weeks on a return voyage to England."

Perhaps the girls heard an implied threat in her reminder, for a chastened hush fell over them.

Jocelyn seized the moment. "Speaking of sleep, I think we had all better get some. Tomorrow will be a busy day. The governor has offered us the use of his summer estate just outside of town."

When some of the girls grumbled at the thought of lodging in the country, she added, "His Royal Highness, the Duke of Kent lived there for several years when he was stationed in Halifax."

"Royal lodgings?" Lily sounded suitably impressed. "What an honor for us! And how very kind of the governor."

Was it kind? Jocelyn wondered, even as she nodded. She had won Sir Robert's agreement to let them stay in Nova Scotia, but she knew better than to suppose he would give her his full support. Did he hope that by settling her and her charges on the edge of town, they would be out of sight and out of mind?

What she had not told the girls about the Prince's Lodge was that the Duke of Kent had lived there quite openly with his French mistress. The place must have a rather tainted reputation on that account. And what sort of housekeeping arrangements would they find there tomorrow? Did the governor hope to make their stay so unpleasant they would be forced to leave?

Those worries plagued Jocelyn through the night, but her spirits lifted as soon as she stepped out on deck the next morning. Golden spring sunshine had burned off the fog. Now it shimmered on the dark waters of Halifax Harbor and warmed the air to a pleasant enough temperature that she was inclined to linger outside for a look around.

For the first time since her arrival in Halifax, she took a moment to survey the town that would be her home for the next few months. Behind the solid ironstone warehouses on the docks, buildings ranged up the steep hillside in tiers that reminded Jocelyn of Bath, back in England. Though, instead of golden stone town houses, most were wooden cottages with barnlike gambrel roofs. Some were painted in bright colors while others had been left to weather to a soft gray. The bustle of ships in the harbor and the looming presence of Fort George on the summit of the hill gave the town an air of excitement, even danger.

There was a sense of suppressed excitement aboard the bride ship, too, when it cast off and sailed a few miles deeper into Bedford Basin. Jocelyn did her best to prevent the girls from swarming all over the deck and getting in the way of the crew, but it was hopeless.

"Oh, very well!" She threw up her hands at last. How could she expect them to contain their eagerness when she could scarcely curb her own? "Only don't all crowd on one side of the deck—you'll make the ship list. And anyone I catch pushing will be sent below!"

The last thing she needed was to fish some sodden young woman out of the frigid water. That would do nothing to dispel Sir Robert's negative opinion of them.

Jocelyn was so busy keeping an anxious eye on her charges she hardly noticed the settlements on shore giving way from town buildings to scattered farms to trees, trees and more trees. Most were still bare of foliage but scattered evergreens lent the rural landscape a little color.

"Look!" Hetty Jenkins pointed toward a spit of land jutting out between two coves. "D'ye reckon that's the place?"

Jocelyn shaded her eyes and peered in the direction Hetty was pointing. Nestled among a pretty grove of slender beech and birch trees stood a curious-looking building. It appeared to be circular with a domed roof. A colonnade of pillars ringed the central structure, creating a shallow cloister. Sunshine glittered off a large golden ball atop the dome. While it looked an altogether charming little place, it was far too small and in every other way unsuited for…

"Don't be a bigger fool than you can help, carrothead!" Vita Sykes gave a snort of scornful laughter. "That's likely just the prince's privy. Up the hill is a house that might hold us all in a pinch."

"As long as I don't have to share a bed with you," Hetty shot back before Jocelyn could intervene. "Be afraid of catching some vermin, I would."

"I'll box your ears for that, see if I don't!"

Fortunately the chief troublemakers were far enough apart that neither could land a blow. Jocelyn half wished that pair *would* lean too far over the deck railing and tumble into the basin. She could think of several girls who would gladly give them a shove.

"That will be quite enough from both of you." She glared at Hetty, who hung her head, then at Vita, who stared back bold as brass. "Any further such behavior and you may find yourselves toting all our luggage up to the lodge. Is that understood?"

They muttered something that might have been "Yes, ma'am."

In Vita's case, Jocelyn wondered if it was a choice bit of profanity. Whatever had persuaded Mrs. Beamish to give that little vixen a berth on the bride ship, Jocelyn could not guess. To test her skills as a chaperone, perhaps? If that was Vita's purpose, she excelled at it!

Having averted a full-blown catfight on deck, Jocelyn turned her attention to the larger building Vita had pointed out in the distance. The place did look as though it might suit their needs. A pleasantly proportioned country villa, it had a pillared veranda that ran the full width of the ground floor topped by an equally wide balcony. Above that, a single large dormer jutted out from the center of the roof. It had one vast window that no doubt provided a splendid view.

The girls would have to sleep several to a room at first and eat their meals in two shifts. But as some left to get married the crowding would ease. Jocelyn imagined how pretty the grounds would look once the trees and flowers began to bloom. Why, they would rival anything on her father's estate back in Norfolk. She stifled a pang of longing for the bright spring daffodils that grew around Breckland in such profusion.

"Drop anchor!" bellowed the captain. "Prepare the boats!"

"Vita, Eleanor." Jocelyn pointed to several girls. "Mary Parfitt, Sophia, Charlotte and Eliza Turner, go below and fetch as much of your luggage as you can carry. You will come with me on the first boat."

She turned to Lily. "Send the rest after us in small groups. Keep Hetty with you until the last."

Lily cast a wistful glance at the little domed building on shore, but bobbed an obliging nod. "Anything else, Mrs. Finch?"

"That will be quite enough for the moment." Jocelyn patted her arm. "Thank you, my dear."

If anything, Lily deserved to be one of the first to disembark, but Jocelyn did not trust any of the others to keep order after she left. And it was necessary for her to lead their party to the lodge. While it looked an agreeable-enough place from a distance, who knew what state they might find it in?

Governor Kerr did not seem the type of man who indulged in country idylls when there were documents to sign and reports to write. Heaven only knows how long it had been since anyone occupied the place. No matter, though. If Prince's Lodge had to be cleaned from cellar to attic, it would give her charges a useful occupation during their early days in the colony.

The first party was lowered gingerly into a boat and rowed to shore. Then the oarsmen lifted each of the passengers out onto dry ground. Vita clung to the sailor who hoisted her ashore far longer than was proper.

Jocelyn grabbed her by the arm and hauled her away. "The others would like to disembark before nightfall." She picked up a couple of bags and thrust them into Vita's hands. "Now make yourself useful for a change."

The girl's full lower lip jutted out in a sulk as she looked around her. "Prince or no prince, it's all a bit rustic for my taste. Too bad we couldn't have stayed in town."

"I shudder to think what mischief you might get up to in town." Jocelyn hoisted one of her bags and set off across a wide, rutted road toward the gates of the estate. "Unless you start behaving with a little decorum, Miss Sykes, you will find yourself rusticating out here all summer."

She could almost feel an invisible dagger piercing her back from Vita's vicious glare. Pity any poor fool tempted into matrimony by Vita's wanton ways!

They had barely gotten across the road when Jocelyn spotted a man striding down the steep, winding driveway to meet them. Had the governor put aside his everlasting papers for a few hours and ridden out from town to welcome them? She strove not to betray any sign of disappointment when she saw it was Sir Robert's aide, Mr. Duckworth. Indeed, she told herself, she was not disappointed. After all, the young man was far more agreeable and obliging than his master.

"Welcome, ladies!" He pushed open the gate and hurried toward them. "I hope you will find the accommodations here to your satisfaction."

"I assure you," said Jocelyn, "provided the place is dry and the floors do not sway beneath our feet, we shall be quite contented here."

He chuckled. "I believe I can safely promise you both those things, Mrs. Finch. But do not exert yourselves to carry so much." He reached for one of Jocelyn's bags. "The lane up to the lodge is quite steep. I will send a cart down to collect all your luggage as soon as it is unloaded from the ship."

Did Mr. Duckworth enjoy being perpetually hurried and worried? Jocelyn wondered. Or had his service to a martinet like Sir Robert Kerr made him so?

"Do not fret." She let him take one of her bags but clung to the other with no intention of surrendering it. "After our weeks at sea, a little exertion will do us good."

"He's welcome to carry mine if he wants to," Vita muttered, just loud enough for Jocelyn to hear.

"I beg your pardon?" said Mr. Duckworth.

Silencing Vita with a stern frown, Jocelyn answered, "We will be most grateful for a cart to haul the trunks. It was kind of you to come all the way from town to meet us."

The young man cast a shy but admiring glance at the girls who had accompanied Jocelyn. "It is a pleasure and an honor rather than a duty, ma'am. Allow me to show you around the place so you can get settled as soon as possible."

A host of welcome smells greeted Jocelyn when Mr. Duckworth threw open the front door of Prince's Lodge and stood back to let her enter. The faint reek of lye, camphor, brass and wood polish overpowered any hint of mustiness. Someone had given the place a thorough cleaning, and not long ago, either. A faint whiff of wood smoke told her at least some of the fires had been lit. While not strictly necessary on such a mild day, they did dispel any trace of dampness from the air.

While the rest of Jocelyn's charges disembarked from the bride ship and made their way up to the lodge, Mr. Duckworth conducted her on a tour of the place from the locked wine cellar to the rooftop lookout with its spectacular view. As she peered into the bedrooms, Jocelyn found herself reckoning how many girls each would hold and who should share quarters with whom.

"Would it be possible," she asked, "to fetch a few more beds from town and convert the little sewing room on the ground floor to sleeping quarters as a temporary measure?"

"More beds are already on their way, ma'am." Mr. Duckworth looked pleased to inform her of the fact. "They should be here before nightfall. Is there anything else you require?"

"A kitchen would be handy." Jocelyn felt rather foolish having to point it out. They were standing in quite a grand dining room. If the villa was equipped for guests to dine on such a scale, surely it must be equipped to cook for them.

"Of course." Mr. Duckworth beckoned her toward a window that looked onto the grounds behind the lodge. "I should have mentioned it before."

He pointed at the nearest of several trim outbuildings. With its tall, arched windows, it had the appearance of a chapel. "That is the kitchen and the cook's quarters. Because this place was designed as a summer residence, the kitchen is separate so its fires do not overheat the house."

"Clever." Jocelyn spotted a small black woman bustling around the kitchen. "Is that our cook?"

The girls could all share in the duties of housemaids, but having someone to prepare their meals would be a great boon.

Mr. Duckworth nodded. "Miz Ada is on loan from Government House for as long as you need her. She knows the kitchen at Prince's Lodge well. She was part of the household staff when the duke resided here."

"I'm certain she will be a valuable addition to our establishment." Jocelyn strove to sound poised and gracious, though part of her wanted to dance around the dining room. When she and her charges had set out for Nova Scotia, she'd never dared hope they would find such excellent accommodations.

Mr. Duckworth lingered at the window for a further moment. "Once you get settled in, you and your young ladies must explore the grounds. They are quite lovely, and will only grow more so in the weeks to come."

"I daresay we will make good use of them." Jocelyn pulled out the chair at the head of the dining table and sank onto it for a moment. She found herself looking forward to being mistress of a fine house again, even if it was only temporary. "After all those weeks cooped up aboard ship, we will be anxious to stretch our legs and enjoy some fresh scenery."

Just then Lily appeared in the dining room doorway, looking flushed and flustered. "I beg your pardon, Mrs. Finch. Sir. All the girls are here, now. Some of them are arguing over which rooms they will get. Can you come?"

"I'll be along directly." Jocelyn stifled an exasperated sigh as she rose from the chair. Clearly it was too soon to think of rest yet. Her mission had barely begun. "Tell them I am on my way. That may settle things."

"Very good, ma'am." Lily disappeared as quickly as she had come.

Jocelyn turned to the governor's aide. "Thank you for the tour of the house and for all your help, Mr. Duckworth." If his master had been half so obliging, their stay in Halifax would have gotten off to a far more pleasant start. "If there is nothing else, I beg you will excuse me to begin organizing our household."

"I will not detain you, ma'am. I should be getting back to town. There are only two more matters I meant to mention."

"And they would be…?" She tried not to sound impatient. Much as she enjoyed the young man's company, she needed to get the girls settled. She did not want him to see how firm a hand she might have to use, in case he carried word of it back to the governor.

"Colonel Carmont will be sending a small guard detail from town, ma'am. The first should be here before nightfall. They will be relieved every twelve hours."

"Armed guards? Is that necessary? This looks like such a peaceful spot." Would their mission be to keep trespassers out or to keep Jocelyn and her charges virtual prisoners on this secluded estate?

"His Excellency has ordered it, ma'am." Mr. Duckworth looked regretful but resolved. "And I believe it is necessary. The road at the foot of the hill is the coach route to Windsor. There is often considerable traffic on it and not always of the best kind. A house full of young ladies might pose an attraction to undesirable company."

"Oh, very well." Never let it be said she lacked the wit to bow to the inevitable. "If His Excellency decrees we must be guarded, then I suppose we have no choice."

Hearing raised voices in the distance, she asked, "What was the second matter you wished to mention?"

"Governor Kerr asked to be informed how soon you wish to begin conducting interviews with men in the colony who are seeking wives. Would you like notices placed in the *Gazette?* His Excellency suggested a system of written applications might be useful, similar to the way land patents are granted."

Interviews? Newspaper notices? Applications! Why not just hold a cattle market and be done with it?

With great difficulty Jocelyn mastered her outrage. After all, none of this was Mr. Duckworth's idea. "I believe I should discuss those details with His Excellency myself. Once we get settled, I shall pay the governor a call to review my plans."

Perhaps Mr. Duckworth sensed the indignation her temperate words masked. "Are you certain that will be necessary, ma'am? I should be pleased to convey any messages you might have for His Excellency."

She should make every effort to avoid that disagreeable man, Jocelyn told herself. Why then did a sense of anticipation race through her at the prospect of confronting him?

"Thank you for your kind offer, sir, but I believe this is a matter the governor and I should settle face-to-face."

Sir Robert set aside the preliminary survey for a series of canals to link Halifax Harbor with the Bay of Fundy. He dragged one hand down his face.

Two days had passed since his chess match with Mrs. Finch and Government House had never been quieter—like a lull in the wake of a storm. Yet the governor could not concentrate on his work. A strange restlessness gripped him, propelling him out of his chair to pace his study. It felt as if he were waiting for something…or something was missing. Ridiculous notions, both.

Duckworth hurried in just then, bearing more documents for Sir Robert's attention.

The young man gave a start to find him out from behind his desk. "Is everything all right, sir? Is there anything you require?"

Some medicine to cure him of this unaccountable malaise, perhaps. But Sir Robert had no idea what form that remedy might take. "Nothing is wrong. I thought it might do me good to stretch my legs. I don't walk half enough these days."

Perhaps that was his problem.

"Mrs. Finch said much the same thing, sir." Duckworth slid the documents he had brought beneath the pile already lying on the desk awaiting Sir Robert's attention. "Yesterday, when

I told her how fine the lodge grounds are. She said after being cooped up on that ship for so many weeks, she and the young ladies would be very glad to stretch their legs."

Once again Sir Robert congratulated himself on settling Mrs. Finch and her charges at Prince's Lodge. Out of sight, out of mind. At least she should be.

"You say they approved of the place?" Sir Robert knew he had already asked this at least twice and both times been assured it was the case. He did not know what made him ask again. It was not as if he doubted Duckworth.

Diplomatic fellow that he was, Duckworth gave no sign he had answered the same question twice already. "Mrs. Finch seemed to think it would suit them very well, sir. A pity you could not have stayed yesterday to see how well she liked the place."

"Er…yes…duty called, I'm afraid." Strangely enough, it had decided to call at the very moment he spied the *Hestia*'s sails from the lodge's rooftop lookout. "I'm sure you gave them a much more congenial welcome than I could have."

He could hardly have done worse than calling them a pack of harlots in front of half the town. Sir Robert writhed with shame whenever he recalled it. Yet part of him wished he *had* lingered at Prince's Lodge to give Mrs. Finch a more courteous welcome.

"Will there be anything else, sir?" asked Duckworth.

Sir Robert thought for a moment. "Could you fetch me a cup of coffee? It might help me concentrate better on my work."

With that he returned to his desk and picked up the canal survey. The matter required his most diligent attention and that was what he would give it.

His aide headed off in search of coffee. A few moments later, Sir Robert heard a tap on the door. Thinking Duckworth must have his hands too full to turn the knob, he rose and strode to the door.

But when he pulled it open, there stood Jocelyn Finch looking beautiful but vexed. All Sir Robert's restlessness left him. Could *she* be what he'd been waiting for, what he'd been missing? Perhaps he'd grown so accustomed to his work being interrupted by her that he could not settle down to it properly until he'd dealt with her daily intrusion.

"Madam." He bowed and beckoned her into his study. "I am surprised to see you in town so soon. I thought you might still be getting settled into your accommodations. Pray what can I do for you today?"

She looked around his study with an air of vague disapproval. "Perhaps you are surprised to see me in town so soon because you know I lack any conveyance to make the journey. Was that your intention—to isolate us in the country where we might not disturb the peace of your colony?"

Why must she always assume the worst about him? "I assure you it was an oversight for which I apologize. I will place a carriage and team at your disposal right away."

His aide returned with the coffee and received a most cordial greeting from the lady. Sir Robert wished he'd ordered something stronger to drink.

"Duckworth, it seems I have been remiss in my hospitality. Can you arrange suitable transport for Mrs. Finch? We do not want her stranded out in the country, after all."

"Of course not, sir." Duckworth handed him the cup of coffee. "I shall see to it at once."

As he passed Mrs. Finch, she favored the young man with a smile of such luminous warmth it took Sir Robert's breath. "My sincere thanks to you, Mr. Duckworth, for all you have done to make us comfortable out at the lodge. Once we have some means of getting to town, our situation will be quite perfect."

Duckworth acknowledged her praise with a self-conscious nod then hurried away.

Sir Robert barely suppressed a huff. Did the silly creature suppose his young aide had undertaken all those tasks on his own initiative? Perhaps it was easier for her to believe that than to expect any consideration from him. The notion hit Sir Robert like the sharp swat of a schoolmaster's cane.

"I hope you were not obliged to walk in all the way from the lodge." He pulled out a chair for her.

She did not appear flushed or out of breath, and what he could see of her shoes did not look soiled by spring mud.

"I am more resourceful than that, sir." She sank onto the chair. "When our guard detail returned to town this morning, I sent a note with them to Mrs. Carmont, who kindly drove out. She offered to keep an eye on the girls and lent me her carriage so I might come and discuss the matter with you."

Sir Robert resumed his seat behind his desk. "I do not doubt your resourcefulness, Mrs. Finch." He took a sip of his coffee then remembered his manners. "I beg your pardon. Can I offer you some refreshment?"

"No, thank you, sir. This is not a social call. Nor did I come here only to request a carriage."

He'd feared there might be more to it. What else had he done wrong? He raised his eyebrows in a mute question.

Mrs. Finch inhaled a deep breath, as if bracing herself for a distasteful task. "I wished to speak to you about the means by which we will arrange matches between the young ladies in my charge and the eligible men of your colony."

Was that all? Sir Robert felt on firmer ground. "Splendid! Perhaps Duckworth told you what I proposed? I believe the most efficient strategy would be to post notices in the *Gazette* asking interested parties to make written application. Each man could explain his circumstances and outline his requirements for a wife. Then you could choose a suitable candidate from among your young ladies and arrange an introduction."

He was so pleased with the idea that, when Mrs. Finch did not make an immediate reply, he charged on. "No doubt there will be far more applicants than available brides. That will allow you to choose the most desirable men in terms of prospects, situation and habits. Should we ask them to submit a character reference as to their sobriety, temperament and so on?"

Mrs. Finch sprang to her feet, obliging Sir Robert to rise out of respect. "Why do we not just set up an auction block in the Grand Parade and sell the girls to the highest bidders? Get it all over with in an afternoon."

"You might be on to something there." The words were out of his mouth before he registered the look of outrage on the lady's face. "Oh. You're joking, aren't you?"

"On the contrary, sir." She planted her hands on the edge of his desk and leaned forward. "What I suggested is only slightly more outrageous than your proposal. I find nothing amusing in either."

Sir Robert shook his head. "I confess I do not understand the difficulty. The system has worked most efficiently for granting land patents."

"You truly do not understand, do you?" Her indignant glare muted to a softer look…of pity? "We are not talking about land or livestock but the future happiness of a man and a woman. I will tolerate nothing less than true love matches for the young women in my charge. If you cared anything for the men of your colony, you would accept nothing less for them, either."

How dare the woman imply he did not care about his colonists? Sir Robert planted his hands on the opposite side of his desk, mirroring her assertive stance. "May I remind you that we are not in some Mayfair drawing room. Parts of Nova Scotia are little better than wilderness. The lives of the colonists are difficult—sometimes dangerous. They do not have time for romantic fancies out of storybooks. Marriage here is a practical matter and should be approached in a practical manner."

As he traded glares with her over his desk, Sir Robert was possessed of a mad urge to lean even closer, seize Jocelyn Finch by the shoulders and crush his lips against hers with furious passion!

Chapter Six

Good heavens! The man was looking at her as if he wanted to reach across his desk and throttle her. With a smothered gasp, Jocelyn stepped back. But she could not allow his outrageous assertion to go unchallenged.

"You have never been in love, or you would not talk such rot. True love may be romantic, but it is far more than a fancy. It has the power to lighten toil and make hardship more bearable."

The governor flinched, almost as though he had feelings capable of being injured.

Before she made the mistake of feeling sorry for him and before he could draw upon his arsenal of cold, practical logic to contradict her, Jocelyn pressed on. "A true love match is not contrived from notices, applications and interviews. It requires a special atmosphere to flourish—merry music, dancing, congenial company…magic."

Sir Robert fixed her with a dazed stare. "Are you suggesting we should mount a *Season* in Halifax?"

For one delirious instant Jocelyn forgot all her grievances against the man. If his very substantial mahogany desk had not stood between them, she might have thrown her arms around his neck and kissed him!

"Of course! Why did I not think of it? You are a perfect genius, sir, when you focus your mind in the proper direction!"

"I am not certain I deserve your praise, ma'am." He looked positively staggered.

"But you do!" Ideas frolicked through Jocelyn's mind. Each new one buoyed her spirits higher. "Just think of it. My young ladies can be presented to the King's viceroy in Nova Scotia, just as if they were making their debut in London. Then there will be a succession of entertainments at which they can be introduced to the men of your colony. Balls, routs…picnics when the weather gets warmer! I daresay your colonists will enjoy the opportunity to socializc."

"I believe they ought to socialize less and put their energies to better use."

For some reason, the governor's protest only made Jocelyn laugh. The poor man was quite impossible, but she was determined to have her way. "Do not be so severe, Sir Robert. A little more socializing might do *you* good. Now, how soon can you host a levee at which my young ladies may be presented?"

When he started to sputter about how infeasible that would be, she reminded him, "The sooner we get started, the sooner my work will be done and the sooner you will be rid of me."

"Yes, yes!" Sir Robert cast his eyes heavenward. "Might as well give up now as waste more time fighting a rearguard action doomed to fail. I will consult with Mr. Duckworth to see how soon we can arrange a levee."

"Why thank you, sir!" Jocelyn tried not to gloat over her victory. "I am certain it will be a great success. May I make one further suggestion?"

"Is there anything I could say to prevent you?"

She chuckled at his humor. "This is for your benefit, I

promise. I do not believe we should restrict the presentations to my charges alone. That would likely cause some resentment toward us. Instead you should issue a general invitation to all eligible young ladies. It might win you some goodwill from local families of consequence."

"You might be on to something there." The governor stroked his chin as he pondered her suggestion. "I could use a little goodwill for a change."

Mr. Duckworth returned just then. "With your permission, sir, I have arranged to dispatch your small gig out to Prince's Lodge for Mrs. Finch's use."

Sir Robert nodded. "I seldom have need of one carriage, let alone two. The gig will do well enough for me, come to that. Let Mrs. Finch have the loan of my town coach and driver. He is always grumbling about not having enough to do. No doubt the ladies can keep him well occupied."

Had she heard right? Jocelyn wondered. Was Governor Kerr granting her a favor she hadn't been obliged to badger and battle him for? Perhaps his initial failure to provide her with a carriage had not been deliberate after all.

"That is very generous of you, sir." She swept him her most elaborate curtsy. "Now I will not keep you from your work any longer. I must get back to relieve Mrs. Carmont."

The governor bowed. "Good day to you, madam. My coach will be in your possession by nightfall. I trust you will make good use of it."

When Mr. Duckworth moved to escort her to the door, Jocelyn shook her head. "I can find my own way out. I do not want to keep the governor from consulting you about plans for the levee."

As she breezed out of Sir Robert's study, she heard Mr. Duckworth say, "Levee? Are you hosting a levee, sir?"

She paused in the anteroom to retie her bonnet.

Sir Robert's exasperated sigh wafted through the half-open door to his study. "It seems I am. Though I'd just as soon attend a hanging…as the convict."

After a moment of silence, Mr. Duckworth gave a forced-sounding chuckle. "Ah, you're joking again, aren't you, sir? 'As the convict.' Ha-ha. Very good."

"Believe me, Duckworth, unless you think bearbaiting jolly sport, there is nothing amusing about the torment I suffer at social functions of that ilk."

She was not eavesdropping, Jocelyn insisted to her conscience as she lingered, fussing with the bow of her bonnet.

"You find them tiresome, sir?" Mr. Duckworth sounded as surprised by his master's revelation as Jocelyn was.

"Not tiresome, so much as just…damned awkward. I always manage to say the wrong thing or stand about dumb because I have no idea what to say. When my blasted foot acts up, I'm a menace to the toes of any poor lady unlucky enough to dance with me. But if I refuse to dance, I appear arrogant and unsociable."

"Then why are you hosting a levee, sir?"

"Because I've been a soldier," the governor growled, "and I know when surrender is my only option."

"Oh, I see!" This time the young man's laughter sounded sincere. "She's quite a lady, isn't she, sir?"

"She'll be the ruin of me before she's through."

As Jocelyn skulked in the anteroom, feeling more ashamed of her behavior every minute, she wished she could be certain this was only one of Sir Robert's jests.

On the drive back out to the Prince's Lodge, she tried to concentrate on making plans for the weeks ahead. The Carmonts could be counted upon to host a ball for the officers of the garrison. Not wanting to be outdone, the admiral would probably do the same for his men. And Mr. Power—Sally claimed he had an enormous fortune. All the better to host a truly lavish evening's entertainment.

With a little assistance, Jocelyn might be able to host a gathering at the Prince's Lodge. If ever there was a place to foster romance, that was surely it. All those winding paths for courting couples to stroll while the little waterfall splashed in the background and music wafted uphill from that pretty domed music pavilion by the shore. Could there be a more picturesque spot for a marriage proposal than beside the heart-shaped pond?

If only poor Ned were still alive and they could stroll those paths arm in arm, exclaiming over the miniature Chinese temple or gazing down at the magnificent view of the basin. But Ned was gone, rest his dear soul, and with him all Jocelyn's romantic dreams. Instead, she must take vicarious delight in the courtship of her charges. Many of them had grown so dear to her, they were almost like the younger sisters she'd once longed for, or the daughters she and Ned might have had. She wanted to see them all wed as happily as she had been—though not so briefly.

Sally looked relieved to see Jocelyn when she arrived back at Prince's Lodge. "You do have your hands full with this position, my dear. Why, you must feel like the mother of an enormous family!"

"Very like." Jocelyn gave a warm but weary chuckle as she removed her gloves and doffed her bonnet. That was part of what had drawn her to the post.

"The girls are all occupied with unpacking and exploring the grounds." Her friend drew Jocelyn into a small sitting room. "Let me call for a nice pot of tea. Then you and I can have a proper chat."

"That sounds like a splendid idea." Jocelyn sank onto the settee. It would be pleasant to converse with a woman her own age rather than one of the girls in need of correction, comfort or reassurance. "Have I told you yet what a godsend it has been to find you here? What would I have done without you?"

"You tell me so almost every time we meet." Sally signaled to one of the girls who happened to be passing and sent her off to fetch tea. "Of course I am delighted to have been of service, but I fancy you would have prevailed, even without my help."

She crossed to the settee and sat down beside Jocelyn. "So tell me what brings the daughter of a marquess to Nova Scotia as the chaperone of a bride ship?"

Jocelyn stiffened at the mention of her father. "I am no longer the daughter of a marquess, Sally. I stopped being that when his lordship disowned me for marrying against his wishes."

"When I heard that your husband had been killed, I felt for you with all my heart." Sally clasped Jocelyn's hands. "I remember how I feared for my dear Will during the battles. Did your father not relent even after you were widowed?"

Jocelyn gave a bitter, mirthless chuckle. "Oh, he made the magnanimous gesture of offering his wayward daughter a roof over her head, if that is what you mean."

"That's something at least," said Sally.

It galled Jocelyn to hear anyone defend her father. "I assure you, His Grace's motives were not admirable. He simply wanted to cloister me at Breckland so my activities would not cause further gossip. And to make certain I showed proper remorse for my *sins*."

Her hand clenched into a fist as tight and unyielding as her resentment. "I vowed I would starve before I'd accept his penance masquerading as pity."

"You were fortunate not to starve." Sally gave a mild shudder. "You must have had some money put by."

"Precious little. Some jewels I was obliged to sell. My

true good fortune was to fall in with Mrs. Beamish, bless her heart. I appealed to her seeking assistance for two young widows of Ned's junior officers. One thing led to another until I found myself aboard the *Hestia* sailing for Halifax."

"I only wish I'd known." Sally shook her head. "Surely you had other friends who would have been happy to assist you."

"Perhaps they would, but I am determined never again to be dependent on anyone else for my living. It gives others far too much power over one."

Sally did not look comfortable with that thought. "You're here now. That's what matters. Tell me, did you manage to bully a carriage out of Sir Robert?"

Had she *bullied* the governor? A few hours ago Jocelyn would have scoffed at the notion. Now she was not so sure. "Sir Robert has agreed to provide us with a carriage."

"You know," said Sally, "for all the man is no favorite of mine, I do not believe he meant to strand you out here with no means of getting into town."

"I expect you're right." Could Jocelyn feel more ashamed of her behavior? "It was probably an oversight."

"And who could blame him, poor fellow, with all the other preparations he had to make for your arrival?" Sally's gaze swept the room. "I must say, the crew he hired did a fine job in such a short time. Of course, Sir Robert would never tolerate a slipshod effort."

"Do you mean Governor Kerr had the house cleaned for us?"

Before Sally could answer, another voice drew Jocelyn's attention to the doorway.

"That's true, ma'am." The cook shuffled in with a tea tray. "Mr. Governor, he told me to round up a bunch of gals who could work hard for a good night's pay. We lit the fires and opened the windows to air the place out. Then we scrubbed and swept and dusted from suppertime till breakfast."

"You all did a fine job," said Sally. "This place had been closed ever since the last governor left for Quebec. I feared Mrs. Finch and the young ladies would find it in a sorry state."

Jocelyn remembered her own anxiety on that score…and her suspicion that Sir Robert might have offered them unsuitable accommodations out of spite or in hopes that they would leave Halifax in disgust.

Miz Ada set down the tea tray on a table in front of the settee. "Mr. Governor knows how to put in a good night's work, too. Him and that young Mr. Duckworth fetched us water and toted wood for the fires."

"Thank you, Ada." Jocelyn willed her hands not to tremble as she commenced to pour tea. It seemed she had only begun to plumb the depths of shame. "I fear I have misjudged Sir Robert very badly indeed."

Why had he gone to so much trouble on her account when he did not want the bride ship in his colony? And after she had done nothing but badger him and rally opposition against him?

"I must find a way to make it up to the poor man. But how?"

Two days of hard rain left the Windsor coach road in a sorry state, but on the third day the sun elected to give Halifax a tantalizing foretaste of summer. For some unaccountable reason, those golden rays streaming through Sir Robert's study window provoked a restless itch to be out in the fresh air.

Almost before he knew it, he found himself riding toward Prince's Lodge with an invitation card in his pocket. The rational part of him wanted to turn around and head back to Government House. But he'd had no word from Mrs. Finch since the day she'd stormed into his study demanding a carriage and a levee. Perhaps the bad weather had kept her from traveling. Still, he felt a responsibility to make certain all was well with her. He was the lady's host…in a manner of speaking.

By the side of the road, a plump robin in his jaunty red waistcoat grubbed a meal of worms from the wet ground. Other birds chirped and trilled from the branches of trees that were beginning to bud. Drops of moisture sparkled on the bright green shoots of undergrowth. The air had a pungent, fertile aroma of new growth rising up from the decay of the old, all faintly seasoned with the ever-present whiff of brine.

When Sir Robert urged his chestnut gelding to a brisk canter, its hooves sent tiny gobbets of mud flying, some of which spattered his boots. Just then, he did not care. After a dark, cold, colonial winter, a ride in the fresh country air and warm spring sunshine was exactly the tonic he needed. Indeed, he felt as if he'd taken a tonic—a bracing, potent one.

"Good morning, ma'am!" He doffed his hat to a woman beating a mat on the doorstep of the Rockingham Inn.

She gave him a suspicious look, but when he was a little way past her she called out, "Morning to you, too, sir!"

A short while later, Sir Robert spied the pale green dome of the prince's music pavilion through the surrounding trees. As he drew nearer, he noticed a number of young women walking around the building and peering in its many windows.

"I beg your pardon," he called. "Would Mrs. Finch happen to be down here with you?"

The lasses started at his question and flocked together. After a bit of nudging and whispering among them, a tall girl with very dark hair and brows answered. "No, sir. You'll find her up at the lodge."

Sir Robert thanked her for the information then turned his mount toward the open gate at the foot of the lane.

"Please, sir?"

He glanced back, brows raised.

"Are you the governor of Nova Scotia?"

Though he tended to be uncomfortable in the presence of

so many females, something about their wide stares made Sir Robert smile as he doffed his hat. "At your service, ladies."

Most of the party hid their faces and tittered. Perhaps they were unused to being addressed as *ladies.*

The dark-headed girl was not so easily ruffled as her friends. "Is it true you're going to host a ball for us at Government House, where we'll be presented...like debutantes?"

"That is correct." Sir Robert patted his vest pocket. "I have come bearing an invitation for all of you."

This news caused a great flutter among them.

"Good day, ladies."

He had almost reached the gate when one of them called out, "Are *you* married, sir?" That caused a riot of squeals and giggles to erupt around the pavilion.

Pretending not to hear, Sir Robert kept on riding. But a fierce blush rose from the top of his collar to warm his cheeks.

Fortunately, it had faded by the time he reached the house. All the same, it left him wary of approaching any of the groups of young women strolling the grounds. Some looked to be enjoying their leisure while others were clearly busy with chores.

Mrs. Finch was nowhere in sight, but Sir Robert noticed Miz Ada bustling around her kitchen. Climbing down from his horse, he tethered the beast, then strode toward the cook. She was one of the few women he could talk to without any awkwardness. Her forthright manner and vast capacity for hard work reminded him of his Scottish mother.

"A very good morning to you, Ada." He took off his hat and bowed to her as he would have to Mrs. Carmont or the bishop's wife. "How are you getting on out here? Ready to come back to Government House, yet? I expect it would feel like a holiday after cooking for such a crew."

"Morning, Mr. Governor." Ada wiped her hands on her

apron. "I'm content to bide here a spell longer. You know I hate being idle. I like to feed folks and these poor gals need feeding after being on that ship so long. I hardly need to wash the plates after a meal, they're picked so clean."

"I'm glad to hear it." Sir Robert noticed a pair of girls carrying wood. "And I'm pleased to see the young ladies are helping out. I'd thought I might need to hire some maids."

"No, sir," said Ada. "Mrs. Finch put them right to work. They all have their chores to do and most of 'em are real willing and respectful."

"How are you getting on with Mrs. Finch? Not finding her too overbearing, I hope?"

Ada thrust out her lower lip. "We get on just fine, sir. Oh, she says what she wants and expects to know why if she don't get it. But she's got to, or these gals would run wild."

"Indeed." His years as an army officer had taught Sir Robert the necessity of a firm hand and a decisive will when it came to maintaining order and discipline in the ranks.

He also knew that civilians often found military men too direct and domineering. Was it possible part of his annoyance with Mrs. Finch stemmed from their being too much alike in that respect? The notion gave him pause.

"Speaking of Mrs. Finch—" he still saw no sign of her "—would you happen to know where I might find her? There are some matters we need to discuss."

The cook pointed back toward a wooded area of the estate. "I told her to get herself out for a walk while the weather was fine. She was looking a little peaked. I thought some fresh air and quiet would do her good. You never heard the like of the noise in that house when all those gals get to chattering."

Sir Robert barely suppressed a shudder. Accustomed as he was to the dignified hush of Government House, the thought of forty women all talking at once horrified him. He did not envy Mrs. Finch her duty. Why had she undertaken it? he wondered. And why did she pursue it with such single-minded passion?

He bobbed a parting bow to the cook. "If you will excuse me, then, I must go in search of the elusive Mrs. Finch."

"Have a good walk, Mr. Governor." Ada waved him away, clearly eager to get back to work. "You could use a little sunshine, yourself."

Her tone of fond scolding warmed Sir Robert as he headed into the woodland behind the lodge. He hoped he would not have to wander its winding paths long to find Mrs. Finch. The work he'd left unfinished on his desk had begun to weigh on his mind.

He had not gone far when he rounded a bend to find himself almost on top of her. She sat on a rustic bench beneath a dainty arbor, its roof supported by trellises. It must be a pretty spot in the summer when wild woodbine or ivy twined up the open frame. For the moment, Sir Robert did not regret its bareness, which gave him a better view of its occupant as she stared off toward a small stand of fragrant cedar, lost in thought.

Jocelyn Finch was a beautiful woman, with her mass of rich, dark hair and her features which managed to appear both lush and delicate. Something more drew Sir Robert to her, quite against his will, as he had never found himself drawn to a woman before.

While he stood there, blatantly gaping in admiration, she suddenly turned his way and gave a violent start upon seeing him. He expected a forceful rebuke for intruding on her privacy without announcing himself.

She sprang from the bench and flew toward him, her greeting quite the opposite of anything he had expected. "Oh, Sir Robert, I am so glad you have come!"

He struggled to quell the ridiculous surge of elation her words provoked in him.

* * *

Jocelyn had been deep in thought about Sir Robert Kerr when she'd glanced up to find the man himself standing there watching her. An irrational spasm of worry gripped her that he could somehow read her mind.

When their eyes met, he seemed to steel himself to speak. Had she given the poor man reason to dread every encounter with her? The remorse that had stewed inside her for the past two endless days came suddenly to a boil. She could not let another moment pass without unburdening her conscience.

When she seized Sir Robert by the arm, his features tensed, as if he feared she meant to strike him.

"My dear sir." She drew him down to the bench where she had been sitting. "I must beg your pardon for my behavior when we last met. It was wrong of me to assume you had neglected to furnish us with a carriage on purpose. And I had no right in the world to demand that you host a ball for us. I cannot blame you if you think very ill of me."

The governor looked bewildered by her apology. "I…do not, I assure you."

He was only being civil, of course. She had overheard his true opinion of her. "I fear I have let my eagerness to succeed in my mission get the better of my good sense and my manners. It is a feeble excuse, I know, but it is the only one I have."

Suddenly aware that she still clutched his arm, Jocelyn let go abruptly, but with a vague sense of regret.

Sir Robert frowned. "Given my strenuous opposition to your presence in the colony, it is hardly surprising you felt the need to demand my cooperation and entertained doubts about my hospitality."

"Your hospitality!" Jocelyn cried. "I never even thanked you properly. I had no idea you'd put yourself to so much trouble to prepare this place for us. I must confess, I am at a loss to understand what prompted you. Why go to such lengths to insure our comfort, when you do not want us here?"

His brow furrowed, as if the question puzzled him, too. But when he replied, he sounded confident of his answer. "I did oppose your staying, and I still have doubts about the effect it will have on the colony. But I could not let those considerations make me neglect my duty as a host."

Duty. That loathsome word almost made Jocelyn grimace. Yet Sir Robert's use of it took her aback. She had always been made to think of duty as a burdensome debt she owed to her father and her family at the expense of her own happiness. Never as an obligation someone else might feel toward her.

"Your efforts went far beyond the call of duty, sir. I insist you let me reimburse you for any expenses you have incurred on our behalf. I have funds from Mrs. Beamish for our food and lodgings."

"Very well, I shall have Mr. Duckworth prepare an accounting for you."

That relieved Jocelyn's feeling of obligation, though not entirely. "I hope you will accept my apology for thinking ill of you. You have my word that from now on, no matter how strenuously you may oppose my plans, I will treat you with the respect you deserve."

He seemed to believe her. The tightness of his jaw relaxed and the anxious creases around his eyes eased. "Perhaps we have both been too hasty in judging one another, ma'am. Though we may not see eye to eye, it does not follow we must be enemies. Shall we declare the matter closed and agree to make a fresh start?"

Something about his earnest expression and his frank willingness to share the blame touched Jocelyn's heart. She shook his hand vigorously. "I should like nothing better!"

The instant she let go, Sir Robert rose from the bench. "Now we have that settled, shall we walk? I have something I wish to tell you...or rather...give you."

"Indeed?" Jocelyn scrambled up. "And what might that be?"

"This." Sir Robert pulled out a card, folded and secured with an official-looking wax seal. He handed it to her.

Jocelyn looked the card over with a degree of apprehension before tearing it open. A tiny bubble of laughter burst out of her when she read the message written in a flowing decorative script. "Our invitation to the levee, of course! How very kind of you to deliver it in person."

"Yes...well..." The governor shrugged off her praise. "I wanted to be certain you received it and to see for myself how you were getting on out here."

He took a few long strides, then slowed his pace when he noticed her struggling to keep up with him. Unlike the day they had walked to Government House, she did not ask to take his arm. Nor did he offer.

"We are managing very well." She tried not to sound too winded. "I never expected to be quartered in such luxury."

"I have long thought it a shame that such a pleasant little estate should sit deserted." With a sweep of his arm, Sir Robert indicated their scenic surroundings. "But it is far too large for my needs and too far removed from town to be convenient."

"And you have no French mistress to keep here." Jocelyn could not resist the quip. The governor's reserved, earnest manner fairly begged to be lightened with a little teasing.

She repented her glib jest when she saw how it flustered him. His face grew painfully red as he huffed, "I should think not!"

A pity, for the right kind of mistress might do him the world of good. Jocelyn managed to keep that scandalous opinion to herself. But the most amusing image popped into her mind, of Sir Robert Kerr en dishabille with a saucy little minx perched on his lap, kissing him into a frenzy of desire. Her whole body trembled and her eyes watered with the effort to contain an unseemly spasm of laughter.

"Is something the matter, Mrs. Finch? Are you unwell?"

His tone of sincere concern pushed Jocelyn over the edge. She exploded in fit of mirth so wild she could scarcely catch her breath.

"Pray what do you find so comical?" Sir Robert demanded.

"Forgive me!" Jocelyn gasped as she fanned her face with his invitation card and struggled to curb her laughter.

But it was like trying to stuff a cannonball back down the barrel of a gun once the fuse had fired. The governor's severity only added power to the blast.

"Should I leave you to recover your composure?" Sir Robert tried to mask his embarrassment with gruffness, but he did not quite succeed in fooling Jocelyn.

Remorse smothered her runaway laughter. What an ungrateful way to repay the poor man's awkward attempts at kindness and to atone for how she had treated him!

"Please don't go!" Jocelyn struggled to catch her breath. "Truly, I am sorry for making a fool of myself, just now. I don't know what came over me. You have my word I will endeavor to restrain myself."

He did not answer right away, but his bristling stiffness began to ease and his stern mouth quivered with the elusive hint of a smile. "Something tells me you do not take kindly to restraint. From yourself or anyone else."

So he was having a jest at her expense was he? Jocelyn did not begrudge him a little tit for tat. "I admit I have never been one to sit by meekly while others decide my fate and my happiness."

Something in his expression made her challenge him, "You do not approve?"

He shook his head. "It is not for me to dictate anyone's conduct but my own."

"But your feelings are always restrained by reason?" Jocelyn persisted. "And your actions ruled by… duty?"

What business did she have talking to him like this? They were strangers of only a few days' acquaintance and that short time had been marred by suspicion and hostility. Yet here they were, speculating about each other's fundamental characters. For her part, Jocelyn could not help it. She found herself curious about Sir Robert Kerr in a way she had not been about any man for a long time.

"My dear lady." Once again he looked guardedly amused. "You speak that word as if it were a profanity."

All her best intentions could not keep a waspish tone from Jocelyn's voice. "Perhaps it only seems that way to you because you regard duty as sacred."

Sir Robert did not appear to mind her sharp retort as much as he had her earlier laughter. "I believe you will find it an occupational hazard among soldiers, ma'am. And a good thing, too, in my opinion. If a charge is ordered, one cannot have half the men suddenly deciding their personal fate or happiness is more important than doing their duty."

Though her sides still ached from laughter, Jocelyn felt her throat tighten and a sob swell in her lungs. "Perhaps more of them should. For it is not only their own fate and happiness they surrender to the cruel demands of duty."

For the first time since his death, she allowed herself to feel a sharp stab of anger toward Ned.

"Forgive me." Sir Robert produced a handkerchief from one of his pockets and handed it to her. "I did not mean to distress you with painful memories. I have the most lamentable habit of saying the wrong thing."

Jocelyn remembered what she'd overheard him tell his aide. She sensed his frustration and impatience with himself.

"Do not fret for me." As she strove to regain her composure, she pressed Sir Robert's handkerchief to her upper lip and caught a subtle trace of his scent—clean, astringent and thoroughly masculine. She drew a deeper breath to savor it. "You raised a valid point, sir. If I were a man, I fear I would make a very poor soldier."

She had not even made a good soldier's wife. She'd resented the duty that had called Ned away from her too often, the last time never to return. Other military widows she knew had accepted their losses in a better spirit than she, taking pride in their husbands' sacrifices for King and country.

"It is impossible to imagine you as a man, my dear." Sir Robert sounded as if he were voicing a private thought. "But it is not difficult at all to picture you as a soldier. I suspect you would make a fine general."

"You mean that as praise, I suppose?" She gave him back his handkerchief. "The first part is quite flattering all on its own, but the latter part spoils the compliment entirely."

By this time the meandering path had brought them to the heart-shaped pond that lay in sight of the lodge. Sir Robert stooped and picked up a small stone, which he pitched into the water with considerable force, shattering the serenity of its surface. "I told you I always say the wrong thing."

"Tush." Jocelyn imitated one of her governesses. "Flummery and chitchat come easily to some people. Others need to learn and practice them, like any other skill. I expect you never bothered when you were a soldier because you didn't need them."

"Quite the contrary." Sir Robert tossed another stone into

the pond, causing more ripples in the water the way his blunt words might cause ripples of gossip in company. "Imagine what would happen if the enemy charged a line and the officer said to his men, 'My dear fellows, you're deuced crack shots. How about having a go at that lot?'"

Jocelyn sputtered with laughter. So the man did have a sense of humor under that gruff, dutiful crust! Might there also be a long-smothered ember of affability she could coax to blaze?

"Bravo, sir! Jest can make a point quite forcefully without giving offense. You should use it more often. Tact may be a liability to a soldier, but it is a vital advantage for a governor."

When he grimaced, she added, "Whether you like it or not."

"You may be right about the necessity," Sir Robert grumbled. "But I am not convinced it is a skill that can be learned."

Ah! Here was the opportunity she had been looking for to make amends to Sir Robert. True, he had accepted her apology, borne some of the blame and declared the matter closed. But that did not lessen her sense of obligation.

She fixed him with a smile that she defied him to resist. "Would you permit me to tutor you in the social graces?"

Chapter Seven

Instruct *him* how to be tactful and charming? As he prepared for the levee, Sir Robert grimaced at himself in the looking glass. Jocelyn Finch might as well instruct a tiger how to hide its stripes! He was what he was—diligent and dutiful, not affable and outgoing. To pretend otherwise, even if he were able, would feel deceitful somehow.

But he had learned better than to deny the redoubtable Mrs. Finch anything on which she had set her mind. If he indulged her in this whim, it might keep her from undertaking anything more troublesome. Besides, some tiny, foolish part of him had enjoyed her initial efforts.

It had felt strange, the other day at Prince's Lodge, being with her in such a romantic spot—strange in a rather pleasant way. Despite his doubts, he had exerted himself to absorb her instruction. Tonight he would endeavor to put it to use.

Hurried footsteps approached the door to his private quarters, followed by an anxious-sounding knock.

"Come in, Duckworth!" he called.

The door swung open and his aide entered.

"Is everything in order down below?" the governor asked. "Musicians all in tune? Plenty of punch?"

Duckworth began to nod even before Sir Robert had finished his questions. "All is ready, sir. Most of your guests have arrived."

"Mrs. Finch and her young ladies?"

"Not yet, sir."

"But Admiral Porter did send his sloop for them?"

"So I understand, sir."

What made him so anxious for their arrival?

"It wouldn't be much of a ball without our guests of honor would it?" Though he addressed the question to his aide, Sir Robert hoped he had found the answer he was looking for.

He adjusted the sash bearing his modest array of medals then assumed his best parade-ground posture. "Will I pass muster, do you think? Suitably viceregal?"

"You look splendid, sir." Duckworth gave an approving nod. "I just came to make certain you were ready. I'll return to fetch you once *all* the guests have arrived."

"Very good," said Sir Robert, though it was quite the opposite of how he felt.

He detested viceregal protocol, which dictated he must always be the last to arrive at any event, so as to make a grand entrance. Until his appointment to this post, it had been his habit to slip into any social gathering with as little notice as possible. Being the center of attention made him painfully self-conscious and irritable. Which made it all the more likely he would say or do something to give offense to whomever he met.

His stomach clenched and his palms grew moist just thinking about it. A decanter of port in his private sitting room tempted him with its innocent promise to soothe his nerves. But he dared not imbibe. The last thing he needed was for a guest to smell spirits on his breath at the outset of an official function.

Sir Robert selected a copy of Smollett's *The Life and Adventures of Sir Launcelot Greaves* from the bookshelf beside the door, but put it back again when he found himself rereading the same sentence for the fifth time. With no other distraction available, he fell to pacing his sitting room. From a little way up the hill, he heard the bell of Saint Peter's toll eight. Surely all his guests would be assembled soon, even the habitual stragglers like Chief Justice Sherwood.

The final reverberations of the church bell had just faded when another noise from outside caught Sir Robert's attention. It sounded like a large flock of birds, chirping, squawking and flapping their wings at one another.

He strode to the window and drew back the curtain to peer out onto the front driveway. It was chocked with carriages—every fine rig in town and several from the country estates beyond. Coachmen and a few footmen had collected in small knots, to pass the time. Small clouds of smoke rose from their pipes into the air above them.

They all turned toward the source of the sound that had lured Sir Robert to the window. Up the driveway, in orderly ranks that would have done credit to a military parade, marched the young ladies from the bride ship in their modest finery. Sir Robert's gaze came to rest upon their chaperone, bringing up the rear.

When he caught sight of her, the tightness in his chest eased a little and one corner of his mouth arched upward. It must have taken a great effort to get so large a party all dressed, groomed and loaded aboard the admiral's sloop to bring them here. He hoped this evening would provide the young ladies with a more auspicious welcome to the colony than they had received from him a week ago.

Determined to make amends for that scandalous gaffe, he took several slow, deep breaths and vowed to do everything in his power to make the evening a success. After all, it couldn't be *that* much worse than charging into battle. Could it?

He was about to step back and close the curtain when Mrs. Finch glanced up. A wide, luminous smile set her whole face aglow. Sir Robert's pulse, which had begun to slow from the rapid throb of alarm, suddenly picked up speed again. But this time it felt invigorating.

Mrs. Finch lifted one gloved hand. For an instant Sir Robert thought she meant to wave. Instead she lofted a jaunty salute his way. The gesture made him chuckle. Until she disappeared from sight, he could not take his eyes off her.

As a small but skilled group of musicians from the regimental band struck up the strains of "God Save the King," Jocelyn watched Sir Robert Kerr stride the vast length of the Government House ballroom. When he reached the bowed end of the room, he mounted a low dais and executed a crisp turn. She could not help but admire his dignified bearing.

"I declare," whispered Sally Carmont, who had edged her way through the crowd to Jocelyn's side. "The man's expression would sour milk. It is clear he is hosting this ball against his will and begrudges us every minute of it."

"Nonsense." Jocelyn raised her fan to screen her lower face. "This is a solemn occasion and he is representing the King, after all. Would you rather he grinned like a monkey?"

Though she would not admit it to her friend, Jocelyn wished the governor could look a trifle less severe. She knew it was only a bluff to hide his lack of confidence, but other guests might take it as Sally had.

"I will say one thing for Sir Robert." Sally gave a soft, rustling chuckle. "At least he looks more interested in the proceedings than His Majesty did when we were presented at court. Do you remember?"

Jocelyn gave a nod then touched her forefinger to her lips. The first of the young ladies from Halifax was about to be presented. She was attired grandly enough for the court in London, as were most of the other local ladies—all silk and plumes. It made Jocelyn acutely conscious of her charges and their pretty but simple gowns. She hoped they would not be too intimidated by this grand occasion. Back home in England none of them could ever have dreamed of being presented at court.

When the chief justice's daughter performed her well-rehearsed curtsy to the governor, a faint spasm of worry gripped Jocelyn. Would Sir Robert remember her coaching and put it to good use? Or would he let his nerves get the better of him and say the worst possible thing? Remembering the way he had greeted the bride ship, she knew that was no exaggeration.

She strained to hear what he would say. Around her, she sensed others doing the same.

The governor bowed to Miss Sherwood and spoke a few words to her. It was all very conventional—one of the remarks he had practiced with Jocelyn. She doubted anyone else in the crowd would guess, though, for his resonant voice rang with sincerity, perhaps even a touch of warmth.

A sense of triumph lifted Jocelyn's spirits. It was nothing like the spiteful satisfaction she'd taken in beating Sir Robert at chess, but a soft glow of fulfilment. Savoring the approving buzz that rippled through the crowd, she shared in the governor's obvious relief over his first hurdle successfully cleared.

When he searched the sea of faces and locked on hers, she smiled and nodded her approval.

"Oh, no!" whispered Sally as a lanky, nervous-looking girl approached the dais to be presented. "It's the bishop's daughter. I vow she must be the clumsiest creature in Halifax, if not the whole colony."

The way Miss Foster wobbled her curtsy, she appeared in grave danger of toppling sideways to land in a tearful heap at the governor's feet. Fortunately, Sir Robert had not lost his soldier's quick reflexes. Instead of the customary bow, he lunged forward and caught the young lady by the hand, steadying her until she regained her balance. When he raised her gloved fingers to his lips and murmured what appeared to be words of reassurance, Jocelyn nearly burst into applause.

Having averted a minor disaster with his quick thinking seemed to bolster Sir Robert's confidence further. He appeared more and more assured as the presentations continued. Jocelyn ceased to worry on his account, fretting instead about how her charges would conduct themselves. The last thing she needed was for Vita to make some brazen remark or Sophia to dissolve in a fit of giggles before the governor.

Fortunately her fears proved groundless. The formality of the occasion seemed to subdue the girls' high spirits and even quench the worst of Vita's perpetual impudence. The governor helped, too, making a special effort to relieve their jitters and bid them a sincere welcome.

"That came off far better than I expected." Sally echoed Jocelyn's very thought when the last of the girls had been presented. She sounded vaguely disappointed there had been no mishaps for her to gossip about in the coming days.

Mr. Duckworth gave a signal and the music swelled once again, this time an old dancing tune called "Shepherd's Holiday." Jocelyn was pleased to see Colonel Carmont's officers and the young gentlemen of Halifax rushing to invite her charges to take the floor.

"My dear." Sally tapped Jocelyn's arm with her fan.

"What is it?" She turned toward her friend. "Oh!"

There stood the governor, regarding her with a hopeful look. "Mrs. Finch, if you are not otherwise engaged, will you grant me the honor of the first dance?"

Jocelyn hesitated for a moment. She'd had neither the occasion nor desire to dance since Ned's death, though it had once been among her favorite pastimes. It dismayed her a little to find herself so eager to accept the governor's invitation.

She swept him an elegant curtsy. "The honor will be mine, Your Excellency."

Why should a perfectly innocent dance make her feel disloyal to her husband's memory? She had danced with plenty of other men when Ned was alive and he'd never seemed to mind. Besides, she still did not feel she'd atoned sufficiently for the way she had treated Sir Robert. She was determined to put him at ease and help him enjoy the evening.

As they took their places as head couple of a long line of dancers, she murmured just loud enough for him to hear, "You did very well indeed. Mrs. Carmont and I both thought it was much better than our own presentation at court."

The dance began with an exchange of bows and curtsies, then each pair of partners turned side-on to one another, clasped hands and took three steps forward.

"I was only parroting what you told me to say." Sir Robert dismissed her praise, but Jocelyn could tell it pleased him more than he would admit.

"Parroted? Nonsense!" she insisted as they took three steps back and exchanged places. "You selected a proper acknowledgment for each young lady. And you delivered each with perfect sincerity. I congratulate you upon your performance."

"I fear none of this will ever come naturally to me." Sir

Robert's glance flickered to the gentleman beside him for a cue to the next figure. "Any more than dancing does."

"What you lack in natural aptitude, you are quick to pick up with study and practice," said Jocelyn, as she and Sir Robert slipped down between the second couple. "I reckon that is more admirable than some fortunate accident of nature."

The words had scarcely left her lips when she experienced another pang of disloyalty to her late husband. For Ned had been one of those fortunate mortals possessed of natural grace and charm. The effortless ease with which he'd done so many things was part of what had drawn her to him. Having to work for a living had since taught Jocelyn the value of effort.

"I think you give me too much credit, ma'am." With a very uncertain look, he led the three gentlemen of their set to circle to the left while Jocelyn led the ladies circling to the right.

After a rather complicated shuffling of couples, they returned to their original places.

"I apologize in advance," said Sir Robert, "in case I should tread on your toes." They stepped toward each other, circled and stepped back to exchange places.

Jocelyn did not let her gaze waver from Sir Robert's. "I have trod on your toes more than once since my arrival in Halifax, sir. You have shown me uncommon forbearance. Toes are apt to recover from a minor assault more readily than pride."

The two long rows of ladies and gentlemen took hands and moved two steps back then two forward. After that each set of three couples joined hands to dance in a circle.

Sir Robert never did injure Jocelyn's toes, nor those of the other ladies in their set. As the dance progressed, he seemed to grow more confident, moving with stately, meticulous grace that suited the music very well.

Jocelyn abandoned any further efforts at conversation, giving herself instead to the enjoyment of the dance. The music seemed to frolic through her veins as her limbs remembered the familiar movements. Something inside her that had long lain frozen began to stir. At length the dance concluded with a final exchange of bows and curtsies. Jocelyn would have been content for it to go on all evening.

To cool her flushed cheeks, she raised and opened the fan that had dangled from her wrist during the dance. Then, seeing Sir Robert also looked a trifle flushed, she waved it in front of his face for a moment. "There, now. That was not so bad, was it? I thought you acquitted yourself quite—"

"Adequately?" The silvery twinkle in his eyes set Jocelyn's insides fluttering like her fan.

"Quite *admirably* I was going to say," Jocelyn teased, as they drifted to the edge of the ballroom. "My but you have trouble accepting a compliment."

"I do not get much practice." This time she sensed he was not in jest.

"I must endeavor to correct that during my stay in your fine colony." A week ago Jocelyn would have vowed there was nothing to recommend the man…except perhaps his looks. Now she wondered if he might not possess many more admirable qualities than she had ever suspected.

"Do not trouble yourself on my account, ma'am." Sir Robert did not look in the least eager to become the object of her flattery. He wasted neither time nor subtlety in changing the subject. "May I fetch you a cup of punch?"

"I would be much obliged to you, sir." Closing her fan, she gestured with it toward an empty Turkish sofa beside the white marble hearth. "I shall take a seat and await your return."

Sir Robert headed off to fetch the punch just as the musicians began to play a lively air that had long been one of Jocelyn's favorites. Humming the tune and taking mincing little steps in time to it, she made her way to the Turkish sofa and lowered herself onto its brocade upholstered seat. She was gratified to see so many of her charges dancing and conversing with the gentlemen of Halifax.

Soft, rosy candlelight reflected off the tiers of crystals that graced three handsome lusters hung from the ceiling. The rich olive wallpaper and draperies made a handsome background to the bright colors of the ladies' gowns and officers' scarlet dress tunics. A melodious blend of music, laughter and conversation filled the air. Through the soles of her slippers, Jocelyn could feel a faint vibration in the floor as so many feet rose and fell together following the rhythm of the dance. Even Sir Robert must sense an aura of magic at work that evening!

A bit of that magic shattered for Jocelyn when, without warning, Barnabas Power strode out of the crowd and dropped heavily onto the sofa beside her. "Good evening, Mrs. Finch."

"Why, Mr. Power." She edged away from him as far as the width of the sofa would permit. The merchant's forceful presence overwhelmed her. "What a...pleasant surprise. Are you enjoying the ball?"

"I am now." He smiled at her with blatant admiration. "All these pretty debutantes are well and good for the young cubs, but a beautiful, unattached *woman* is a rare commodity. Will you do me the honor of this dance?"

What made her hesitate? It was one of her favorites. "It has already begun."

"But there is plenty of music left." Mr. Power rose and held out his hand to her.

A man of his wealth and influence could prove very useful in furthering her mission. Yet Jocelyn could not overcome her reluctance. "I danced the last, you know, and I was rather looking forward to—"

"Don't tell me you are too delicate to undertake two dances

in a row." Unwilling to accept her excuses, the merchant seized her hand and hoisted her to her feet.

"But the governor—"

"Hang, the governor!" Mr. Power drew her toward the other dancers. "I'll wager a crown this ball was your idea, not his."

Jocelyn recalled something she had overheard Sir Robert tell his aide, about knowing when surrender was one's only option. Now she was getting a taste of how he must have felt when she browbeat him into hosting this levee. She joined the dance at Mr. Power's insistence, but her heart was not in it.

"I did suggest to His Excellency—"

"I knew it!" The scorn in Mr. Power's hearty laugh grated on Jocelyn's nerves. "You owe me a crown, but I shall claim another dance in lieu of it."

Not if she had to sell everything she owned to pay a wager she had not even accepted! At that moment Jocelyn was more concerned with defending the governor. "Sir Robert was quick to endorse my idea."

"*That* I do not believe." Mr. Power made a sweeping gesture around the grand ballroom. "I know to the last shilling what this place cost to build and furnish. Hate to see it not earning its keep."

No question, the merchant was a far more confident dancer than Sir Robert. He spoke more, smiled more and laughed more. For all that, Jocelyn found him a much less congenial partner. None of his frequent smiles brought a merry sparkle to his eyes, which were hard and gray as the ironstone walls of his warehouse. She sensed a coldness in them, as if he were calculating her worth to the last shilling. When he took her hand or brushed against her in the course of the dance, a clammy chill of aversion slithered through her.

Every interminable moment in his company raised her opinion of Sir Robert Kerr. Better a frosty manner masking an amiable heart than the other way around. The better acquainted she became with Mr. Power, the less she liked him.

The merchant's forceful voice intruded upon Jocelyn's thoughts. "I told Kerr the right wife could be of use to him. She could manage all the social doings and leave him to his canal schemes and land patents."

"I wonder if one of my charges might do for him?" Somehow, the words left an unpleasant taste in Jocelyn's mouth. Having a bride-ship girl as the governor's lady would insure the future of the program in Nova Scotia. And yet…

"You must be joking," Mr. Power made no effort to disguised his contempt. "One of these raw chits, mistress of Government House?"

Jocelyn struggled to hide her mounting vexation. It would not do to provoke a man of Mr. Power's wealth and influence. "I assure you I am perfectly in earnest. Some of the girls come from very respectable families and have received a superior—"

Mr. Power interrupted her. "What about you, my dear? Given any thought to marrying again?"

Was he thinking of *her* as a prospective wife for the governor? Jocelyn found herself blushing.

"Why you cannot be above six-and-twenty," Mr. Power continued. The hint of a leer in his smile told Jocelyn it was not Sir Robert he had in mind for her. "Plenty of good breeding years left, eh?"

The indelicacy of his questions stunned her speechless, which was probably a blessing, or who knew what she might have said to the odious man?

Fortunately her sense of discretion had asserted itself by the time she found her voice. "I was most fortunate in my first marriage, sir. It was a true love match and a very happy one.

Since I could never be satisfied with anything less, I have no interest in taking another husband."

Mr. Power did not appear daunted by her assertion. "If a man had enough to offer, he might change your mind, my dear."

She was not his *dear,* nor would she be, for every penny of his fortune! But how could she rid herself of him without making an enemy she could ill afford? His vulgar reference to her breeding years gave Jocelyn a clue.

In the upsurge of conversation following the dance she lowered her voice and met his granite gaze with one of flint. "Even if I were inclined to wed, Mr. Power, my childless first marriage might make most gentlemen think twice before offering *anything* for my hand."

The dazed look on his face went a little way toward easing the familiar ache of regret in Jocelyn's heart.

Sir Robert's heart sank a little when he returned with two cups of punch only to find the sofa beside the hearth empty. That was ridiculous, of course. A few days ago, he'd have given anything never to set eyes on Jocelyn Finch again. When and how had he come to feel at ease in her company as he did with few other women?

Perhaps it was because she had seen him at his worst yet still appeared willing to give him another chance. Or perhaps having seen a less pleasant side of her character, he knew she was as fallible as he, not some flawless paragon. Whatever the reason, he'd enjoyed their dance tonight and had been looking forward to a little more of her company.

He'd hoped Mrs. Finch might feel the same, but now he was not so sure. Had she sent him off to fetch punch so she could slip away in search of more congenial company?

Sir Robert turned and scanned the crowded ballroom. It surprised him how quickly he picked her out of the throng.

He told himself it was her rich claret-colored gown that had drawn his eye.

For a moment he was too busy admiring the sprightly grace of her dancing to take any notice of her partner. Then he recognized Barnabas Power. His fingers tightened around the handles of the cups he'd forgotten he was holding. The well-honed edge of some potent emotion stabbed him, but he was not certain what it could be. Indignation, he decided after a moment's thought.

He recalled with perfect clarity what Power had said about his interest in Jocelyn Finch as a prospective wife. But the man was too old for a vibrant woman in her prime, and far too mercenary for a woman who had abandoned fortune and position in pursuit of love.

When the dance concluded, Sir Robert found himself striding toward Mr. Power and Mrs. Finch, keeping a tight grip on the punch cups so as not to spill any on his guests. Prudence warned him he should not interfere with the most influential man in the colony, but for once in his life, he paid it no heed.

"Mrs. Finch?"

She started at the sound of his voice and spun about.

He handed her a cup of punch. "I apologize for taking so long to fetch the drink you requested. No doubt some refreshment will be even more welcome after a second dance."

"Your Excellency!" Her splendid eyes seemed to light up at the sight of him. "How kind of you to seek me out. It was not my intention to abandon you—"

Before she could finish, Barnabas Power snatched the remaining cup of punch from Sir Robert's other hand. "Thank you, sir. Most hospitable of you. Now if you will excuse us..."

He pointed toward the bowed alcove at the far end of the ballroom and addressed himself to Mrs. Finch. "It looks less crowded over there. Shall we find a spot to rest and partake of our drinks?"

Sir Robert clenched his mouth shut and prepared to make a dignified retreat. He did not dare spit out any of the words that crowded on the tip of his tongue.

But Jocelyn Finch caught him by the arm with surprising strength for her size. "Later, perhaps, Mr. Power. There is an urgent matter which I must discuss with Sir Robert."

"Can it not wait?"

"No, I'm afraid it cannot."

Sir Robert nodded as if he knew what she was talking about.

Barnabas Power looked from the lady to the governor. "I hope you will be able to resolve the matter to your satisfaction." His tone sounded doubtful.

Mrs. Finch took a sip of her punch. "I'm certain we shall. Sir Robert has proven himself most accommodating."

Power retreated after a barely civil bow. "Later, then."

Mrs. Finch raised her cup to him then drew Sir Robert toward the bay end of the ballroom.

"So what is this urgent matter we must discuss?"

"Shh! Not so loud, if you please." She lowered her voice until he was obliged to bend very close to hear her. "The only urgent matter is my need for you to keep me from falling into the clutches of that obnoxious man again."

Had he heard properly? Sir Robert's heart felt as if it were beating to the jaunty rhythm of the dance music.

Mrs. Finch looked up suddenly. Her bewitching gaze captured him. "If I have to suffer another five minutes in his company, I may say something that will land me in a great deal of trouble."

He would not put it past her. "Worse than challenging me to a duel?"

"Much worse."

"We cannot have that, can we?"

She shook her head slowly. "I believe it is your duty as our host to prevent it."

By spending the rest of the evening in her company? Never before had his duty promised such great pleasure!

Chapter Eight

The evening after the governor's levee, Jocelyn stole away to a quiet corner of the sitting room at Prince's Lodge with the small rosewood writing box she had brought from England.

Of the finest craftsmanship, it was just large enough to hold a supply of paper and her writing implements—quills, ink, blotting sand and a tiny knife for trimming pen nibs. In the absence of a table, she could even rest her paper on the gently slanted cover to write. It was one of her last possessions of any value she had not sold after Ned's death.

Now she drew out a sheet of paper and prepared to draft her first report to Mrs. Beamish. The captain of the *Hestia* had paid a call that morning to inform her he had secured a cargo for the return voyage and expected to sail two days hence. If she had any messages she wished to send back to England, he would be pleased to deliver them for her.

She had intended to start her report earlier, but the girls were so keyed up after being presented at Government House and dancing the evening away with the young officers and merchants of Halifax, she had been obliged to supervise them more closely than usual. Vita Sykes alone had been more than a handful. Her striking looks and forward manner had made her rather too great a favorite among the gentlemen at the levee.

Once too often since then, she'd gloated to the other girls of how she had not sat out a single dance. She'd boasted she would be the first and best wed of them all—she would choose the richest and handsomest of her suitors, then the others could console themselves with inferior brides.

Jocelyn had been obliged to intervene in the ensuing scuffle. As punishment, she'd assigned Vita to the scullery giving the others duties that would keep them as far from her as possible. Vita had complained bitterly of the unfairness of it, but Jocelyn had turned a deaf ear. No doubt the men of Halifax wanted Vita, but not as a wife. If she was not careful, the little minx might land herself in some scandalous scrape that would bring the whole bride-ship scheme into disrepute.

Forcing thoughts of Vita from her mind, Jocelyn trimmed the nib of her pen, then uncorked her bottle of ink. She marshaled her thoughts and began to write of their long, difficult Atlantic crossing.

We did not arrive in Halifax until the first week of May, but we thanked the Almighty that we had been spared to reach our destination at all. I fear our letter of introduction met a worse fate and never arrived. There was some…

Jocelyn paused, pen poised over the paper, trying to work out how she would phrase the next part of her report. After a moment's consideration, she began to write again, her lips pursed in a devious little grin.

There was some small difficulty, at first, about our arrangements, since our arrival had not been anticipated. We were most fortunate in the kind hospitality of His Excellency the governor, who placed at our disposal a very pretty little estate just outside town.

In this spirit of well-intentioned duplicity, Jocelyn went on to tell how Sir Robert had hosted a levee for the girls to make their debut in Halifax society.

Colonel Carmont, the commander of the garrison, and his wife will be hosting another ball for us next week. The chief justice has promised us a garden party as soon as the flowers bloom. And Mr. Power, a merchant of great consequence, says he will host a picnic this summer for us on his island in the harbor. At the rate events are progressing, I fear there may not be many of my charges still eligible for matrimony by then.

Her lips puckered in a grimace of distaste when she thought of Mr. Power. He was very obliging, and he had proven a valuable ally in her early disagreement with Sir Robert. Yet there was something about his manner that made her uneasy in his presence as she had never been with the governor, even at the height of their hostilities.

I hope you will make favorable mention of His Excellency to any friends you may have in the Colonial Office. I have found him a most diligent servant of the Crown and of his colonists.

That part was scrupulously true, Jocelyn told herself. A commendation to Sir Robert's superiors in London should relieve her conscience of any lingering remorse for the way she had browbeat him. No doubt it would mean more to him than her efforts to put him at ease last night.

She was tolerably certain she'd succeeded. As the evening wore on, Sir Robert had seen for himself how well the leading citizens of the town approved of the levee. That had helped him relax, as had her observation that his guests were too much absorbed in their own merry-making to take much notice of him. Provided he did not take it into his head to swing naked from the lusters—some imp of mischief compelled her to add.

He'd sputtered and blushed almost as red as his splendid uniform, but for the rest of the evening his behavior had been livelier and more convivial. Perhaps he was convinced at last that the bride ship could be a boon to his colony, not the trouble he'd predicted.

Trouble? Jocelyn lifted her pen from the paper so her silent laughter would not make her hand shake and spoil her writing. What manner of trouble did Sir Robert reckon a shipload of marriageable girls could make for his colony? Once she had mastered her amusement, Jocelyn returned to her report. She had scarcely written another sentence when she heard hurried footsteps approaching.

Lily Winslow appeared at the door looking very agitated. "Mrs. Finch, you must come! One of the soldiers said you must."

With an exasperated growl, Jocelyn rose from her chair. "What has Vita done now? I vow, that girl is the most—"

"It isn't Vita." Lily caught Jocelyn by the hand, fairly dragging her out of the sitting room.

In the entry hall, a number of the girls were clustered around one of the young soldiers Colonel Carmont had sent to guard the lodge. Some of them were wide-eyed and pale, clinging to their friends. Others were exchanging urgent whispers.

But with what cause? Prince's Lodge was the most peaceful place.

Jocelyn shook off Lily's hand. "You wished to speak with me, Corporal? Is there some difficulty?"

"Yes, ma'am, there is. Leastways there could be. I spied a crowd gathering down at the foot of the lane, so I barred the gate and told them to be on their way."

"Crowd?" Out here? Jocelyn could scarcely imagine it. "What sort of crowd?"

"Men, ma'am. Not gentlemen. Some farmers, by the look of them. Fishermen. Woodsmen. Laborers. That sort."

"I see. And what did they do when you asked them to leave?"

The young soldier clutched his musket tighter. "They... laughed at me, ma'am."

A whisper of fear made the fine hairs on Jocelyn's nape rise but she strove to appear unruffled. "And where is your partner, pray? Down keeping an eye on the gate?"

The corporal shook his head vigorously. "No, ma'am. I can't find him nowhere. You don't reckon *they* got him, do you?"

Louisa gave an anxious whimper.

"The men at the gate, you mean?" Jocelyn fixed the young soldier with a dubious look. "They have proven themselves impolite, but nothing worse. I'm sure your partner is somewhere about. Girls, look around the house for him."

When no one moved to obey, she raked them with a forceful glare. "Now, if you please!"

After a swiftly murmured consultation, they split up in groups of two or three and headed off in different directions.

Jocelyn turned to Lily. "Go outside and summon the rest of the girls in. None of them were down by the shore, were they?"

The little music pavilion was a favorite destination for groups of the girls to take short strolls.

Lily shook her head. "I don't think so, ma'am. Not at this time of day."

That thought relieved Jocelyn's mind…a little. "Once our second sentry has been found, tell everyone they are to go to their rooms and wait there. That way we can count heads and make certain everyone is accounted for."

"Good idea, ma'am." Lily hurried off.

It was a sensible precaution, Jocelyn assured herself, nothing more. There was probably no cause for alarm. Perhaps the men down on the road had just happened to gather there on their way someplace else.

The young soldier cleared his throat. "What should I do, ma'am?"

He looked fearful she might order him back to hold the gate single-handedly against an invasion. Jocelyn wondered if he had ever seen military action. Probably not, she decided. The boy didn't look as if his cheeks had yet felt the scrape of a razor.

She beckoned him toward the stairs. "Let's go have a look from the attic dormer. Perhaps the men have gone already. They may not have meant any harm. Even if they did, they might have reckoned you left to fetch reinforcements and run off."

"I hope so, ma'am." The lad sounded far from convinced as he mounted the stairs behind her.

A few moments later, they looked out the huge window that protruded from the roof of the lodge. For an instant, Jocelyn was struck by the splendid view. She had never seen the sunset from this window before. The evening sky glowed in vivid hues of orange, red and gold, all reflected in the tranquil waters of Bedford Basin. What a pity that tranquility did not extend to the Windsor coach road!

Even in the fading light, Jocelyn could easily pick out the dark figures of a rather large crowd—she would not permit herself to think of them as a *mob.*

"They're still there, ma'am," the young soldier pointed out, as if she might not have noticed. "I reckon there's more of 'em, now, than there was before."

Suddenly aware of her racing pulse, Jocelyn told herself it must be on account of having climbed two flights of stairs so quickly. "It is a public road. As long as they stay outside the gate, those men have done no harm by gathering. And they can do us no harm. If we ignore them, I expect they will all go home once darkness falls."

As if to mock her fragile hopes, a few lights kindled down on the road, then flared and flickered. While Jocelyn watched in dread, the lights began to move, bobbing through the gate and up the winding carriage driveway toward the house.

"Corporal, you must go for help." Jocelyn fled for the stairs, issuing orders as she went. "Duck out the back, then take the path through the woods heading east. That will lead you to the edge of Hemlock Ravine. Follow it down to the road and you will come out not far from the inn. Our coachman is probably there at this very moment enjoying his evening pint. Get a horse from the inn and ride to town with all haste. Explain to Colonel Carmont what has happened and tell him to send out a party of mounted men."

"Yes, ma'am." The boy sounded relieved at being ordered away. "I'll be right quick, ma'am. I promise."

"Do be careful around the ravine," Jocelyn warned him. "I would rather you reach town a few minutes later than not at all."

With luck the lad would have enough light to make his way safely to the inn. Jocelyn whispered a little prayer under her breath as she watched him go. But how long would it take him to get there, then ride five miles to Fort George? Once he'd delivered her message, how long would it take Colonel Carmont's men to reach Prince's Lodge?

Long enough for a great deal to happen—and none of it

good. Jocelyn had witnessed some of the civil unrest besetting England in the wake of war. Though her situation had made her sympathetic to the plight of the rioters, the explosive violence of their protests had shaken her. It was one of the things she'd been glad to escape by coming to the colonies. Now it appeared she might not have escaped it after all.

She was about to pull the back door of the lodge shut when a trio of girls scampered in. "Whatever is the trouble, Mrs. Finch? Lily said we must all go to our rooms at once. Bossy old thing!"

"I don't have time to explain, now." Jocelyn pointed toward the stairs. "Just do as you were told and don't dally about it!"

"Yes, ma'am!" The three bolted past her.

Lily arrived not long behind them, her pale cheeks flushed and her chest heaving as she gasped for breath, "That's everyone…I could find…outside, ma'am."

"Any sign of the other guard?"

Lily shook her head.

"Did you check the outhouse?"

The girl's flushed face reddened further, but she gave an emphatic nod.

Jocelyn muttered an oath that would have shocked Lily's late father. "We must bar the doors and windows."

It would provide no protection for this wooden house against those flaming torches, but Jocelyn could not bear to dwell on that thought, let alone put it into words. "Go make certain all the girls are in the house. Miz Ada, too. Then send me half a dozen of the strongest and calmest to help shift furniture."

By the time Jocelyn finished speaking, Lily had caught her breath. She dashed away. A while later, several of the girls appeared, looking frightened but not overwrought.

"Heavy pieces in front of the doors," ordered Jocelyn as

she tried to drag the settee out into the entry hall. "Anything tall and solid to bar those big bay windows. Wardrobes or the sideboard. Upend the dining table if you have to."

Hearing the rumble of approaching voices and the tread of feet, she cried, "Hurry!"

The girls scattered like a flock of pigeons set upon by a tomcat. Soon the ominous noises from outside the house were drowned out by the heavy scrape of furniture across the wooden floors of the lodge.

Jocelyn and a hardy Dorset lass named Mary Ann had just finished barricading the sitting-room window when Lily appeared again, looking more agitated than ever. "All the girls are accounted for except Hetty, ma'am. And there's no sign at all of the other guard—I checked everywhere. Eliza Turner claims she saw him and Hetty go off together just after supper."

"Why didn't she say something sooner, the little fool?"

Lily shrugged. "She didn't want to land Hetty on scullery duty with Vita, I expect."

Jocelyn's fists clenched. When she got her hands on Miss Hetty, the little minx would count herself *lucky* to be scrubbing pots in the scullery. Why, she'd be emptying chamber pots from now until autumn!

"At least I needn't worry about her," Jocelyn muttered. "Wherever she is, she's probably a good deal safer than we are."

She peered through a chink in the barricade of furniture piled in front of the sitting-room window. Their *callers* had reached the house at last. The men ranged about the lawn, talking together in smaller groups. It appeared they needed to work up their nerve for every step they advanced. Jocelyn welcomed any delay.

But the size of the crowd dismayed her. It was becoming more and more difficult to keep from thinking of it as a mob.

If those men decided to storm the house, a few piles of furniture would scarcely slow them down.

She turned to Lily again. "Move all the girls up to the attic. Then take your helpers and barricade the top of both staircases behind you. Do you understand?"

Lily gave a jerky nod, like a marionette in the hands of an unskilled puppeteer. "Anything else, ma'am?"

"Once the heads of both stairways are barred, I want you to collect everything you can find that is small enough to throw, but heavy enough to hurt if it hit someone on the head."

"D-do you think that will be necessary, ma'am?"

Jocelyn reached for the girl's hand and gave it a reassuring squeeze. "I pray it will not, but we must be prepared. I know if the worst happens, I can rely on you to what must be done. We need only stall for time. I sent the corporal to fetch help from town. I expect he is riding to Halifax at this very moment."

Why had she let him take his musket away with him? Jocelyn cursed herself. He could have traveled more quickly without it, and the tenants of Prince's Lodge needed the weapon far more than he did. She thrust the thought from her mind as quickly as it had come. There would be plenty of time to indulge in self-blame later. At least she hoped there would.

"You *can* rely on me, ma'am." Lily spoke with the solemnity of one swearing a sacred vow. "But where will you be while I'm doing all those things?"

Jocelyn inhaled a deep breath and squared her shoulders. "I shall be where one would expect to find a good hostess—out on the veranda, bidding our guests welcome."

What sort of welcome would he receive from Mrs. Finch if he paid a call at Prince's Lodge this evening? For the second time in far too few days, Sir Robert found himself riding along the Windsor Road, not certain what had drawn him here.

From the reedy shallows of Bedford Basin, frogs serenaded him with their shrill twilight chorus. The sun had almost set behind the rugged hills to the east, painting the sky in the vivid shades of a driftwood bonfire.

Might Jocelyn Finch be persuaded to take a stroll down to the music pavilion with him, to watch the last shimmer of sunset reflected on the water? He wanted to thank her for what she had done last night—making the levee at Government House pass so quickly and enjoyably for him. In the bustle of departures, he had not been able to find a private moment to express his gratitude.

A gloating grin tugged at the governor's lips as he rode along, recalling how Mrs. Finch had shown a marked preference for his company over that of the wealthiest man in all the northern colonies. Or perhaps she'd only been pretending out of pity for his lack of social graces. If that was the case, Sir Robert did not resent it.

He could not recall when he'd enjoyed himself more. The pleasant memory of it had made his step lighter, his appetite keener and his disposition more amiable. The weight of responsibility for his colonists sat lighter on his shoulders, more a satisfaction than a burden.

He knew he could be stubborn, even rigid, at times. But Sir Robert prided himself on having a mind not entirely closed. He was willing to admit he might have been mistaken about Jocelyn Finch and her bride ship. The young ladies' behavior at his levee had been perfectly decorous. The foremost citizens of Halifax had received them warmly and appeared to welcome the excuse they provided for livelier society than the town had seen in quite some time.

To think he had denounced them as strumpets and feared

they would wreak havoc in his well-ordered colony! Sir Robert shook his head and had a derisive chuckle at his own expense. He was still scoffing at his own foolishness when his horse whinnied and shied toward the edge of the road.

Sir Robert bent forward and gave the beast a firm, reassuring pat on the neck. "What's the trouble, old fellow? Catch the scent of a wolf, did you?"

In spite of bounties on them, the creatures still roamed these woods near town. They tended to prey on stray sheep from farms in the area, which must be easier to catch than the watchful, fleet-footed deer in the forests.

"Help!" A breathless cry erupted from an alder thicket on the opposite side of the road. The brush rustled furiously for a moment then a soldier staggered into view.

Sir Robert slid from his saddle. "What's the matter, man? And what the devil are you doing out here?"

"Pardon, sir," the young soldier gasped. "Which way is Rockingham Inn?"

Sir Robert pointed back down the road. "Half a mile that way. Why? Are you not supposed to be on guard duty at Prince's Lodge?"

Perhaps the young soldier did not recognize the governor in the twilight shadows, but he responded to the voice of command when he heard it.

Shouldering his musket, he stood tall and saluted. "Aye, sir. Corporal Jack Henshaw, sir. Could I borrow your horse? Mrs. Finch sent me to fetch help from town."

Sir Robert felt his flesh crinkle—not just on the back of his neck, but over his whole body.

"What sort of help?" he cried. "And why does she need it?"

Corporal Henshaw was too winded and agitated to give an account that was both quick and coherent. If he could only have one of the two, Sir Robert elected to settle for speed. He hoped his mind was nimble enough to make sense of the young soldier's disjointed explanation. He did not waste precious time by interrupting with questions.

"By all means take my horse, Corporal." He helped hoist the young soldier into his saddle. "Tell the officer on duty that you have orders from Governor Kerr to send an armed, mounted detail as fast as they can get here."

"The governor?"

"The governor." Sir Robert tapped his chest. "Me. Now hand over your musket and be quick about it!"

"What are you going to do with it, sir?" The corporal loosened his grip on the musket stock when Sir Robert reached for it.

"Head to the lodge and do what I can until help arrives." He should have insisted on a larger guard detail, but he hadn't reckoned they might have to fend off a mob. "Powder and shot, too. Come on, man—we haven't got all evening!"

In the process of switching riders the horse had got turned around, so it was headed toward town. Once Sir Robert had his hands on all available weaponry, he struck the beast a firm blow on the rump and cried, "Hurry!"

The gelding gave a shrill whinny and bolted for town, the young corporal clinging to the reins for dear life. As the muted thunder of flying hooves retreated, Sir Robert loaded the soldier's musket. Then he slung the canister of powder and shot over his shoulder by its long leather strap and headed into the brush from whence the corporal had emerged.

Daylight was fading fast. Sir Robert prayed it would last long enough for him to scramble up the ravine and find a path that led to the lodge. As he surged up the hill, plowing through the alders, stray branches struck stinging blows to his face, almost like the slap of a woman's hand.

If any harm came to Mrs. Finch or her young ladies, he would never forgive himself. Guards or no guards, he should not have consigned a group of women to so remote a place. He had reckoned they would be less trouble to him out here than billeted in town. Instead he should have asked himself what trouble might arise *for them* being all the way out here.

By the time he had pushed through the dense thicket of alders, his hat had been knocked off and his chest heaved from a mixture of alarm and exertion. The ravine presented new challenges. Though the way was clear, Sir Robert found his footing treacherous, made worse by dwindling daylight. The moon was more than half-full, but it hung too low on the horizon to do more than deepen the perilous shadows at his feet.

He followed the bed of the ravine for some distance, keeping watch for a less steep spot on the western face of the rock wall that he might climb. At last he spied a promising location. There appeared to be a gap in the trees above it, too. If he could find a clear, smooth path through the woods, it would not take him long to reach the lodge.

His first few steps were deceptively easy. Then without warning a large stone shifted beneath his right foot, throwing him off balance as it tumbled down into the ravine. Its fall dislodged several other rocks, which rolled over Sir Robert's left foot—the one that had been wounded at Corona. He flailed about for something to break his fall.

He dropped the musket, which discharged with a deafening blast that echoed off the walls of Hemlock Ravine. Sir Robert fell backward, striking his head. As he lay there, dazed and in pain, he heard the distant baying of a wolf.

Chapter Nine

A surprised, expectant hush fell over the crowd in front of Prince's Lodge when Jocelyn stepped through the front door.

Behind her, she could hear Lily and Mary Ann pushing the settee back in place as she had instructed them. Something about the slow, muted rumble sounded reluctant.

Then, from off in the distance, came another sound—the sharp report of a musket. Had the corporal got into trouble? Dread tightened its grip on Jocelyn. She'd hoped the young soldier would have made his way much farther than that in the time he'd been gone.

Hearing the shot, the intruders exchanged questioning mutters. They almost drowned out another distant sound, one Jocelyn had only read about until now—the chilling howl of a wolf. Given a choice between facing that creature or the hard-faced men at her doorstep, Jocelyn was not certain which she would have picked.

The wolf's howl seemed to trouble the intruders less than the shot, as if it explained the other sound in a way that posed no threat to them. Jocelyn overheard someone say, "Old Fred Clayton guarding his sheep pen."

Once the distraction had passed, the men turned their attention back to her.

Jocelyn swallowed the lump in her throat and clasped her hands together to still their trembling. "Gentlemen, to what do we owe the honor of your visit? The hour is rather late for paying a call, is it not?"

She took care to moderate her tone. The last thing she wanted was to provoke these men, yet neither did she wish to betray her fear of them. Resolute civility held the greatest promise for safely biding time until help arrived.

If help arrived. After hearing that shot and the howl of the wolf, Jocelyn was far less certain anyone would be riding to their aid soon.

The men shuffled and muttered among themselves, until finally one of them stepped forward. He was not a tall fellow, but straight and strong looking with an unruly shock of dark hair. A darker beard covered his lower face, giving him a somewhat savage appearance. His clothes and boots were the coarse, serviceable type worn by farmers and laborers.

"Ma'am." He nodded but did not bow. "I reckon ye must be the Mrs. Finch that was writ about in the paper."

He must be an Irishman, Jocelyn guessed by the lilt of his deep, husky voice. That did not soothe her trepidation. His countrymen were not above resorting to violence when they reckoned themselves hard done by.

Still, his greeting was civil enough to shore up her precarious hopes. "I am Mrs. Finch. But I fear you have the advantage of me, sir. Whom have I the honor of addressing?"

Her words were met with some sputters of laughter from the Irishman's friends. One of them mimicked her in an exaggerated falsetto. An ember of outrage began to smolder deep in Jocelyn's belly—its heat burned in her cheeks. But she did not have the luxury of venting it.

The spokesman rounded on the mimic and let fly with his thick fist. Jocelyn could not suppress a savage flicker of satisfaction at the wail his blow produced.

Glaring at the rest of his mates, the Irishman growled, "Any more o' that and ye'll all be laughing out yer arses before I'm done with yez."

His threat provoked a low hum of stifled protest, but no one dared talk back to their fierce spokesman, who turned to face Jocelyn again. "Me name don't matter, ma'am, on account of it's not meself alone I'm speaking for."

"Indeed? For whom do you speak then? And what business can you have here?"

"I speak for the bachelors of the Nova Scotia colony, ma'am. Not the officers and rich traders and government lackeys in Halifax. Not half of them will be here ten years from now, ye mark me."

"What makes you say that?" At last, Jocelyn began to understand what had brought these men to her door. But she continued to pretend ignorance to stall for time. "And why do the bachelors of Nova Scotia need you to speak on their behalf?"

The Irishman ignored her first question in favor of the second, which clearly gave him the opening he desired. "On account of they're being cheated, ma'am, same as always, by the swells in town."

"I am sorry to hear that." Jocelyn interjected the comment to prolong their exchange. "But I fail to see what it has to do with me or with your coming here this evening."

"I reckon ye know better than ye want to let on, ma'am."

The man might be uncouth, but he was also perceptive. Too perceptive for Jocelyn's peace of mind. She hoped he would not divine her reason for keeping him talking.

"Perhaps I do, at that, sir." She managed a pallid smile.

"But would you kindly indulge me by making it quite plain. That way there will be no misunderstanding between us."

After a moment's consideration, he nodded. "If it's plain ye want, it's plain I can be. Me and the lads read in the paper about ye coming to Nova Scotia with this here bride ship. We thought it was fine idea altogether—lasses for the settlers to woo and wed."

One of the others called out, "'Cept they wasn't ever to be for the likes of us, was they?"

The man's voice had a belligerent slur that suggested he'd taken a detour past some tavern on his way here. Jocelyn caught a sour whiff of spirits on the night air.

The Irishman ignored the interruption. "Then what do we hear tell but all the lasses are being presented at Government House, followed by a fine ball to dance the night away with the officers and town gents. Somehow the lads and me got overlooked on the governor's invitation list."

His sour jest hit Jocelyn harder than she expected. Mrs. Beamish had devised this scheme to provide wives for men like these, who truly needed them. Somehow, in her eagerness to relive the carefree days of her first Season, Jocelyn had lost sight of that.

"You must realize the governor's levee was only the first of many gatherings at which I hope to introduce my young ladies to Nova Scotia society. And I do not mean only high society."

The Irishman crossed his arms in front of his broad chest and stared at her, as if weighing her sincerity.

"I give you my word—" Jocelyn swept her gaze over the whole group, trying not to quail at a glimpse of the odd hatchet or crowbar in their hands "—you and other men in your position will have an equal chance to court the young ladies in my charge."

"Ye wouldn't just be saying that to appease us, would ye?"

The man *was* far too perceptive. "Would you rather I made no effort to appease you, sir?"

Immediately she regretted her sharp retort. The honor, and perhaps the safety, of her girls was in peril and she could not help feeling partly to blame. She must not jeopardize them further by letting her temper get the best of her.

But the Irishman only laughed. "If yer lasses have half yer cleverness and spirit, ma'am, they'll make fine wives for the likes of us."

His brazen flattery emboldened Jocelyn to risk saying something she hoped might defuse the whole situation. She spoke in a gently chiding tone. "If they refuse you, gentlemen, you will have only yourselves to blame after frightening them by calling here so late and in such a large, menacing group."

A look of doubt crossed the Irishman's rugged features. Behind him the other men exchanged words in hushed tones. From the snippets of conversation Jocelyn overheard, it sounded as though the sober members of the group were having second thoughts about the whole enterprise.

"Ye swear the lasses won't all be wed off to the swells from town?" The spokesman appeared to be searching for a means to retreat from the situation with honor and a sense of moral victory.

Though practicality urged Jocelyn to say anything that would get rid of them, some streak of perversity and a sense that she owed them the truth made her reply, "I cannot promise you whom the young ladies will choose. Some may elect to make advantageous matches if they are offered. But I believe most did not come to this colony with that in mind."

Sensing something more was needed to sway the men, she added, "You may have read in the newspapers that I am the daughter of a nobleman. Yet I married a man without title or fortune and we were very happy together. I believe with all my heart that affection must be the first consideration for marriage. The officers and merchants of Halifax have no monopoly on that."

"Ye speak true, ma'am." The Irishman made an awkward bow to her. "I reckon we can be satisfied with that. Tell the lasses we never meant ye or them any harm. We had a complaint and we wanted ye to hear it firsthand, is all."

Relief swept through Jocelyn with such force it made her knees weak. The men were going to leave peaceably and everything would be all right.

Then, from the balcony above, came the last words in the world she wanted to hear.

"Seeing as ye've come all this way, gents," called Vita Sykes, "why don't ye pop in for a proper visit? The cellar's full of good wine. We could have a grand time!"

Jocelyn wished the other girls would push the little minx off the balcony!

Intemperate from drink, a number of the men were eager to accept Vita's invitation, even if it meant forcing their way into the house. Their sober companions, including the Irish spokesman, tried to restrain them. Before Jocelyn's eyes, a full-fledged brawl broke out on the front lawn.

Fists flew. Jocelyn prayed the men would have more sense than to use their hatchets and crowbars against one another. She also feared what might happen if a torch got dropped in the wrong place. She longed to retreat into the safety of the house, but the door had been barricaded behind her, on her own orders.

The darkness and shifting torchlight made it difficult to see exactly what was going on and who might have the upper hand in the fight. At the foot of the steps, two men were trying to restrain a third, but could not lay hands on him because of the crowbar he swung in a most erratic fashion. If he'd been less drunk, he might have done one of the others a serious injury. As it was, he managed to evade them and make a lunge for the door of the lodge.

Hurriedly trying to decide whether to stand her ground or flee, Jocelyn glimpsed a blurred movement out of the corner of her eye. One of the other men must have scrambled up over the balusters. Pressing her back to the door, she clenched her lips together. She would not frighten the girls any worse by screaming, nor would she give these intruders the satisfaction.

Less than a yard from her, the man with the crowbar came to an abrupt halt, the barrel of a musket pointed at his chest. Glancing over, Jocelyn discovered Governor Kerr standing beside her, the musket stock in his hands and his forefinger finger upon the trigger.

"Drop your weapon!" he roared. "Or I will blow a hole in your chest big enough to pass a cannonball through!"

A bar of blackened iron clattered onto the deck of the veranda.

"Bloody shite!" one of the intruders gasped. "It's the gov'ner."

"Well spotted," said Sir Robert, his tone as grim as his countenance. "There is a mounted detail of soldiers not a mile from here and riding fast. If you slip away before they come to arrest you, I promise you will not be hunted down. Any of you still left on this property when they arrive will be lucky to get off with a public flogging!"

Was it true? Jocelyn wondered. Could Colonel Carmont's men be that close? Perhaps it did not matter, as long as the intruders believed it.

A moment of tense, unnatural stillness followed. Jocelyn held her breath, silently praying these men would make the right decision, and hoping the other girls would have the good sense to stifle Vita Sykes so she could not stir up more trouble.

After what seemed like an unbearable length of time, but

could not have been much more than a minute, the man at the wrong end of Sir Robert's musket spun around and fled into the night. The others followed hot on his heels.

With a cry of relief, Jocelyn turned toward the governor to throw her arms around him.

Instead he thrust the musket into her hands. "Hold this."

She'd barely grasped the weapon when his hands fell slack. With an obvious effort, the governor hoisted one arm up and around her shoulders. Then he slumped sideways against her.

"Sir Robert?" Jocelyn struggled to hold the musket and keep from collapsing under his weight. "What's wrong? Are you injured?"

"Sore foot. A knock on the head. My own fault—should have waited to load the musket until I climbed *out* of the ravine. I'll know better next time...though I hope there will not be one."

Jocelyn tried to piece together his disjointed words. "The shot? That was you? And you hit your head in the ravine? Good Lord, we must get you into the lodge and seen to at once!"

When she lowered the musket barrel, the governor growled, "Not yet! Wait until we're certain this lot have gone."

"To blazes with them! You said yourself, Colonel Carmont's men will be here any moment."

Sir Robert gave a rusty-sounding chuckle. "To think I never prided myself on being a convincing liar."

"You've probably never tried until now." Jocelyn could well believe it. The man had a rare fault for telling the unvarnished truth. "Are there *any* soldiers coming from town?"

"There'd better be or I will have that corporal's head."

Now Jocelyn understood. "This is his musket?"

"Traded it for my horse." The governor's voice had the peculiar rasp of someone trying to talk while in pain. "Don't worry, it isn't loaded."

"You *are* a good liar!" She could have sworn he'd meant to shoot the intruder. "Can you hold yourself upright for a moment?"

"I can try." Sir Robert pulled himself erect, though his balance looked precarious.

No longer burdened by his weight, Jocelyn turned and pounded on the door with the butt of the musket. "Lily, they've gone! Open up!"

After a moment, Mary Ann called down from the balcony above, "Lily's on her way, Mrs. Finch! As soon as they can clear the stairs."

Jocelyn tossed down the musket just in time to catch Sir Robert as he swayed toward her. "Please stay awake!" she begged him. "At least long enough for us to get you inside."

"Shall make...every effort...to oblige...a lady." By the sound of him, it took a considerable effort just to heave out those words.

As Jocelyn waited for the girls to unbar the door, the governor's scent overwhelmed her as much as his weight. He smelled of clean sweat, shaving soap and the faint, dangerous pungency of gunpowder. Together they stirred something in her that she would rather let sleep. She had not experienced such close, prolonged contact with a man in a great while. She had almost forgotten how much she missed it.

Just when Jocelyn feared she would crumple beneath Sir Robert's weight, she heard the heavy scrape of the settee being pushed away from the door.

An instant later, Lily burst out, followed by Mary Ann and Eliza Turner. "Mrs. Finch, are you all right? This man hasn't harmed you, has he?"

"No! This is the governor and he's injured. Mary Ann, help me get him inside."

"Aye, ma'am!" The girl wedged her shoulder under Sir Robert's other arm, lightening Jocelyn's burden.

The governor had not entirely surrendered consciousness, it seemed, for his feet moved when they bore him into the lodge.

"Lily, fetch that musket," Jocelyn called over her shoulder, "then bar the door again in case those men come back before Colonel Carmont's soldiers arrive."

While Lily did as she'd been bidden, Mary Ann asked, "Where do you want to take him, ma'am?"

Jocelyn quickly considered and discarded several options. "Keep going down to my room. We'd never get him up those stairs."

Upon arriving at Prince's Lodge, Jocelyn had converted a tiny sewing room on the ground floor into a bedchamber for herself. She treasured the slight sense of privacy it gave her but she could not justify taking a larger room when the girls were so crowded. Now she was grateful to have a bed near at hand where they could rest Sir Robert and tend his injuries.

"Someone fetch Miz Ada!" she called.

The little cook had proven herself calm and capable in the demanding task of feeding the girls thrice a day and keeping them productively occupied between meals. Perhaps she knew a useful thing or two about compounding poultices and salves.

"Here we are, Sir Robert." Jocelyn wasn't certain he could hear her, but for her own peace of mind, she had to pretend he could. "You'll be able to rest, now, while we look after you."

A swift glance at his face revealed closed eyes and slack features. Jocelyn's stomach churned with worry.

"He told me he hit his head." She spoke half to Mary Ann and half to herself. "Let's lay him facedown so I can get a good look."

One *good look* at Sir Robert's torn, swollen scalp and his blood-matted hair made her grimace and suck in a breath between clenched teeth.

"How did you make it all the way here from the ravine in the dark with *that?*" she whispered, now quite certain he could not hear her.

By the time she and Miz Ada had cleaned the wound and bound Sir Robert's head, Colonel Carmont's men had arrived, led by the colonel himself.

He grew livid when Jocelyn informed him of the governor's promise not to hunt down the intruders. "I will have my men make a thorough search of the grounds and woe betide any of those scoundrels we find skulking about."

Was she daft, Jocelyn wondered, to hope Colonel Carmont's men did not find any of the intruders? While she did not condone their manner of protest, she could not dispute their complaint. Only a few of her charges had come from the kind of background that would allow them to mix with ease among the best families of Halifax. And Mrs. Beamish had intended the bride-ship scheme to benefit the colony as well as the girls.

Colonel Carmont glanced toward the bed where his friend lay senseless. "Unless he makes a swift and full recovery, I will not be bound by his promise. I will find and prosecute the men responsible for his injuries. If I have my way I will see them hanged!"

"I fear you are being too harsh," Jocelyn protested. "None of those men raised a hand against Sir Robert."

"He would never have been clambering around that ravine at dusk if it had not been for them." The colonel clenched his fists as if they itched to throttle someone. "What the devil was he doing out of town at this time of day?"

The Colonel's words jarred Jocelyn. Sir Robert would never have charged into danger if it had not been for *her* and her charges. "I have no idea what brought him out here, though I am grateful for his intervention. Now, will you please send to town for a doctor to examine him?"

"I have already dispatched one of men to Rockingham Inn. Dr. Pemberton often dines there at this time of year, unless he has a call."

Jocelyn hoped with all her heart this would be one such night. "In that case, there is another matter I must discuss with you, Colonel."

She lowered her voice so it would not carry above the noise of footsteps, furniture being dragged across the floors and the soft, urgent buzz of gossip being exchanged between the girls. "One of my charges is missing."

Seeing the colonel glower with outrage, she hastened to assure him. "The men who came here tonight had nothing to do with it, I am certain. But one of our sentries is gone, too. I believe he may have something to do with Hetty's disappearance…or she with his."

Colonel Carmont gave a growl that boded ill for the foolish young sentry. "The girl will be found, ma'am. If you will excuse me, I must go start the search."

Once the colonel had departed and Sir Robert was as comfortable as she could make him, Jocelyn left Miz Ada to sit with him while she sent her charges to bed. The last room she checked was the one Vita shared with three other girls. They were all whispering and laughing together when she looked in.

"Bring your nightgown, Vita, and come with me." Jocelyn spoke with a severity that would have done credit to the governor himself. "For tonight, you will be sharing a room with Lily, Louisa and Mary Ann."

Vita made a sour face, which set the other girls sputtering with laughter. They quickly swallowed their mirth when Jocelyn snapped, "I had planned to wait until tomorrow to switch all of you to other rooms. Would you prefer I do it now?"

"No, ma'am," muttered Mazie. Fanny and Kate shook their heads.

Vita took her time sauntering to the door, dragging her nightgown behind her. Jocelyn refused to be provoked.

When the girl finally stepped into the hallway, Jocelyn pushed the bedroom door shut and exploded with rage. "What in the devil possessed you to call out to those men? Do you have any idea what might have happened if Sir Robert had not arrived when he did?"

Vita stared at her with a sullen sneer and shrugged a single shoulder, as if employing both for the purpose would not be worth her trouble. "Maybe ye should think twice about sticking me in that stinking scullery again."

"I will indeed." Though probably not the way Vita intended. "I will deal with you in the morning. Now get to bed and do not let me hear a peep from you tonight or you may find yourself *sleeping* in the scullery."

The girl shot Jocelyn an insolent glare but had sense enough to hold her tongue.

Hearing hurried footsteps on the stairs, Jocelyn turned back to find Lily rushing toward her. "The doctor's come, ma'am. He's with the governor now. Miz Ada sent me to fetch you."

"Thank you, my dear." Jocelyn clasped Lily's hand. "I do not know what I would have done without your help tonight. Now you must get some sleep." She lowered her voice to a whisper. "Tell Eliza I want her to exchange beds with Vita. Just for tonight, I promise. I need someone I can trust to keep an eye on her."

"Very well, ma'am." Lily did not look overjoyed at the prospect, but resigned to do what was needed.

Jocelyn raised her voice again as a warning to Vita. "If she gives you any trouble, come and tell me at once and I will deal with her."

With a grim nod, Lily beckoned Vita to follow her. Meanwhile Jocelyn hurried back to her bedchamber to find the doctor working over Sir Robert. She recognized the tall, gangly man from the ball at Government House.

After thanking Miz Ada for sitting with Sir Robert, Jocelyn ordered her away to get some sleep. Then she quizzed Dr. Pemberton about the condition of his patient.

"You did an excellent job cleaning and binding the wound, ma'am." The doctor put away his pocket watch after taking Sir Robert's pulse. Then he rummaged in his satchel and produced smelling salts. "But it is vital we revive him and keep him awake for the next several hours."

"If you think he should be moved back to town," said Jocelyn, "I have a carriage I can put at your disposal for the purpose."

The doctor shook his head as he unstopped the vial of smelling salts. "A jolting like that could be very bad for him. He must not be moved until morning at the earliest, and then I recommend he return to town by water."

"You mean he must stay here all night? In *my* bed?" Those words conjured up a scandalous image, one that shocked Jocelyn almost as much as it intrigued her.

Chapter Ten

The sickening reek of ammonia wrenched Sir Robert from a place of darkness and silence to painful consciousness. He groaned and tried to turn his head away. But the movement only made it throb worse, which prodded him more fully awake.

His eyelids fluttered open for an instant to reveal Jocelyn Finch hovering over him, waving the horrible-smelling concoction under his nose.

"Where am I?" His mouth felt dry as ashes and his voice sounded hoarse. "What happened?"

To his mounting confusion, a vaguely familiar masculine voice answered. "You're at Prince's Lodge, sir. It seems you fell and knocked yourself on the head. In the ravine, we gather. Wake up, now. It's not a good idea to sleep after a head injury. How do you feel?"

"Vile." Sir Robert forced his eyes open and tried to focus them toward the sound of the voice. He made every effort to hold his head still, though. The pain had dulled to a heavy but bearable ache. He did not want to provoke it to a worse pitch. "Oh, it's you, Doctor. I should have known."

"Natural for you to be a trifle confused," the doctor assured him. "Now, can you sit up if we pile a few more pillows behind you? I do not want to place any additional pressure on your skull until that wound has had time to heal."

"I'm a bit dizzy." Sir Robert understated matters. He felt as if he were trying to stagger across the deck of a ship in heavy seas. "But I reckon I can sit up if you say I must."

Dr. Pemberton chuckled as he heaped more pillows behind Sir Robert. "Soldiers make good patients. They seldom balk at following orders. There, how is that? Still dizzy?"

"Not as bad as it was."

He found the room did not lurch and spin so violently if he kept his eyes open and focused on a single object—the face of Jocelyn Finch. Even drawn with fatigue and worry, her features were among the loveliest he had ever beheld.

Her gaze flittered under the intensity of his. "I'm so relieved you are awake at last, Sir Robert. I blame myself for your injury."

Why? What had she done to him? He forced himself to think back on the events of the evening and managed to piece them together, though some bits were rather hazy.

"It is not your fault." He started to shake his head, but a stab of pain and a wave of dizziness stopped him. "I am glad I got here in time to be of some assistance."

"Some assistance?" She lifted her eyes to meet his once more. The warm brown depths glowed with admiration. "I shudder to think what might have befallen us without your timely intervention. How did you come to be so far out of town at so late an hour?"

Perhaps if the doctor had not been present, Sir Robert might have confessed the truth. "It seemed a pleasant evening for a ride. And the country is very pretty out this way."

The doctor gave a disparaging grunt. "Point Pleasant has a much finer view."

Sir Robert continued to gaze at Mrs. Finch. "With respect, sir, I must disagree."

"To each his own, I suppose." Dr. Pemberton retrieved his satchel from the floor and rose. "Now, if you will excuse me, I must get back to town. Mrs. Andrew McGrath is past her time and I anticipate a call at any hour to attend the birth."

Among the merchants of Halifax, Mrs. McGrath's husband was second in wealth only to Barnabas Power. The expected child would be heir to that fortune. The doctor could anticipate a handsome fee for his assistance.

"Of course," said Sir Robert. "Has my carriage been summoned to fetch me back to town?"

The doctor shook his head. "As I told Mrs. Finch, that is quite out of the question tonight." He explained the necessity for Sir Robert to remain at Prince's Lodge. "To be quite safe, I would suggest staying put until you are able to stand and walk without further dizziness."

"Stay here?" The notion appealed to him far too much. "I cannot impose upon Mrs. Finch. She has her hands full already. And I have work back in town that will not wait."

"Have it brought to you, then," the doctor suggested. At the same moment Mrs. Finch protested, "Imposition—nonsense!"

"Very well." Sir Robert lifted his hands to signal surrender. "I see I am overruled by a margin of two to one."

The doctor chuckled. "I commend your democratic principles, sir. I know we can both rely on Mrs. Finch to tend you well. It was she who dressed your wound before I ever got here."

Though he was certain it would have pained like the very devil, Sir Robert almost wished he had been awake to experience the lady's gentle but deft touch.

"Thank you for coming so quickly, Doctor." Mrs. Finch

walked toward the door with him. "You have eased my mind greatly. Here, do not forget your smelling salts."

"Keep them." Pemberton nodded toward the bed. "Use them on your patient if he slips into unconsciousness again within the next six hours. After that, I reckon it will be safe to let him sleep for a while."

"May I give him a drop of brandy to ease the pain?"

The doctor shook his head. "Nothing of a soporific nature. Tea is permissible if he will take it."

When Mrs. Finch tried to follow him from the room, Pemberton waved her back. "I will return tomorrow to see how the governor is recovering, provided I am not detained at the McGraths'. In the meantime, if he takes a turn for the worse, send for me."

Once the doctor had departed, Mrs. Finch returned to her chair beside the bed. An uneasy silence settled over the room. For his part, Sir Robert was acutely conscious of being alone in her company at a very late hour of the night.

"*Would* you care for some tea?" she asked at last. "I could send for some."

"Later perhaps. At the moment, I fear I would slop it all over myself."

"I'm sorry the doctor forbade me to give you wine. Are you in much pain?"

"Some."

"That must mean your head feels ready to explode." Mrs. Finch rolled her eyes. "A soldier can be in agony before he will admit to the slightest discomfort."

Her words made Sir Robert laugh. The laugh made him groan.

"Hardly *agony*," he protested, though the notion of her fancying him stoic held considerable appeal. "However, I would welcome some distraction to take my mind off it. Why don't you tell me what those men were doing here, brawling on your doorstep? While you are about it, explain to me what you were doing out there with them."

It would take more than a knock on the head to make him forget the fear that had clutched his heart when he'd seen that drunkard with the crowbar in his hand lurching up the steps toward her.

Briefly Mrs. Finch explained who the intruders were and the grievance that had brought them to Prince's Lodge. "It seems you were right after all in claiming the bride ship would cause a disturbance in the colony. And in ordering sentries to guard the lodge. I should not have doubted you."

"Believe me, I take no satisfaction in being right. I only regret I did not insist on a larger contingent of sentries. From now on, I promise you and your charges will be properly protected."

"And I promise you, from now on the girls will be properly chaperoned." She told him about the disappearance of one of the sentries and a girl called Hetty. "I fear they have eloped, the young fools. Though they are no more foolish than I for presuming I could supervise such a large group on my own."

She raised her hand to rub her tired eyes. "Now there is sure to be a scandal that may taint the reputations of all the other girls. Then no respectable men will want them and my whole mission will end in…failure."

Her voice broke and her slender frame began to shudder with silent sobs.

Sir Robert could not bear to witness her distress. He sensed she was not the kind of woman to blubber over every minor misfortune. She must be exhausted after a long day and her recent fright. Did some worry on his account also contribute to her vulnerable state?

Though it aggravated the pain in his head to an almost unbearable degree, Sir Robert pulled himself upright and reached for her. Once he had grasped her free hand, he sank back onto the pillows, drawing her toward him. She was too tired and troubled to resist, any more than she could resist the sobs that racked her. She came to rest on the edge of the bed, with her head cradled against his chest, his arms encircling her.

"There, there," he murmured. "I'm sure it won't be as bad as you think. I promise you will have my full support. I know I had some…reservations about this bride ship of yours, but I am beginning to recognize its possible benefits."

He was quick to recognize how pleasant it felt to hold a woman in his arms. But not just *any* woman. The pain in his head eased. Or perhaps he had just succeeded in distracting himself from it. Though he felt suddenly light-headed, he doubted it had anything to do with his injury.

Almost against his will, his hand rose to stroke her hair. "You have done a remarkable job under difficult circumstances. These latest troubles may set you back a little, but I cannot imagine you will let them discourage you for long… any more than you let my opposition daunt you."

Her weeping eased to a sniffle or two, but she made no effort to forsake the shelter of his arms. "That was different. You were wrong. At least, I believed you were. The men who came here tonight may have chosen an offensive way to present their grievances, but what they had to say was true."

"You think so?" He was still too shaken by his glimpse of that violent fray on the doorstep of Prince's Lodge to credit the intruders' protests. Their actions felt like mutiny and he was still too much a solider to condone rebellion.

Jocelyn nodded vigorously, making her head rub against his chest and her hair whisper against his chin. It took all his powers of self-discipline to concentrate on her words when he wanted to relish every sensation of her nearness.

"The bride ship was intended to aid men in their situation."

She inhaled a deep, moist breath. "But I let my desire to relive my own first Season get the better of my…duty." She spit the last word as if it had a disagreeable flavor in her mouth. "Now I fear it may be too late to set matters right."

"I make it a practice never to give in to the demands of a rabble," said Sir Robert. "But if we put our heads together, surely we can come up with a solution to benefit all concerned."

Mrs. Finch gave a final sniffle then abandoned his embrace to sit up again. Her eyes searched his. "You think so?"

Even with a red nose, swollen eyes and disheveled hair, she stirred potent feelings within his guarded, sensible heart. "I am certain of it."

Perhaps that fall in the ravine had temporarily knocked the caution and good sense out of him. Just then he wanted very much for the two of them to put their heads together…starting with their lips.

Jocelyn's heart raced faster than it had when she'd faced the crowd of intruders a few hours ago. Her breathing grew rapid and shallow as she stared into the governor's cool blue eyes. No doubt he would be scandalized if he knew how much she wanted to kiss him at that moment.

The firm restraint of his lips lured her in a way a more lively or sensual demeanor could never have done. It challenged her to both rouse and subdue him. To provoke him into a passionate outburst. Yet it was he who had provoked her… without even trying.

At first she'd welcomed the steady, reliable solace she found in his arms. He had charged to her rescue tonight, like some knight errant of old, exciting her admiration. Then his injury had made him vulnerable and in need of her help, stirring all her best feminine instincts. Finally he had relaxed his accustomed reserve to offer her comfort and sympathy.

Besides all that, the act of lying on a bed, once again in a man's arms, stirred a host of tantalizing memories. She was still a young woman, after all, with a young woman's desires and needs. Jocelyn reminded herself that the man who had held her with such tender strength was the last man in the colony she could hope to gratify those desires.

"I beg your pardon, sir!" She dashed away the last traces of moisture clinging to her lashes and returned to her chair by his bedside. "I am supposed to be taking care of you, not imposing upon you when you are injured and in pain."

"You did not impose, Mrs. Finch." Was it her imagination, or did he place an emphasis on her married name? "I offered."

"It was kindly done. I thank you." She lapsed into a weary smile. "If you claim we can find a way out of this predicament, I believe you. I will put the matter out of my mind until morning and direct my energies to diverting you, instead. Shall I fetch a book and read to you?"

Sir Robert's nose wrinkled at the suggestion. "Not if you aim to keep me awake, ma'am. Most nights I read a little after I go to bed. I seldom get through many pages before I am obliged to snuff the candle. I fear persistent habit has made me associate books with sleep."

"Cards, then? Draughts? Chess?" Glimpsing a quicksilver twinkle in his eyes, she added, "I will not have you let me win this time, however."

"I promise you, your victory in our first match was altogether your own doing. The only way I contributed was by underestimating your ability and allowing my arrogance to get the better of me. That you were able to recognize and exploit my errors is to your credit."

That guarded scrap of praise kindled a pleasant glow within Jocelyn. "Shall I fetch a board, then?"

"I beg you to postpone a rematch until I have all my wits about me. I know I shall have need of them."

Who would not shrink from taxing their brain in his condition? Jocelyn gave a resigned nod. "You do make yourself difficult to entertain, Sir Robert. How will I ever keep you awake until morning at this rate?"

He thought for a moment. "Perhaps we could use the opportunity to become better acquainted. If you would not find that too tiresome?"

"Indeed not!" She knew almost nothing about him except that he'd been a soldier before being appointed governor…and that he had never been wed. "I should like it very much."

"Good. Then what if you start by telling me about this first Season you are so eager to relive? I expect it is a far more engaging story than most works of fiction."

Jocelyn dismissed a momentary stab of disappointment that her curiosity about him would not be appeased. There were plenty of hours to fill between now and sunrise. Sooner or later he was certain to lower his guard and tell her something about himself.

"I marvel that you should be interested in such frivolous tales, sir. My first Season was nothing but balls and evenings at the theater and visits to the pleasure gardens—all the sorts of events you claim to detest. Why ever would you want to hear about them?"

He gave a cautious shrug, as if too vigorous a movement might jar his sore head. "I do not enjoy taking part in such activities—at least, I did not until recently—but I have no objection to hearing about them. Especially from someone for whom they do afford pleasure."

At least, I did not until recently. Was that a roundabout way of saying he had enjoyed her company the other evening?

"If that is the case, I shall be happy to oblige you with an account. Let's see—it all began with my presentation at court. Having overheard a number of sensational accounts from my father about the King and his spells of madness, I was heartlessly disappointed to find our sovereign such an unremarkable gentleman."

"Indeed?" A look of amusement softened the tense set of fatigue and pain around Sir Robert's eyes. "I felt rather cheated when the Prince of Wales had to deputize for His Majesty to confer my title upon me. Now I discover I was not missing much after all."

This was just the kind of opening Jocelyn had hoped for. "How did you earn your title?"

"In battle, of course," Sir Robert replied in a tone of wry deprecation. "Chance put me in a critical spot on the field, then I managed to survive the carnage. My men won the victory, not I. None of them received a knighthood."

This was not a subject on which they should dwell, Jocelyn knew. But she could not let it drop before offering one observation. "Soldiers do not win victories without able leadership."

Sir Robert did not acknowledge her implied praise. "Speaking of able leadership, pray give me an account of what happened this evening after all those men arrived. You dispatched Corporal Henshaw through the woods and the ravine to fetch help. What then?"

"I summoned the girls inside and sent them to their rooms so we could account for all of them. That was when we discovered Hetty missing." Jocelyn related the events of the evening up until the moment Sir Robert had appeared by her side with an unloaded musket and put the intruders to flight with his bold bluff.

He did not interrupt her story, but stared at her with an increasing look of disbelief. When she had finished, he demanded, "What on earth possessed you to go out there by yourself and talk to those men? Did you not know how dangerous it might be?"

A few days ago his scolding tone would have provoked Jocelyn to a sharp retort. Tonight, she sensed his fear for her safety and it touched her.

"I had to go—don't you see? These girls are my responsibility. I had a..." She searched for the proper word.

"A *duty* to protect them?" Sir Robert suggested. "Even at risk to yourself? Call it what you will, it is clear to me you have a stronger sense of duty than you care to admit."

Did she? The notion rather shocked Jocelyn, but she could not dispute it altogether. Besides, it was evident Sir Robert meant his remark as a compliment and she found herself suddenly anxious to secure his good opinion.

"Perhaps if you had been brought up as I was, you would not think duty such a great virtue, sir."

"How were you brought up to despise the very word?"

The late hour, the dim light of a single candle and Sir Robert's stillness all conspired to draw Jocelyn out. "I was but seven years old when my mother died *doing her duty* to my father and the family by providing him with a second son."

"So you have two brothers?"

"Had," Jocelyn corrected him. "Little Charles did not survive our mother long, poor babe. My brother Lord Thetford is dutiful enough for any ten children. He wed an heiress of our father's choosing, rapidly sired two fine sons of his own and is a conscientious member of the King's household. How can one expect even the DeLacey family to produce two such marvels?"

Sir Robert seemed to understand that her bitter query did not require an answer. "I have two brothers, as well. Both living, thank God. Gavin is a captain in the Royal Navy and Alec is studying at the University of Edinburgh to become a physician. I was eight when we learned that my father had been killed in India, doing *his* duty for King and country."

"I am sorry." Jocelyn's throat tightened. She'd had trouble enough surviving on her own after Ned's death. How would she ever have managed with three small children? "You and your brothers have all got on well in the world. Your mother must be an extraordinary woman."

"Aye, she was." For the first time since she'd met him, Jocelyn detected a trace of the Scottish burr in Sir Robert's speech. "She expected a lot of us—mostly me, because I was the eldest. *Man of the family* at eight years old." He gave a soft chuckle that sounded somehow wistful.

Jocelyn remembered the sorrow of her mother's death as if it were yesterday. So many things in her life had changed because of it, and not in agreeable ways. But at least she'd never wanted for material necessities. "It must have been even harder for you than for me."

"Oh, I didn't mind most of the time. Mam worked so hard to provide for us, I was anxious to help her out any way I could. She was so proud when I took up my first commission. I wish she'd lived to see me appointed governor. I'd have brought her with me to live at Government House. Though I don't know how I'd have kept her from polishing the furniture and helping Miz Ada in the kitchen."

Was he still a bachelor because he'd never found a woman who could measure up to the high standard his mother had set?

"I would have been honored to meet her," Jocelyn murmured. "How long have you been without her?"

Sir Robert thought for a moment. "Three years. The winter after Alec went away to school, she took sick for the first time I can remember. It was as if she'd kept some sort of promise to my father, so she could rest at last."

His words wrung a sigh from Jocelyn. "How tragic! To have struggled so hard then not been able to enjoy the fruits of her labors."

Sir Robert contradicted her with a wave of his hand. "Mam would have scoffed at the notion of her life being tragic. You may not believe it, but a person can take great satisfaction and pride in fulfilling their duty. Even when they do not reap the benefits directly. Even when the results may not appear satisfactory to others."

He was right in one particular—she did not believe it. And yet…the grave sincerity of Sir Robert's words touched her and made her wonder if they could be true.

He seemed to sense her uncertainty. "What did you stand to gain for yourself by going out alone to face that angry crowd of men, this evening?"

The soft glow of admiration in his eyes kindled the beginning of a blush in Jocelyn's cheeks. She hoped the dim candlelight and flickering shadows would conceal it. "You give me too much credit, sir. I did not fancy myself in any great danger until a few moments before you arrived. Indeed, I thought I had convinced the men to leave peaceably once they'd made their complaints known to me."

She went on to tell him how Vita had incited the riot he'd witnessed. "I mean to send the little wretch back to England on the *Hestia* before she ruins everything, if she has not already."

Sir Robert endorsed the idea.

"You do not think I have a duty to reform her?" Jocelyn teased him. At that moment she found herself anxious to coax forth one of his reluctant smiles or even a grudging chuckle.

He rewarded her with both. "On the contrary, I would say you have a duty to the other girls. You should rid them of a rotten apple before she spoils the whole barrel."

They continued to talk late into the night on every conceivable subject. At Jocelyn's prodding, Sir Robert related his adventures in the army, including his service in Egypt and later in Spain. In turn he demanded more stories of her merry social doings, which led to an account of her courtship with Captain Edward Finch.

"My father refused to countenance the match." Jocelyn could not keep the bitterness from her voice. "He intended me to wed a neighbor of ours, a particular friend and political ally of his—a widower not many years younger than himself. I vowed I could never marry one man when my heart belonged to another. Father insisted it was my duty to the family."

"Ah." Sir Robert sounded as if he had just gained some fresh insight into a baffling mystery.

Jocelyn was not sure she liked the idea. "I suppose you think I should have martyred my heart by going along with my father's wishes?"

"Well..." A troubled look came over Sir Robert's face and his right hand clenched in a tight fist. "No."

"You do not sound very convinced of it."

After a moment's hesitation, he replied, "There are some who might call *your* situation a tragedy. You severed all ties with your family to make a love match, only to lose your husband a short while later. Then you were left without the support and comfort of your kinfolk."

Jocelyn bristled. "The only tragic part of all that was my husband's death. The rest I do not regret for a moment! I would have rued it bitterly if Ned had left this world without having shared the brief happiness of our marriage."

Sir Robert thought for a moment. "I reckon we all make the choices we can best live with. Or perhaps we convince ourselves that is what we have done because we cannot bear to live with such regrets."

Of course she had made the only choice she could live with!

In marrying Ned, certainly. But in refusing to reconcile with her family after his death? Of that Jocelyn was not so sure.

A strained silence fell over them, now and then broken by yawns. Jocelyn cudgeled her brain to think of a safe topic for further conversation. One that promised to keep them talking until morning without trespassing into private territory.

Then suddenly it *was* morning. Jocelyn jolted awake to find herself slumped forward, her head resting on the bed. She wrenched herself upright. "Sir Robert, you should have woken me—"

The words stuck in her throat as she glanced at the governor to find him lying pale and still. Was the poor man even breathing? After he had injured himself coming to her rescue last night, she had failed in the simple but crucial task of keeping him awake as the doctor had ordered.

"Sir Robert?" She clasped his hand, faint with relief to find it warm to the touch. Fear chilled her again when the sound of her voice failed to rouse him.

"Please wake up!" She chafed his hand with increasing agitation.

When he remained unconscious, she perched on the edge of the bed and began to slap him gently on the cheek. "Please, Sir Robert, you must open your eyes. I'm so sorry I did not keep you awake as I promised I would."

She leaned closer, her pleas growing more and more desperate. Without conscious intention, her touch muted from light blows to beseeching caresses. He must wake up. He *must*. How would she live with herself if he did not?

Her heart was fluttering like a small wild bird imprisoned within the cage of her ribs when suddenly Sir Robert gave a soft moan and opened his eyes.

"Thank God!" Jocelyn gasped. Overcome with relief, she leaned forward and pressed her lips to his.

Chapter Eleven

For the second time in twelve hours, something coaxed Sir Robert awake against his will. Jocelyn Finch's sweet voice and the tender caress of her fingers were a far more agreeable inducement than the sickening reek of ammonia. Still pleasantly fuddled from sleep, he wondered what it might be like to waken every morning in such a way.

But the delightful sensations that had beguiled him back to consciousness were soon overpowered by a most unpleasant one—the nagging ache of his head. It felt even worse than last night! The pain wrung a moan from him.

He opened his eyes with some reluctance. Once she realized he was awake, Mrs. Finch would probably stop stroking his face and murmuring his name. But she sounded so anxious, he could not bring himself to distress her for another instant.

His small sacrifice was rewarded with the closest view of her face he'd ever been permitted. Her brown eyes radiated the most tender concern. Something in him melted beneath their attentive warmth.

"Thank God!" she cried with a catch in her voice that made his throat ache in sympathy.

Before he knew what was what, her lips were on his. Their lush softness made him almost forget he *had* a head, let alone that it hurt. Her nearness overwhelmed him in the most pleasurable way. Her delicate hands cradled his face. Her warm, moist breath whispered against his skin. Her subtle feminine scent tempted him to inhale more deeply. A lock of her hair fell forward to tickle his cheek.

Her lips moved against his, puckering, parting, then closing again as if she were nibbling on a sweet, juicy morsel of fruit. For his part, he'd never consumed fruit or confection that tasted as delectable as her kiss. It made him ravenous for more.

He raised his arms and folded them around her, plunging one hand into the silken swirl of her hair. Straining toward her, he explored her mouth with his. He suckled on her full lower lip, then ran his tongue over it with hot, greedy gusto. Desire crackled through his veins like flame racing along a line of gunpowder to cause a dangerous, shattering explosion. He could hardly wait for the fireworks!

A sharp gasp from the doorway brought Sir Robert to his senses in a way Jocelyn Finch's earlier pleas had not. If anything, they had driven him *out* of his senses. The sound made Mrs. Finch start, too. She pulled away from him so abruptly that she almost tumbled to the floor.

"Pardon me!" cried Duckworth. "I did not mean to intrude."

"Nonsense! Come in at once," Sir Robert ordered, his voice rasping with unsated desire. "Mrs. Finch was just—"

"—just checking." She hastened to fill his awkward hesitation. "To make certain His Excellency was not running a fever." The breathless quality of her voice did nothing to subdue his inflamed passion.

Duckworth advanced a few cautious steps into the room. "Pray what did you discover, ma'am? Is he feverish?"

The young man's manner betrayed no suspicion that events might be other than what his master and the lady claimed.

"A trifle warm, perhaps," Jocelyn lied. Surely she must have sensed he was on fire…though not from any ordinary fever. "But I do not think he is any danger. Are you in much pain, Sir Robert?"

"Some." In truth, the ache in his loins had made him forget the one in his head. "But I do not feel quite as dizzy."

"Colonel Carmont told me what happened," said Duckworth. "He asked me to inform you that his men were unable to apprehend any of the trespassers, but they did locate Corporal Miller and Miss Jenkins. It seems the pair eloped to town, where they persuaded Father O'Neil to witness their vows. It is not proper in the eyes of the law, but I daresay it might have been worse."

"Not legal?" Jocelyn pressed her fingers to her lips. No doubt she was recalling the fears that had driven her to weep in Sir Robert's arms several hours earlier.

He sought to explain. "Betrothed couples in the colony are required to file a marriage bond stating their intention and swearing there are no impediments to the proposed union."

Jocelyn greeted the news with a dispirited shake of her head. "I suppose there is no chance of having the marriage quietly annulled."

Even in the faint light of early morning, Sir Robert could make out the blush that mottled Duckworth's face. "Colonel Carmont seemed satisfied the union had been…consummated."

Jocelyn muttered an oath. "Did the colonel say what has been done with the young fools?"

"I believe Miller has been confined to barracks. They fetched Miss Jenkins back here. She is out in the kitchen building at the moment."

"I must go speak to her, I suppose." Jocelyn winced as she rose. "And try to refrain from wringing her neck."

"Wait." Sir Robert hesitated. What he was about to propose was highly irregular, perhaps not even strictly legal. A few hours ago he would never have contemplated it, but now he could sympathize with the young couple smitten by desire. No one would be well served by their disgrace. "Can you fetch some paper and writing implements, Mrs. Finch?"

"Of course, but—"

"Duckworth, I'm sure you are familiar enough with the customary form of such documents to draw one up for the signatures of Corporal and Mrs. Miller."

His aide looked mildly shocked by the request but soon rallied. "If…that is what you wish, sir."

"It is. I expect Colonel Carmont can vouch for Miller and Mrs. Finch for the bride." Both would surely want to avoid the kind of scandal to which this situation might otherwise lead.

Jocelyn gave an eager nod. "Once I've had a quick word with Hetty, I shall bring everything Mr. Duckworth needs."

After she had hurried from the room, Sir Robert made one final request of his aide. "Be a good fellow and date the document for yesterday, will you?"

Late that afternoon, Jocelyn wilted onto a chair in Sally Carmont's private sitting room. "I cannot stay long. I've only come to beg you for the strongest cup of coffee you can spare. Otherwise, I may fall asleep during the ride back to the lodge."

Sally wagged her finger. "You shall not have it. A nap is the very thing you need. Or are you planning to cry off the assembly ball tonight?"

"I dare not." Jocelyn rubbed her throbbing brow. If Sir Robert's head hurt as much as hers, the poor man had her most profound sympathy. "Have you seen the *Gazette* today?"

"Not yet. Will always brings the newspaper home with him and tells me if there is any worthwhile reading in it.

Why? Is there some adverse report about what took place last night?"

"More than one." A bilious spasm gripped Jocelyn's belly. "And a scathing editorial. Mr. Wye seems now as strongly opposed to my mission as he was in favor of it at first. He called for the governor to send the bride ship and its cargo back to England before we cause any more disturbances in the colony."

"That is outrageous!" Sally pounded her fist against the arm of the settee. "What happened last night was not your fault."

Jocelyn wished she could convince herself of that. Every time she remembered her first glimpse of Sir Robert's blood-matted hair, remorse overwhelmed her. "The ball at Government House was my idea, Sally. And I failed in my responsibility to supervise the girls as closely as I should have. Otherwise Hetty could never have run off with Corporal Miller."

"Shh!" Sally hurried to the doorway and gave a furtive look into the next room. When she turned back toward Jocelyn she lowered her voice to an urgent whisper. "You must be careful what you say about that whole business. In a place this size, gossip travels faster than in London. There are only a handful of us who know what truly happened and we must keep it that way. Otherwise yours is not the only removal Mr. Wye will be calling for."

"You're right, of course. I am so tired I scarcely know what I'm saying." Jocelyn had not even trusted Lily Winslow with a true account of Hetty's elopement. The girls had all been assured that she and her besotted corporal were properly wed by Nova Scotia law—a cause for celebration, not scandal.

"I see now what Will means about Sir Robert being a good fellow to have on hand in a tight spot," said Sally. "There have been a few incidents with the garrison of late and this would have looked very bad for Will. Fancy Sir Robert coming up with a plan to make it right—injured as he was. Have you heard how he is faring?"

"Quite well, I think, all things considered." Jocelyn tried to sound as if the governor's condition was of only the most casual concern to her. She wondered what Sally would have thought if she had been the one to catch them kissing this morning, instead of Mr. Duckworth. "He insisted on returning to town this afternoon aboard the admiral's sloop. I understand the doctor has given him strict orders to rest for a few days."

His idea of *rest* would likely entail sitting up in bed, reading reports and petitions, then dictating replies to Mr. Duckworth. The thought brought a smile of fond exasperation to Jocelyn's lips. She was amazed the governor had gone to such lengths to give her a second chance. He might easily have used the riot and Hetty's elopement as excuses to be rid of them all.

But what had made him do it? Was he trying to atone for responding when she'd kissed him this morning. If so, he had no cause to repent. She was the one who'd initiated it, in an outburst of relief. A man would have to be made of stone to resist such an ardent assault upon his lips. Contrary to what she'd once believed, Sir Robert Kerr was not made of stone.

He was a man of flesh and blood—blood he'd shed coming to her defense and flesh that had roused to her kiss. She could not deny that *his* kiss had roused her in turn. She had never imagined him capable of such passion.

Sally's tart tone pierced the bubble of Jocelyn's bemusement. "What have you got to smile about, pray? You haven't slept for the better part of two days, you had a riot on your doorstep and all the support you had from the leaders of the colony seems to be turning into opposition."

"That is not all." The reminder of her lack of sleep made

Jocelyn yawn. "I have also just come from packing off one of the girls back to England, on account of her constant defiance and troublemaking." She told Sally how Vita had provoked the riot at Prince's Lodge.

Her friend's jaw dropped. "After that you put her on a ship back to England? I'd have *drowned* the brazen hussy!"

"Don't suppose I wasn't tempted. If I smiled just now, it was from relief at being rid of her. I can handle the others once they are free from Vita's bad influence and example." It was as good an excuse as any. And perhaps true, in part.

"Which reminds me why I came here," she added.

"For coffee?"

Jocelyn chuckled, though she wasn't sure why. Giddy from lack of sleep, perhaps? "Besides that. I wondered if you could introduce me to some respectable women of mature years who might be willing to assist me in chaperoning the girls? I was foolish to imagine I could do it all myself."

"Let me think." Sally tapped her chin with her forefinger. "There's Mrs. Langford. She's a most agreeable soul and rather lonely in that big house since her niece left to get married."

"I remember, you introduced me to her the other night at Government House. She seemed very pleasant."

"What's more," said Sally, "she was a Brenton before her marriage. They are a large family and vastly clannish. If you can enlist her help, I fancy we won't hear another murmur against you from any of them."

Sally proposed several other women of her acquaintance possessed of even tempers, good sense and sterling reputations. Finally the mantel clock interrupted her by chiming the hour of four.

"Oh dear!" Jocelyn jumped from her chair. "I must get back to the lodge and ready the girls for this evening!"

As Sally ushered her out to her waiting carriage, Jocelyn

tried to curb her mounting dread of facing the censure of Halifax society. "You must introduce me to all those women, tonight, so I may call upon them soon. If I had time, now, I would drop in on Mrs. Langford, but I fear that must wait."

"Do not fret." Sally seized her hands and gave them a heartening squeeze. "You faced down that rabble last night and you overcame the governor's opposition. I have every confidence you will prevail again."

Jocelyn was in too great a hurry to contradict her friend, but she could not share Sally's optimism.

A censorious silence fell over the Halifax assembly hall that evening when Jocelyn and her charges made their entrance. If it had not been for the presence of Will and Sally Carmont, she might have turned tail and fled the place in shame.

The Carmonts greeted her warmly as if nothing had changed since the evening of the governor's levee, when she and her girls had been the toasts of Halifax. Colonel Carmont's officers hastened to invite a number of the girls to dance. Were they acting on the colonel's orders, Jocelyn wondered or were they eager to take advantage of less competition for pretty partners?

Not all the young gentlemen of the town were daunted by the disapproval of their elders. Before long, a few of the bolder ones took to the dance floor with more of Jocelyn's charges. Meanwhile, several clutches of townsfolk gathered around the perimeter of the ballroom, speaking together in low, grave tones. Now and then someone would look up to glare at Jocelyn then return to the conversation with fevered whispers.

Giving a defiant toss of her honey-colored curls, Sally Carmont took Jocelyn's arm and led her toward one such group. It dispersed in a flutter before they reached it. The members of the clique scattered to join up with others in different parts of the room.

Sally raised her fan and spread it open to mask her mischievous grin. "I could not resist seeing what they would do if we approached them. The cowards!"

"Well, don't let's do it again," Jocelyn whispered back. "They might decide to stand their ground next time. Open hostilities with the leading citizens of the colony will not do my reputation or my mission any good."

"I overheard something interesting just before you arrived." Sally checked to make certain no one else was close enough to overhear *her*. "It seems the doting mamas of Halifax were rather dismayed to discover how all the officers and young gentlemen flocked to your girls at the governor's levee. Those with daughters fear all the eligible beaux will be stolen away. The ones with sons are worried the lads might decide to marry dowerless English girls, rather than wed within their own purse-proud circle."

"I see." Looking around the ballroom Jocelyn spied one elegantly dressed young lady watching with longing eyes from the fringe of the dance floor while an equally elegant gentleman twirled Charlotte Reynolds around to the lively strains of "Chelsea Reach." Another young fellow was dutifully dancing with one of the local ladies. But his focus kept straying from his partner to Jocelyn's vivacious charges, who seemed blissfully unaware of the baleful glares being directed at them by the matrons of Halifax.

Both the gentry and the working men of this colony seemed to have the same quarrel with the bride-ship scheme. The people attending tonight's assembly were expressing themselves in a less threatening manner, but the young Irishman and his comrades had made their objections a good deal more plain.

How could Jocelyn convince the matrons of Halifax that

she did not mean to threaten their matchmaking plans for their sons and daughters?

One dance concluded and another began. This time more of the young merchants and professional men ignored the frowns of their parents and invited the newcomers to take the floor. The buzz of conversation from the fringes of the ballroom swelled in volume, like a hornet's nest that had just been shaken.

"Sally, did you get a chance to speak with any of those ladies you mentioned as potential chaperones?"

"Not yet. The truth is I've hardly been able to get near them. Since I'm known to be a friend of yours, I have been cut this evening quite as pointedly as you."

A sense of frustration churned inside Jocelyn. She'd thought the governor stubborn and unreasonable at first, but at least he had been willing to hear her out. "What about Mrs. Langford? She didn't seem like a woman easily cowed by popular opinion. Do you suppose if I spoke to her, she might spread the word among her relations."

"She might." After her earlier burst of audacity, Sally was beginning to look more and more intimidated by the spiteful stares directed at her and Jocelyn. "I haven't seen her here this evening. I'm not sure she attends the assembly balls much. I'll go ask after her…if I can find anyone willing to speak to me."

Before she could beg her friend not to desert her, Sally had slipped away. Jocelyn decided not to chase after her. It might look as though she had been routed. Instead she stood her ground, her attention fixed on the dance floor while her lips froze in a counterfeit smile. She fluttered her fan in front of her face to cool a self-conscious flush that burned in her cheeks.

If only some gentleman would ask her to dance, she might not feel quite so awkward. Colonel Carmont would make an ideal partner. Even a dance with that bothersome Mr. Power would be preferable to standing here alone, the target of so much censorious scrutiny.

She would have given anything, just then, to take the floor on the arm of Sir Robert Kerr. But the governor would be laid up in bed at Government House for some days yet. No doubt he would welcome any excuse to keep him away from the social gatherings he so detested.

Out of the corner of her eye, Jocelyn glimpsed someone approaching. She turned toward the kind soul with a grateful smile. It hardened on her face when she recognized Mr. Wye, the editor of the *Gazette* who had written such horrid things about the bride ship in his newspaper. His glowering countenance warned her he had not come to apologize.

"Good evening, Mrs. Finch." The editor's tone implied he did not truly wish her a *good* evening, but was only paying the barest lip service to civility.

"Mr. Wye."

"I am surprised to find you in attendance this evening, ma'am."

Though she knew the man was baiting her, Jocelyn could not resist asking, "Indeed, sir. And why is that?"

The editor's eyes took on the gleam of a hunter's with prey firmly in his sights. "I assumed you would not want to run the risk of provoking more riots here in town or more of your charges running off with young soldiers."

Fie! Better a hundred stubborn governors than one weather vane of a newsman! At least Sir Robert had been honest and frank in his opposition and sincerely concerned for the welfare of his colonists. Not to mention that he had turned out to be right in several particulars. The governor was a far worthier opponent, yet she could not back down from Mr. Wye's challenge. It would be an insult to Sir Robert if she yielded to an inferior adversary.

"Upon my honor, sir." She prepared to throw down the gauntlet. "I always thought you gentlemen of the press prided yourselves upon the accuracy of your reports."

"Indeed we do!" Mr. Wye bristled. "Are you telling me I have been misinformed? Was there not a riot on the grounds of Prince's Lodge last evening, provoked by the presence of so many unattached young women? And did not one of those young women elope with a soldier assigned to guard the estate?"

Jocelyn sensed several onlookers drawing closer to overhear their conversation. Across the ballroom, she glimpsed Colonel Carmont urging the musicians to play louder. "I cannot vouch for what information you received, sir. It may be that the facts were correct, but the wrong conclusions were drawn from them. I did receive a deputation at the lodge last night. And I cannot deny it grew somewhat…disorderly before it dispersed."

Before the editor could mount a counterattack, Jocelyn hurried on. "But from what those men told me, their actions were prompted by stories in *your* newspaper. Early accounts of the bride ship led them to believe the girls would wed working men like themselves. Then your reports about the levee at Government House convinced them their future brides were being stolen by officers and merchants. One can hardly blame them for wanting to voice their objections."

For all her brave words, she had never felt so cornered or bereft of allies. Where was Sally? Or the colonel? Anyone with a word to say in her defense? She braced for Mr. Wye to demolish her with the stinging wit she had read in his editorial.

But before he could speak, another voice rose from behind her—a familiar and most welcome voice. "Answer the lady, Mr. Wye. Do you advocate the suppression of free speech in Nova Scotia? I have never known you to refrain from voicing *your* objections on any matter."

Sir Robert's comment drew chuckles from several officers and a number of the young gentlemen of the town who happened to be within earshot. Jocelyn turned to reward him with her warmest smile of gratitude. If they had not been in such a public place, she might have repeated her actions of the morning by throwing her arms around his neck and kissing him soundly.

Her first glimpse of Sir Robert startled her. He looked so formal in an old-fashioned powdered wig. Then she understood. He must have donned it to hide the bandage over his head wound. Her relief turned to dismay. The poor man should not be out of bed so soon!

"Humph!" The editor's thick brows bristled. "You cannot hold me responsible for how those young fools acted. I only reported what took place. They drew their own conclusions."

The governor considered for a moment then gave a judicious nod. "I agree, sir. You are no more to blame for the actions of those men than is…Mrs. Finch."

"Er…well…I suppose…" Mr. Wye sputtered.

The governor was not done with him yet. "If you could have witnessed the self-possession and courage with which this lady handled the encounter, I feel certain you would have offered a toast in her honor."

"Indeed?" The editor appeared to realize he had been neatly outflanked. "I received no account of that."

"If you were to," said Sir Robert, "no doubt you would publish it, to counter the negative impression your previous reports may have created."

As Mr. Wye gave a grudging growl of agreement, Jocelyn sensed someone standing beside her. She glanced over to find Lily Winslow, looking pale and anxious but determined.

"I should be happy to provide you with an account, sir." Lily sounded nervous. For all her capability with the other girls, Jocelyn had noticed she shied away from men, especially men of authority. "His Excellency is correct. Mrs. Finch was magnificent. I'm sure your readers would find it a thrilling and inspiring story."

"No doubt," muttered the editor in a tone of reluctant surrender. "Let us find a quiet corner where you can tell me all about the heroics of your chaperone."

Sir Robert raised his hand to detain them a moment. "You might also tell your readers Mrs. Finch has agreed to let her young ladies accompany me on my forthcoming tour of the colony."

Jocelyn struggled to keep her jaw from dropping. She had agreed to no such thing! Sir Robert had not even broached the idea with her.

But when their eyes met, she sensed a plea in his for her indulgence. After all he had done for her, she owed him her trust, difficult as she found it to grant. While he continued to speak, she held her tongue and nodded in agreement, praying he knew what he was doing.

"Since my arrival in Nova Scotia, it has been my desire and intention to visit other parts of the colony." With each word Sir Robert raised the volume of his voice. "No doubt I will receive a much warmer welcome if I am accompanied by a great many pretty young ladies. Besides, Mrs. Finch and I have discussed the need for marriageable women in rural areas of Nova Scotia."

For the second time in two days Jocelyn heard the governor utter a blatant falsehood. He sounded as convincing as when he'd threatened to blow a hole in one of the rioters with an unloaded musket. Yet she sensed it did not come easy for him to dissemble.

They *would* discuss the matter, she decided, and several others. Including their early-morning kiss. What would Sir Robert have to say about that?

Chapter Twelve

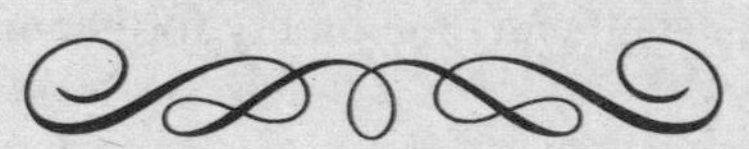

Would Mrs. Finch have his hide? Sir Robert wondered. For publicly committing her to an undertaking she had never discussed with him, let alone agreed to?

He could scarcely blame her if she did. At least she'd had the forbearance to present a united front for Mr. Wye and the crowd at the assembly. More than that he had no right to ask.

He hoped she would understand that he'd had no choice. After reading the *Gazette,* he'd known she would be walking into an ambush tonight. Turning a deaf ear to Duckworth's warnings and pleas, he had risen from his bed, slapped a wig on his wounded head then ventured out to lend Mrs. Finch his support...such as it was.

The effort had set his head pounding again. Beads of sweat prickled on his forehead and at the back of his neck. He wasn't sure if they were caused by the pain in his head or the warmth of the wig. Either way, he did not want to spoil his rout of the belligerent editor by swooning to the floor.

"Come, Sir Robert." Mrs. Finch seized him by the arm and tugged him toward a quiet alcove. "Let us sit for a moment and discuss your plans for this tour of the colony. I have a suggestion to make."

No doubt she did. A suggestion that he stick to the truth from now on, perhaps. Or that he not take advantage of a lady's slip of propriety to kiss her breathless. Still, he did need to sit before he humiliated himself by falling down. And the prospect of a private moment or two with Jocelyn Finch appealed to him, even if it meant enduring her reproaches.

It seemed to take a very long time for them to reach the alcove and sink onto a pair of chairs. Mrs. Finch opened her fan and fluttered it in front of her face, but at such an angle that the breeze cooled Sir Robert, too.

When she spoke, her tone was reproachful, but gently so, prompted by concern rather than annoyance. "Do you call this resting? You should never have left your bed so soon. I must speak to your Mr. Duckworth for permitting it."

Her words acted like the whisper of her fan to revive Sir Robert's spirits. "It's not his fault, poor fellow. I insisted. As you know, I can be rather stubborn at times."

"Stubbornness is a much maligned virtue, in my opinion—one with which I am well supplied, myself. Until you are fully recovered, I warn you I shall be most stubborn in my insistence that you look after yourself properly."

"Are you saying you wish I had stayed away tonight?" No doubt it would have been less awkward for them both if he'd allowed more time to elapse before seeing her again.

Time during which they could have pretended to forget what had passed between them that morning. But how long *would* it take for him to forget that kiss? Far longer than Jocelyn Finch would remain in Nova Scotia.

"For your sake, I do, indeed." The tempo of her fan quickened. "For my own, I cannot deceive you. I have seldom been so happy to hear anyone's voice. This is twice you have come to my rescue, at some cost to yourself. Of course I am grateful, but I hope you do not mean to make a habit of it."

Sir Robert could give her no such assurance.

"Did you mean what you said?" she asked after an awkward pause. "About taking us with you on your tour of the colony?"

"Would you object? I'm sorry I told Wye it was all settled, but I thought the news might take the wind out of his sails. I truly believe the venture could benefit us both."

Her attention never wavered as he told her of his plan to sail around the colony, visiting a number of the larger settlements. "I wish to see for myself the local conditions and hear, firsthand, what the settlers need. Having you and your young ladies along will make the tour more festive, less political. I am certain they'll meet plenty of willing suitors in areas where their presence could do a great deal of good for the colony."

A look of uncertainty creased Jocelyn Finch's features. "But you will not be staying long in any one place. How are my girls to form lasting attachments so quickly? I want them to be happy!"

"I know you do." Sir Robert glanced toward the dance floor, where a number of the young ladies appeared to be enjoying themselves. "But you do not have the power to insure their happiness. The best you can hope is that they will choose husbands wisely and for the right reasons."

"That is true." Her eyes were focused on the dancers, but for a moment her thoughts seemed far away.

Perhaps if Sir Robert made his suggestion now, she would agree without truly hearing him. "What if the eligible men in each settlement write letters of introduction, telling what they want in a wife and what they have to offer?"

One of Jocelyn's delicate brows flew up. "Like the marriage applications you proposed before?"

He should have known better than to imagine he could

sneak anything past her. "Not altogether. The couples themselves would make their choices, but letters might be a useful first step in bringing about compatible matches. Surely even in matters of the heart, one must not lose one's head entirely."

Jocelyn's brow arched even higher. "The way we lost ours this morning, you mean?"

"Yes…I mean, no! Perhaps I misplaced mine, but that is no excuse. I should never…that is, I beg your pardon for what happened!" Of many awkward moments in his life, this was quite one of the worst. Yet when he recalled the lush sweetness of her kiss, Sir Robert could not bring himself to regret it.

"Beg *my* pardon?" Jocelyn raised her fan higher to conceal a teasing grin from everyone but him. "Nonsense! It is I who should beg yours—throwing myself upon you the instant you woke. I fancy any man would have reacted as you did."

"Perhaps so, but…" He should be grateful for the brisk humor with which she dismissed the incident. He *was!* And yet…

She turned toward him. Her incomparable eyes sparkled with daring mischief and her voice dropped to a provocative whisper. "I must confess, I never suspected you capable of such…fervor. You kiss very well, indeed!"

"Madam, please! What if someone should overhear you?" They would likely assume their ears were playing tricks on them.

But he was not certain how much of the lady's playful baiting he could take before being provoked to silence her with another kiss. One that would make this morning's seem subdued and decorous by comparison.

With a mixture of keen anticipation and profound wariness, he found himself looking forward to touring the colony in her company.

* * *

Two weeks later, Jocelyn watched with a mixture of relief and regret as the town of Halifax slowly disappeared into a bank of fog. Sir Robert stood beside her on the aft deck of the *Aldebaran* as it eased out of the harbor, bearing them on their tour of the colony. Nearby, clusters of girls were huddled together, reading and exchanging letters that had reached Sir Robert the previous day from the South Shore town of Liverpool.

"John Sarty?" Mary Ann held up a piece of paper. "Has anybody not read his letter?"

"The widower with two little ones?" Charlotte's tone left no doubt what she thought of a widowed suitor. "Give it to Mary Parfitt. She's always on about wanting a big family. That would give her a head start."

"I've read Mr. Sarty's letter," Mary snapped. "He sounds very amiable and hardworking. I hate to think of those poor babes without a mother."

"Here's one from a shipwright," said Lily. "He claims he goes to church regularly and is temperate in his habits. He writes a very fine hand."

Glancing toward Sir Robert, Jocelyn muttered, "Very well. I'll admit those letters of introduction were a good idea."

The governor did not take his eyes off Fort George, rapidly disappearing into the fog. "I demanded no such admission from you, Mrs. Finch."

"You did not have to. The self-satisfied look on your face spoke volumes." Jocelyn concluded with a soft laugh to let him know she was in jest...at least partly.

Since the evening of the assembly ball, the two of them had discussed, planned and compromised upon their strategy until she was convinced her mission had a far better chance of meeting its objectives. Mrs. Beamish would be pleased with her next report.

Sir Robert nodded toward the girls. "I was beginning to worry we might have no prospective brides left to bring along with us on this tour. I should not have been able to show my face in Liverpool or anywhere else without an armed escort."

"There has been quite a rash of marriage proposals in the past few days." Jocelyn waved her handkerchief one last time at a clutch of girls standing on the wharf with Sally Carmont. "I reckon their beaux were afraid the girls might not return to Halifax if they left on this tour."

Sir Robert nodded. "It was prudent of you to insist their weddings wait until we return."

Prudent? Jocelyn strove not to make a face at the word. No doubt the governor thought he was paying her a great compliment. "After what happened with Hetty and Corporal Miller, I could not abide the prospect of more hasty weddings. I hope the girls will behave themselves for Sally and Mrs. Langford until we return."

Halifax society had relaxed its disapproval of her charges once the governor announced he would be taking them away to the far corners of the colony. Jocelyn did not want any more scandalous incidents stirring up fresh gossip.

"It was a good thing a few stayed behind." Sir Robert scanned the crowded deck. "Otherwise we might be packed as tight as a catch of herring for our voyage to Liverpool."

Though his words conjured up a ridiculous image, Jocelyn could not help wondering what it might be like to share close quarters with the handsome governor. Ever since the morning of their imprudent kiss, her attraction to Sir Robert Kerr had intensified daily.

Whenever he held her hand during the course of a dance, she recalled the seductive way his fingers had tangled in her hair. When he spoke, she could not keep her gaze from straying to his lips. Sometimes she fancied she could feel them upon hers again, moving with sweet, wild urgency.

Often she searched his cool blue eyes for a secret gleam that might betray his preoccupation with similar thoughts about her. But his usual facade of solemn courtesy gave nothing away. Had her kiss stirred anything more than a passing fancy in him? It seemed not.

And that did not seem fair. For it had stirred far too many and far too intense feelings in her. Foremost, it had reminded her how much she missed the feel of a man's arms about her, the breathtaking power of his kiss…even the soft rumble of his snoring in the bed beside her at night. Since Ned's death she had been too numbed by grief, consumed by bitterness and preoccupied with her struggle for survival to think of any man as an object of desire. How she wished that had not changed!

Yet part of her was not sorry it had. Her kiss had roused Sir Robert from a deep and dangerous sleep, like the bewitched princess in one of her favorite nursery tales. But he had woken something in her, too. For all her frustrated longing, Jocelyn felt alive again in a way she had not since Ned's death…and perhaps even before that.

Their reception in Liverpool was everything Jocelyn had expected and hoped they would receive when they'd arrived in Halifax. This time their coming had been announced well in advance. There should be no unpleasant surprises and no unfortunate misunderstandings on either side.

A number of smaller vessels sailed out to welcome the *Aldebaran* when it entered the harbor. They escorted it to the wharf, which looked to be thronged with an even larger crowd than had greeted the *Hestia* in Halifax.

"Do you hear, Mrs. Finch?" cried Charlotte. "They are ringing the church bells for us!"

"I expect the bells are meant to welcome the governor, my dear." Jocelyn bustled among her charges, straightening the bow of a bonnet here, ordering a hanging petticoat hiked up there. "Now, you must all promise me faithfully that you will be on your best behavior. Heaven knows what sort of stories about us have reached here from Halifax. I do not want to give anyone ammunition for more tattle. Is that understood?"

Perhaps remembering how Vita had been bundled off back to England, the girls responded with a subdued "Yes, ma'am."

They soon recovered their high spirits, however. Whatever reports had made their way down the South Shore about the bride ship, the local folk appeared inclined to believe only the favorable ones. Their welcome could not have been warmer.

After a few brief addresses by leading citizens of the town and a general exchange of pleasantries, the governor's party was treated to a fine dinner in the local assembly hall. The men who had submitted letters of introduction were presented to Jocelyn's charges, then seated opposite them at several long tables to become better acquainted during the meal.

Jocelyn was given a seat across the table from the governor, with the local magistrate's wife on one side of her and the sister of a prominent local shipbuilder on the other. Over steaming bowls of chowder and plates of salmon in egg sauce, the men discussed colonial politics and business. Meanwhile the ladies chatted about matchmaking and all the social events they had planned for the governor's visit.

Engaged as she was in their conversation, Jocelyn still could not prevent herself from stealing several covert glances at Sir Robert. He really was a most well-favored gentleman, with his firm, angular jaw, well-shaped nose and frank, penetrating blue eyes. As for the way his broad shoulders filled out his splendid dress uniform—it gave new meaning to the customary address His Excellency.

"...Don't you agree, Mrs. Finch?"

"Yes, indeed," Jocelyn murmured, her attention upon the governor. "Most excellent."

"I beg your pardon?" The sharp tone of the magistrate's wife roused Jocelyn from her blatant admiration of Sir Robert.

It drew his attention to her. "Is there a problem, ladies?"

"None at all." Jocelyn felt like a child caught filching tarts from the pantry. She turned to her dining companion to avoid the governor's perceptive scrutiny. "I was just thinking what an excellent welcome you have extended us. I fear it distracted me from what you were saying."

"A feeble jest, I'm afraid. I was wondering what you and Governor Kerr would do if *all* your young ladies lose their hearts here on the South Shore and you had no brides left to go with you to Yarmouth and Annapolis?"

Jocelyn laughed as if it were the most amusing remark she'd heard in a great while. Across the table, Sir Robert and the other gentlemen chuckled, too.

"I should be obliged to postpone the rest of my tour, naturally." The governor broke apart a biscuit and spread half of it with fresh butter. "Otherwise I would risk inciting rebellion. And that would never do."

The rest of their stay in Liverpool passed in a hectic round of social functions. By the end of the first week, it was clear several serious matches were blossoming between Jocelyn's charges and the bachelors of the South Shore. Before offers of marriage could be made or accepted, Jocelyn insisted each girl pay at least one chaperoned visit to the home of her suitor, to see what sort of life she could expect to lead *after* the wedding.

"Marriage is not all parties and picnics, you know," she warned the girls on more than one occasion. "I hope you will choose a husband for more than his engaging conversation and his dancing ability."

She was pleasantly surprised when Sir Robert asked to accompany her on these visits to the homes of ordinary fishermen and farmers.

"There is more to governing a colony than sitting in council meetings and writing reports." He echoed the tone he'd overheard her use to lecture the girls about marriage. "I want to see firsthand how my colonists live, especially the new settlers."

To her further surprise, Jocelyn found the governor's presence helped ease the initial awkwardness of such visits. His sincere interest and forthright questions coaxed the men to talk about their present difficulties and their hopes for the future.

Once the ice had been broken by his refreshing frankness, Jocelyn employed her subtle tact. "When we came in, I could not help notice what a fine view you have of the bay. Sir Robert, would you be so kind as to escort me for a better look?"

The first time she'd asked, he gave her a mystified look and practically needed to be dragged from the house. He soon came to understand, however.

"This *is* quite a pleasant view," he announced on the fifth such occasion as he offered Jocelyn his arm. "I was amazed that you could keep a straight face, yesterday, when you asked for a better view of that swamp near Mr. Jacobson's place."

"*Marsh,*" Jocelyn corrected him. "And I thought it looked very pleasant with the breeze rippling through the reeds. It reminded me of the fenlands in Norfolk where I grew up. You might not believe it, but I am a simple country lass at heart."

They passed a most enjoyable half hour, trading stories of her childhood on a great estate in eastern England and his in a small town on the Scottish border. Like everything else about them, their upbringings had been quite different. Why, then, did she feel such a growing bond with a man so little like her…and quite the opposite of her darling Ned?

* * *

On the day before their departure from Liverpool, a rash of weddings took place at which Sir Robert was invited to give away the brides. Having little experience with nuptial ceremonies, he was not prepared for his emotions to be stirred so deeply.

As he walked down the aisle of the small Methodist chapel early that evening with a radiant young lady on his arm, his throat tightened and a curious mixture of pride and wistfulness overwhelmed him. He managed to deliver the bride to her waiting groom and force out a gruff "I do" when the clergyman inquired who gave the girl in marriage. Then he retreated to a nearby pew where Jocelyn had saved a seat for him.

Leaning toward him, she whispered, "You are getting good at this. With a bit more practice you will soon be an expert."

The teasing warmth in her voice coaxed a reluctant smile from him. It felt pleasing and proper to have her by his side while the Methodist preacher spoke about the sacred duties of marriage.

For as long as he could recall, he'd intended never to wed. The army had been his destined career and, while he'd been willing to sacrifice his own life for King and country, he could not condemn a wife and children to the hard life his family had endured after his father's death.

With that resolution in mind, he'd taken care to avoid the company of women. Eventually he'd almost forgotten the reason and simply kept his distance from the fair sex as a matter of habit. Then Jocelyn Finch had marched down the gangway of the bride ship and into his life. He'd tried to keep his distance from her, but she had refused to let him. Gradually he discovered that he liked her best at the distance she was now—close by his side.

After the final wedding of the day, a large crowd gathered

to celebrate at the home of Mr. Parker, a shipbuilder who had grown rich from privateering. That evening, the guests all congregated in the garden, which was his sister's pride and joy.

It was a fine warm night with enough of an ocean breeze to keep the mosquitos at bay. Tin lanterns sat at intervals on the low stone wall that enclosed the garden. They cast a flickering fairy light over the beds of flowers that perfumed the summer air. Even Sir Robert, the most practical and unfanciful of men, was not immune to the magical atmosphere that pervaded the place.

Their host served up an excellent punch made from the finest Caribbean rum, sugar, oranges and lemons, all brought to Liverpool by his own small trading fleet. After several rounds of toasts to the various brides and grooms with that potent libation, Sir Robert felt more than usually pleased with everyone and everything around him.

"May I have the honor of proposing one last salute?" he asked Mr. Parker.

"By all means, Your Excellency, but do let me refill your cup first." Parker helped him to a further generous measure of punch while a number of other guests also took the opportunity to procure refills.

The company fell silent when Sir Robert raised his glass, until he could hear the distant whisper of ocean waves washing against the shore. "Tonight we have drunk to the health and felicity of all the newlyweds. Now I wish to propose a toast to the person responsible for making this happy occasion possible."

He turned toward the lady standing beside him—a lady who seemed to grow more attractive every time he looked at her. "I know it has not been an easy task bringing her charges across an ocean and watching over them as they seek worthy partners in a new, young land. Speaking for myself, I would gladly govern a dozen colonies rather than organize such a venture!"

Chuckles of agreement and murmurs of approval rippled through the company.

"Since she first came ashore in Halifax several weeks ago, I have watched her efforts with astonishment and admiration. There have been a few stumbling blocks in her path, and I freely admit to being one of the worst. But she has persevered against all obstacles with a commendable mixture of resolve and charm. Today we have seen the first fruits of her labors and we must acknowledge her success. If I am not mistaken, the years ahead will see a number of little girls in this community bearing the name....Jocelyn."

He savored her name upon his tongue. He fancied it had the sweet, wild tang of fresh strawberries. "Please join me in a toast to Mrs. Jocelyn Finch and her continued success!"

All around the garden, glasses clinked softly and hearty voices echoed the governor's words.

The voice of the lady herself was almost lost in the general acclaim. "I vow, Sir Robert, you are determined to make me blush!"

"And what if I am?" An exhilarating sense of recklessness possessed him. "You look very pretty when you blush."

She laughed. "You, sir, have had too much punch!"

Before he could contradict her, one of the brides appeared with her new husband in tow. "Governor Kerr is right, ma'am! We all owe you our thanks. And I thought I was being so clever intending to name our first daughter after you. No doubt she will have plenty of little playmates named Jocelyn, too!"

"Indeed she will!" Another of the brides threw her arms around Mrs. Finch's neck. "This has been the happiest day of my life and it never would have come about without you!"

Soon Jocelyn was surrounded by several very emotional young women, embracing her and shedding happy tears.

"You *will* all write to me?" She begged with a catch in her voice that touched Sir Robert. "Let me know how you are getting on? Send your letters care of Mrs. Beamish in London."

"Perhaps you will visit Liverpool again next year with another bride ship?" suggested one of the girls. "Then we can all be together again."

That notion appealed to Sir Robert, though the thought of Jocelyn going back to England made him drain his cup of punch rather more quickly than he meant to.

He did not get another opportunity to talk with her until the party dispersed and she had marshaled her remaining charges to walk them back to the houses where they'd been billeted.

"May I offer my services as an escort?" he asked. "You never know when the company of an old soldier might come in handy."

"You are *not* old!" She sounded vexed at the suggestion he might be. "But will it not take you out of your way?"

For the past fortnight, he had been a guest of the magistrate, who lived less than a quarter of a mile from where they were standing.

Sir Robert shrugged. "It is a pleasant night for a stroll in the moonlight...unless you have some objection to my company."

"Don't be absurd!" She gave his arm a playful cuff. "I have always found your company most stimulating—even at first, when we didn't get along."

By heaven, he would like to show her how stimulating his company could be! But it would take more than a little rum punch and the presence of an attractive woman to overthrow a lifetime of restraint and self-discipline.

"Likewise." He acknowledged her praise with a decorous

bow. No one overhearing them would ever guess what a tempest brewed within him.

"In that case, let us go." She took his arm and they set off after the girls, who had already started on their way, engaged in animated chatter about all the weddings and the letters of introduction that had arrived the previous day from Yarmouth.

"What a glorious evening to crown a happy day!" Jocelyn gave a sigh of satisfaction.

"Did all the weddings remind you of your own?" More than once today Sir Robert had glimpsed a wistfulness in her eyes that made him ache to comfort her.

"Hardly!" Her voice held a grating note of bitterness. "Ned could not spare the funds for a special license, and I feared my father would use his influence with the bishop to prevent us getting one. So we ran away to Scotland and had one of those 'anvil weddings,' which may *sound* terribly romantic, but aren't. I am so happy the girls who got married today were able to exchange their vows in proper churches, surrounded by people who care about them."

Fearing he would only say the wrong thing if he tried, Sir Robert reached over and patted her hand as it nestled in the crook of his arm.

"Not that I minded so very much at the time," Jocelyn hastened to add. "At least I tried not to. As long as it meant Ned and I could be together, what did it signify where or how we wed? But later, and especially after…he was gone, I felt cheated somehow. I loved him so much, it should have been a cause for celebration. Eloping felt furtive and shameful."

"Your husband must have been a very fine man." Sir Robert had great difficulty speaking those words. Envy for the late Captain Finch smoldered deep in his belly and no amount of shame could quench it.

"Fine?" said Jocelyn. "That sounds so cold and impeccable. Heaven bless him, Ned was neither of those. He had a hasty temper and he was not always as prudent with our money as he might have been. But he had such a winning way about him, it was impossible to stay angry. Whenever he was around, it felt like a holiday. I'd had such a quiet upbringing, I found his high spirits and charm irresistible."

"I can imagine." Indeed he could. What Jocelyn Finch had described sounded all too much like his feelings for her.

As she continued to talk about her brief but happy marriage, the moonlit magic of the night mocked Sir Robert. How could a man so opposite in every way from her fascinating first husband ever hope to win her?

How could he even persuade himself to try?

Chapter Thirteen

If she had loved Ned Finch as much as she claimed, why did she find herself so potently attracted to a man who was not like him in the least?

Jocelyn stared out at the choppy waves of the Atlantic, her emotions as turbulent as the ocean. After departing from Liverpool on the morning tide, the *Aldebaran* was now headed for Yarmouth, a thriving port on the westernmost tip of the colony. In the overcast sky above, a flock of seagulls glided and wheeled. Their shrill cries sounded like an accusing chorus. *Why? Why? Why?*

Jocelyn had no answer to give them…or herself.

Last night when she'd walked in the moonlight with Sir Robert, clinging to his arm, she had talked continuously about her late husband. But her thoughts and senses had been focused on the man by her side. His nearness brought her a feeling of exhilaration tempered with security. His restrained manner challenged her to rouse the unexpected passion she had glimpsed in him that morning at Prince's Lodge.

Perhaps that's all he was to her—a challenge, the likes of

which she had never been able to resist. And a reminder of everything she missed about having a man in her life.

The sound of firm, brisk footsteps coming toward her drew Jocelyn's attention. She tried not to blush when she saw the governor. She also tried to forget what he had said about her looking pretty when she blushed. Whatever could have prompted that remark…besides Mr. Parker's rum punch?

He showed no sign of thinking any such flattering nonsense this morning. "I have told the captain to take us as far as Seal Island today. Then we can continue on to Yarmouth tomorrow."

After the rough crossing she'd endured from England, Jocelyn did not relish the notion of spending the night aboard ship. "Seal Island? That sounds rather desolate. Is there no town where we could put in for the night, instead?"

"None very near." The governor shook his head, all solemn and businesslike. The flatterer and confidant of last night seemed to have disappeared with the dawn of a new day. "Besides, I want to see the island for myself. I've had a petition to fund a lighthouse there. Before I raise the matter in council, I would like to satisfy myself of the need."

His voice sharpened. "This *is* a working tour, remember, not an excuse for matchmaking from one end of the colony to the other."

Jocelyn's volatile and bewildering mixture of feelings for the governor made his remark sting more harshly than it might have otherwise. Ned, bless his heart, had hardly ever raised his voice to her during their marriage.

"I will thank you not to take that tone with me, sir!" She welcomed her anger. Perhaps it would put a stop to her foolish infatuation with Sir Robert Kerr. "This tour was your idea, if you recall. You invited us to accompany you—something about receiving a warmer welcome if you brought along a bunch of pretty young ladies. Or was that just a ruse to fob off Mr. Wye?"

"In part perhaps, but—"

There, he admitted it! "If you consider me and my charges too great an inconvenience, we will gladly part company with you at Yarmouth. Any of the girls who do not find suitable husbands there can accompany me back to Halifax."

She stormed away from him. Hateful man!

"Mrs. Finch, please," he called after her in an exasperated tone.

Well, he could be no more exasperated than she! It wasn't just what he'd said and how he'd said it, but the unwelcome realization that he had the power to injure her feelings. Yet he still made her pulse race and her senses tingle...even when she was furious enough to throttle him! She dared not speak to him again until she got her wayward emotions under control.

But the Atlantic Ocean had other ideas. At that moment a sudden swell caught the *Aldebaran* amidships. The deck gave a lurch, throwing Jocelyn off balance. Flailing her arms in a vain effort to break her fall, she prepared to make bruising contact with the deck. Instead she found herself caught in the governor's strong arms.

"Are you all right?" He sounded as if he truly cared.

"Thanks to you, I have suffered no injury, except to my dignity." Jocelyn struggled out of his embrace, though the struggle was less against him than against her own inclination to linger in his arms.

He helped her to her feet then released her readily...all except one hand, to which he clung. "Then kindly do me the favor of hearing my apology?"

She did owe him that. And his look of genuine contrition would have persuaded her in any case.

"Very well." She straightened her bonnet and tried to recover her composure, which seemed to have washed overboard. "You have my attention."

He had claimed far too much of her attention, almost from the moment she'd stepped onto the wharf in Halifax.

"I beg your pardon, Mrs. Finch." Sir Robert did not release her hand. And she could not bring herself to pull it away. "You are right in every particular. You and your charges are here by my invitation. It is true the idea first occurred to me as a way of placating Mr. Wye. But I believe our visit to the South Shore has proven the benefits of this tour to both of us. Most of all, to the communities we visit."

"Then why did you say what you did just now?" Jocelyn tried not to sound like a child sulking after being scolded.

But she could not deny her feelings harked back to the few times in her youth when her father had spoken sharply to her. The marquess would never have thought of apologizing, though. Especially not to his daughter.

"I begged your pardon." Sir Robert released her hand at last. "I told you I was wrong. What more do you want from me?"

Before she could reply, he seemed to relent. Perhaps he had decided she deserved an explanation after all. "I have had some disturbing news from Halifax. I made the mistake of venting my frustration upon you. For that I am sorry. I suppose your affable paragon of a husband never engaged in such contemptible behavior."

What disturbing reports from Halifax? Jocelyn wondered. And what did Ned have to do with this? But the governor's words made her think.

"No, he did not, that I can recall. I did, though. Whenever his leave was about to end and he would have to go away again, I would often pick a quarrel…because I was worried he would never come back to me."

Somehow Ned had recognized her ill temper for what it was. She remembered him pulling her onto his knee and saying, "Don't fret, sweet Jo. I've got more lives than a dozen cats. I'll still be around vexing you to pieces when we're ninety!"

"Then you *do* understand." The governor's voice wrenched Jocelyn from her bittersweet memories. "Though I reckon you had far better cause to pick a quarrel than I did just now. You know, whenever I was tempted to regret my decision not to wed, I would ask myself if I could bear to leave behind a wife to wonder and worry when I went off to battle."

A hint of longing in his voice assured Jocelyn he *had* been tempted to regret it. That did not surprise her as it once might have. "I assure you, I would rather have endured the loss of my husband a hundred times than never to have known the happiness of our marriage, however brief."

The governor shook his head as if he could not fathom such feelings. "You are a gallant lady, Mrs. Finch. And your husband was a very lucky man."

"Lucky for us the wind died down." The captain of the *Aldebaran* lifted a long spyglass to his eye and stared toward the coast of Nova Scotia, a distant gray smudge along the western horizon. "It's a foolhardy sailor who wants to risk rounding the Devil's Elbow in rough seas."

"That bad, is it?" asked the governor, who stood beside him on the foredeck.

The captain nodded. "A miserable mess of rocks and shoals. The worst bloody tides in the world to pull you onto them. And fog more than half the time so you can't see what's coming until it's too late."

"Will we be able to make a safe anchorage off the island before sunset?" Sir Robert did not want to risk any danger to Mrs. Finch and her charges, especially after their difficult crossing from England.

"Like I said, sir, it's not so bad on a clear, calm day. We'll be there with a couple of hours of daylight to spare."

Evidently the captain knew his job, for the evening was still young when they dropped anchor in a sheltered cove on the eastern side of the island. Sir Robert and Mr. Duckworth scrambled down into the ship's boat where one of the crewmen rowed them the short distance to shore. Mrs. Finch and some of the young ladies watched from the deck of the *Aldebaran*.

Just as the boat reached the beach, a man appeared. He looked to be somewhere between the ages of the governor and his aide. He wore sturdy work clothes, his shirtsleeves rolled up to reveal muscular, well-tanned arms.

"Welcome to Seal Island, sirs. Is your ship in trouble?" His question and his puzzled look suggested that could be the only reason for anyone to visit the island.

Sir Robert strode forward, his hand extended. "Captain Howell? I am Governor Kerr. I received your petition about…"

"Th-the governor?" The man wiped his hand on his breeches before taking Sir Robert's and giving it a hearty shake. "I'm not Howell, sir. I'm his brother-in-law, Edmund Canning."

He turned and bellowed at the top of his lungs, "Richard, Mary, Jerusha, come quick! It's the governor!"

Another man, somewhat older than Mr. Canning, came running, followed by two young women, one carrying a baby. Sir Robert had never received a warmer welcome in his life.

Once introductions were concluded, he lost no time coming to the point of his visit. "Your petition impressed me, Captain Howell. Since I had to sail past your island, I thought it might be worthwhile to see the place for myself and to discuss your situation at greater length than letters allow."

"A fine idea, sir," said Howell.

He seemed about to say more when his wife laid a small, work-roughened hand on his arm. "Why don't we invite our guests back to the house, my dear? It's a little more comfortable than standing around the beach."

"Do you have time, sir?" Howell asked.

Sir Robert nodded. "We plan to anchor here for the night, if that is agreeable."

"It's an honor, sir. Come, our place is this way. We've all been living in one house, but this summer we're building Edmund and Jerusha a place of their own."

As the party ambled up the beach, Sir Robert asked, "Do I understand you survived a shipwreck in these waters?"

"Aye, sir. It was my good fortune to be rescued by some brave fishermen from Barrington and brought to shore where the Cannings took me in. If I'd ended up on the island, instead, they'd have been burying my bones the next spring."

"They? But I thought the island was uninhabited before you elected to settle here?"

Captain Howell glanced toward his wife. "Why don't you tell the governor? You know more about that part of it than I."

Mrs. Howell did not take any great urging. "Every winter there would be at least one wreck, you see. We'd know because wreckage would wash ashore and sometimes we'd catch a glimpse of lights on the island—fires made out here by the survivors. But it was too dangerous for any boats from Barrington to sail out after them. The fires would burn for a night or two then they'd go out and we'd know those poor souls had starved or frozen or died of their injuries."

By now they had reached a snug house sheltered by a small grove of evergreens, stunted by the relentless Atlantic winds.

Mrs. Howell stared up at Sir Robert, almost challenging him not to be moved by her account. "Have you ever known someone was dying, sir, and not been able to go to their aid?"

Her words conjured up dark memories of one particular battle and a boyish lieutenant who'd looked a bit like Duckworth.

"Now, Mary…" protested her husband.

Sir Robert lifted his hand to indicate he did not mind the question. "I have been a soldier, ma'am."

She gave a solemn nod, as if satisfied. Then she continued her story. "When spring came, we would sail out to the island." She glanced toward her brother. "Our pa's a preacher. He said the least we could do was give those poor folks a decent burial."

Sir Robert winced. The woman scarcely looked old enough to be wed. She must have been little more than a child when she'd first come here on that grim mission. "Your father brought you with him to bury dead bodies?"

Corpses that had lain out in the open for weeks, perhaps month, exposed to the elements. .

"Brought?" Edmund Canning's deep voice rumbled. "Why we could not keep her from coming along, short of tying her up."

They all crowded into the main room of the little house where the women served them tea. Captain Howell gave the governor an account of their first two years on Seal Island. "There was one wreck that first winter and four this past. We still had bodies to bury from folks who drowned, but we saved eight people who would have perished if we had not been here to give them warmth, shelter and food."

"I sincerely commend you." Sir Robert fixed each of them with a look of admiration. "Though I doubt any words of mine can add to the satisfaction you must take from the lives you have saved. If nothing else, I can promise you a grant of money to help defray the costs of your…guests."

Captain Howell set his mug on the table. "That's good of you, sir. I'm sure we'd be glad of the help. But now that we're here, it doesn't seem enough just to save the folks that make it to shore. If we had a good boat, we might be able to rescue more from the sea. And if we built a lighthouse, we might be able to prevent most of those wrecks altogether."

When they finished their tea, Sir Robert asked if they might show him around the island. Mrs. Canning stayed behind to put the baby to bed. But Captain Howell, his wife and brother-in-law gave the governor a thorough tour of the southern part of Seal Island, which was divided from the northern portion by a wide stretch of sand and a large, shallow pond.

Sir Robert's hosts pointed out particular rocks that took their names from the ships that had wrecked upon them. They showed him the graveyard, far more heavily populated than the island itself. At his insistence, they paid a visit to the site where the Cannings' house was slowly taking shape.

"Strange you should not build it closer to the other one," he remarked, surveying the sturdy frame. "In such an isolated place, I'd think you would want to huddle together for company."

Captain Howell pointed out toward the ocean. "That might be pleasant, sir. But we didn't come here for pleasure. If Edmund and Jerusha live here, they can keep watch over a whole section of the coast we cannot see from the other house."

Canning nodded. "We're hoping to convince my wife's brother to come out in a year or two and build a place on the north part of the island. If he does, we should be able to watch over the whole island."

Not even a grant of money and his most strenuous effort to secure funds for a lighthouse seemed enough for Sir Robert to do to help these courageous, compassionate people.

The western horizon was stained a glowing crimson when the crewman from the *Aldebaran* suggested they head back to the ship.

"Red sky at night," said Captain Howell. "You'll have fine weather for sailing on to Yarmouth, tomorrow."

An idea suddenly took root in Sir Robert's mind. Though he knew there might be the devil to pay with Jocelyn Finch, he could not keep from voicing it. "Would you object if we stayed over an extra day and gave you a hand working on the new house?"

When his hosts looked aghast, he tried to forestall their objections. "An old soldier can turn his hand to most anything, and my aide knows the business end of a hammer. Don't you, Duckworth?"

"Indeed, sir. I should be honored to render my assistance. And it would give you more time to discuss the proposed lighthouse. The more intimately you are acquainted with the matter, the better able you will be to persuade the assembly and the council."

"Precisely what I was going to say." Sir Robert patted Duckworth on the shoulder.

They exchanged a covert look that acknowledged he could never have come up with such an eloquent argument.

"I reckon if you insist." Captain Howell still appeared somewhat doubtful. "It would be a great boon to have a couple more men to lend a hand."

Mrs. Howell and her brother bid their guests good-night, while the captain escorted them back to the beach.

"The governor of Nova Scotia," he murmured to himself as if he still could not believe it, "paying a call on Seal Island."

"Thank you for your hospitality." Sir Robert shook his hand. "We shall look forward to a good day's work tomorrow. I can scarcely express the depth of my admiration for what you and Mr. Canning have begun here."

The captain shook his head. "It's not us, sir. I mean, it is, but...we'd never be here now if it wasn't for my wife. She's the one who convinced us we must give it a try at least. And here we are. She insisted I must write and ask you to build us a lighthouse. And here you are. They say the Fundy tides are some of the most powerful in the world, but I reckon they've met their match in my Mary."

As Sir Robert's small party rowed back to the *Aldebaran*, the governor mulled over what Captain Howell had said. He thought about Mrs. Howell, and Mrs. Finch and his mother. The young ladies who had left their homeland to venture across an ocean in hopes of finding love and beginning a new life.

The weaker sex? Sir Robert fancied not.

Duckworth must have mistaken the cause of his pensive silence. "Worried what Mrs. Finch will say when she hears we'll be staying another night, sir? Would you like me to break the news to her?"

The governor stirred from his thoughts. "Kind of you to offer, but I'm not as cowardly as that."

He did flinch, just a little, from the look in Mrs. Finch's eyes—a mixture of disappointment and impatience. But once he told her some of what he had learned that evening, her attitude underwent a complete reversal.

"Of course we must stay! Is there anything the girls and I might do to help? I'm afraid I would be hopeless at any actual construction work, but I would be happy to fetch things for you or run errands."

Sir Robert thought for a moment then began to nod. "Perhaps you *should* come ashore tomorrow. I don't suppose the ladies here get much company. They might enjoy a visit."

"I'll ask the captain if we might borrow from the galley stores to make everyone a nice meal," she suggested.

No doubt the captain would bend over backwards to give her whatever she asked—like most men who came under the influence of her skilful blend of determination and charm.

* * *

The summer sun had barely risen when Sir Robert, Mr. Duckworth and several crewmen rowed ashore. By the time Jocelyn and the girls followed, the pounding of hammers could be heard in the distance.

Some of the girls spent the morning fetching and carrying for the men. Others helped Mrs. Howell and Mrs. Canning with their washing and made a great fuss over the baby. The rest spent the morning preparing a midday meal, which was eaten out of door, spiced by the briny ocean breeze.

After they had eaten, the men returned to work while the ladies spent a pleasant social hour.

"Would you care for a tour around the island?" asked Mrs. Howell when her sister-in-law had taken the baby inside for a long-overdue nap. "It isn't very big, but what's here, I'd be glad to show you."

"Please, ma'am," said Lily. "It's called Seal Island. Do any seals ever come here? All I've seen this morning is sheep."

Jocelyn had been surprised to see so many ewes and lambs wandering at will, grazing on the hardy island grass and shrubs.

With a merry laugh, Mrs. Howell rose and beckoned them all. "Come and see for yourselves."

They rose and followed her to the rocky southern tip of the island.

Jocelyn gave a cry of surprise when several brown-gray lumps she had supposed to be rocks suddenly began to move. Wriggling over the sand between real rocks, they slid into the water and disappeared. But plenty more remained behind.

"Lazy old things," said Mrs. Howell. "They'll lie there sunning themselves for hours on a day like this. I often envy them their leisure."

Was she ever tempted to envy the creatures the society of so many of their own kind? Jocelyn wondered. Life on this windswept parcel of rock and sand must be hard and solitary. Yet Mary Howell seemed more than content in the life she had chosen.

Jocelyn could not help admiring the woman...and envying her a little.

Mr. Duckworth appeared just then, mopping his brow with his handkerchief. "The governor and I will be sore tomorrow, no doubt. But it is gratifying to see the results of one's work so quickly. Reports and documents and meetings seem endless. Once one is done, there are several more to tackle, yet we seldom see what comes of it all."

"Those reports and meetings will be worthwhile if Sir Robert can secure funds for boats and a lighthouse." Jocelyn watched as several of the girls took off their shoes and walked barefoot in the sand to get a closer view of the seals. "I only wish there was something I could do to help."

A scrap of memory suddenly reared in her mind. "Sir Robert told me he had received troublesome news from Halifax, but he did not say what it was about. Could you enlighten me, perhaps?"

When the young man hesitated, she begged him. "I am not asking you to betray a confidence or government secrets. But I owe Sir Robert a great deal and if there is anything I can do to help..."

"Well...we did hear from Colonel Carmont that there were rumblings among the council against this tour. They're worried the governor cares more about the rest of the colony than he does about Halifax. They seem to think Halifax *is* the colony."

Jocelyn nodded as she called out to the girls not to venture too close to the seals. "What a pity the governor could not have brought a few of them along on this tour. No one with a heart could fail to be moved by the sight of that graveyard or Mrs. Howell's stories."

Once again she found herself wishing she could find some way to help Sir Robert.

Chapter Fourteen

"Heaven help me," Sir Robert murmured to himself as he stared at the great stack of documents awaiting his attention.

For the first time in many weeks, he was back behind his desk at Government House. The very number of papers piled upon it seemed to chide him for his neglect. For twopence, he would have lit a fire in the hearth and burned them all to cinders.

Well, perhaps not. He'd taken a holiday from his duties, but he could not abandon them altogether. He must justify Wellington's faith in him and merit the many sacrifices his mother had made to provide him with a proper upbringing.

But even if he had to work twice as hard to get caught up, he did not regret going away. Even if the council opposed every project for which he needed funds, he would not be sorry he had lent Jocelyn Finch his support and taken her charges along on his tour of the colony.

Duckworth entered just then, appearing more than usually anxious. "Can you look through your correspondence, sir, for a report from the National School? They have had such success instructing the boys of Halifax that the headmaster is eager to begin classes for girls as well. He begs leave to meet with you at your earliest convenience to discuss the idea."

"He can expect my full support." Sir Robert began to rifle through the stack of documents. "Send a message saying I shall be pleased to meet with the headmaster tomorrow morning at nine."

His acquaintance with Mrs. Finch and her charges had kindled his sympathy for the plight of girls without resources. Schooling might prove a long-term means to remedy a number of social evils. At the very least, it was a good place to start.

"I'll see to it at once, sir." Duckworth turned to go.

But not before his dispirited tone caught Sir Robert's attention. "Why the long face, man? Not happy to be home after a summer gadding about?"

A weak smile barely lifted the corners of the young man's mouth before letting them fall again. "This isn't really my home, is it, sir?"

What the devil did *that* mean? "Pining for the Thames Valley, are you?"

"No, sir. Any sign of that report yet?"

"Not yet. Ah, yes, here it is." Sir Robert began to read, then set the document aside and called to Duckworth as he tried to slip out of the room. "Get back here, and take a seat."

Some kinds of duty might reflect no honor on his position or reputation. That did not make them any less important.

"I beg your pardon, sir? Do you wish to dictate a letter?"

"I do not." The governor pointed toward the chair on the other side of his desk. "Take a seat and tell me what's bothering you."

"But, sir, we have so much work to catch up on," Duckworth protested, but he did sit down. "The autumn session of the council will be convening soon and—"

"And I refuse to sign another document or draft another report until I find out what is weighing on your mind." If any threat had the power to compel his aide, that one should.

Perhaps a jest would break the ice. "Trouble with a woman, is it?"

"How did you know, sir?"

The governor struggled to hide his surprise. Young Duckworth was no more the type of fellow to enjoy a high time on the town than he. "Always at the top of the list, isn't it?"

"I wouldn't know, sir. I haven't much experience with this sort of thing."

"Well, neither have I, but I'm a good listener—a fellow has to be in this job. So let's hear all about it and see what can be done."

"Nothing can be done, sir! That's the problem. There's no use talking and no use thinking about it, either." Duckworth sprang back up from the chair. "I have been thinking about it far too much, but I won't anymore, I promise you. From now on, I shall keep my mind always upon my duties."

Strange. Since returning from their tour, Sir Robert had been thinking much the same thing about Jocelyn Finch.

He motioned Duckworth to sit back down. "No signatures, remember? No reports. You will not have any duties to occupy your mind unless you start talking. Perhaps nothing can be done, but I believe it will do you good to get the matter off your chest just the same. You could begin by telling me her name."

After a strained hesitation during which he remained defiantly on his feet, Duckworth muttered, "Miss Winslow, sir."

"Do I know her?"

"Of course you do, sir!" Duckworth seemed offended by the question. "She's one of the young ladies from the bride ship. The one Mrs. Finch relies on for everything."

"Ah, Miss *Winslow!*" said the governor, pretending he had not heard correctly the first time. A capable creature. Quite attractive in a modest sort of way. He had never taken much notice of her name. "The one Mrs. Finch relies on…the way I rely on you."

"Yes, sir. Thank you, sir. If I can provide you with as able assistance as she does Mrs. Finch, I would take it as a very great compliment indeed."

"Of course you do." Had he never told the young man how much he valued his able assistance? Or had he assumed it must be self-evident? "But Miss Winslow does not strike me as the sort of young lady who would cause a man problems. What's the matter? Are you in love with her?"

"I think I might be, sir." Duckworth blushed an alarming shade of scarlet. "I mean, I admire her a great deal and I think she's the most beautiful young lady I've ever met. I'm happy whenever she's around and miserable when she's not. The thought of her marrying some other fellow makes me want to go drown myself in the harbor!"

The governor grimaced. "That does sound like love, I'm afraid."

It also sounded too much like his feelings for Jocelyn Finch. He didn't have to worry about her marrying another man, of course. But whenever she mentioned her late husband—the charming wastrel who had lured her to Gretna for an unseemly elopement, causing a bitter breach with her family—Sir Robert longed to thrash the fellow!

"Does Miss Winslow not return your feelings?"

Duckworth stared at the carpet. "I'm not certain, sir."

"You have told her how you feel, haven't you?"

The young man raised his head, anguish twisting his handsome features. "It isn't always that easy, sir!"

"No." The governor sighed. "I suppose it isn't. Perhaps you had better explain your specific difficulty."

"It's like this, sir…" Duckworth sank back onto the chair

as if he meant to stay this time. "I got to know Miss Winslow while we were on the tour of the colony. Often, if you had a message for Mrs. Finch and I couldn't find her right away, Miss Winslow would be kind enough to relay it for me."

Sir Robert nodded. "I can appreciate how the situation would have thrown the two of you into frequent contact."

"Yes, sir. And as she was such a well-spoken and agreeable young lady—not flighty like some of the others—I would often fall into conversation with her when we met. Or ask her the honor of a dance in the evenings."

Now that he thought of it, Sir Robert did recall seeing the two young people together quite often.

"It was after we left Yarmouth, sir, sailing for Annapolis, that I found myself fretting Miss Winslow might meet her future husband there. I wasn't sure how I would bear it if she did. It was the same at Fort Amherst, only worse."

The governor did recall his young aide brooding by times during their tour. He had put it down to all the late nights and rich food and changes in lodging. "If you felt that way, why didn't you tell the young lady?"

"Tell her what?" Duckworth threw up his hands. "That I cannot bear the thought of her marrying someone else, but I can offer her no honorable alternative?"

"You might have told her the last part at least!" Sir Robert did not intend to speak so sharply, but could the lad not understand? His heart might not be the only one engaged and his future was not the only one at stake. "If Miss Winslow returned from our tour unwed, it can only mean she did not give any of those other men the least encouragement. If there is the slightest chance you have engaged the lady's affections, you owe it to her to make your intentions known. Otherwise, she may miss an opportunity to secure a husband while waiting in vain for you to propose."

Duckworth flinched under the rebuke but accepted it. "You

are right, of course. I should have thought what this would mean for Miss Winslow. *Do* you reckon I have spoiled her chances?"

"Damned if I know." He was treading on very thin ice by presuming to give advice in matters of the heart. "More to the point, why can you not ask Miss Winslow for her hand if you care for her?"

"What do I have to offer her? I have nothing beyond my salary and, though I have saved, it would never be enough to keep a wife and family. Besides, I have my duty to you, sir. You need me." Duckworth sounded very certain of that—as well he should. "But the Colonial Office could send you elsewhere at any time. Ireland or India or Jamaica. It is one thing for a bachelor to travel the globe like that, but it would not be fair to uproot my wife every time you accepted a new post."

Sir Robert pressed the tips of his fingers together. "I see your difficulty. Perhaps you had better have a talk with Miss Winslow just the same. If she does not return your feelings, there's nothing to be done, I suppose, but hope your heart will mend in time."

"But if she does?" Poor Duckworth looked as if that might be the more heartbreaking of the two options. "What then?"

He would have to go along to Prince's Lodge for moral support, of course. The intensity of his anticipation surprised Sir Robert. It felt like weeks since he had set eyes on Jocelyn Finch, rather than hours. The distance between Prince's Lodge and Government House seemed like hundreds of miles rather than six.

"Then—" he offered young Duckworth an encouraging smile "—this is what you must do…."

Prince's Lodge felt so quiet with most of the girls gone. A wistful ache tugged at Jocelyn's heart as she stared out at Bedford Basin from the great rooftop dormer. The happy pride and satisfaction she'd felt each time another group of her charges had taken their wedding vows was ebbing fast, leaving a sense of emptiness in its wake.

Was this how mothers felt after their children wed? Even when they were confident the matches would be happy ones? How much worse might a parent feel if she *or he* doubted the suitability of the match? If, indeed, that doubt had caused an irreparable breach with the child? An unwelcome twinge of pity for her father compounded the pain in Jocelyn's heart.

That breach was his fault! she reminded herself. And he had been wrong about her and Ned. Besides, she had no indication he'd ever missed her—except as a tool of his dynastic plans gone astray.

There had been that letter after Ned's death. But she'd been too consumed with grief and anger to do more than glance at it before throwing it in the fire. She could not allow herself to be angry at Ned for dying in battle, so she had focused her rage on the marquess instead. Had she been unfair to her father?

Some movement down on the road drew her attention and provided a welcome distraction from her troubling thoughts. She spied two men on horses—and they were coming up the lane.

The governor! Delight at his unexpected arrival banished all Jocelyn's melancholy. The intensity of it staggered her. When and how had he gained such power over her happiness? Refusing to let that worry spoil her pleasure at seeing him, she raced down the stairs.

"Why, Sir Robert, how good to see you!" She swept him a deep curtsy, though she would rather have embraced him. "To what do we owe the honor of your visit?"

"I don't know that it is much of an honor." The governor climbed down from his horse and swept off his hat as he bowed to her. "I'm surprised you are not sick of the sight of me after all those weeks on our tour."

Jocelyn laughed and shook her head. "Quite the contrary, I assure you."

It had astonished her just how much to the contrary.

Sir Robert nodded toward the other rider. "I came along to keep Mr. Duckworth company. He has a particular errand here."

"Mr. Duckworth, of course." Jocelyn curtsied to the young man, embarrassed that she had not even noticed him. "An errand? How may I assist you?"

"Well, ma'am…" Mr. Duckworth removed his hat and began to toy with the brim in a rather agitated manner. "If you would be so kind as to direct me to Miss Winslow. There is something I wish…to discuss with her, if I may?"

With Lily? Oh!

"I believe you will find her over in the rose garden with some of the other young ladies. They are trying to decide what sorts of flowers to use for their bridal nosegays."

An uncertain look came over Mr. Duckworth's boyish features at the mention of "other young ladies."

"Perhaps," said Jocelyn, "you would be so kind as to tell the others I wish to speak with them. We have several important details still to decide about the weddings."

"With pleasure, ma'am!" The transparent eagerness of the his smile rewarded Jocelyn for her tactful suggestion and banished any crumb of doubt as to the nature of his errand at Prince's Lodge.

As he hurried off to find Lily, one of the sentries appeared, saluted the governor then offered to water the horses. With a word of thanks, Sir Robert turned over the reins.

"Of course you must be busy with plans for the weddings," he said to Jocelyn. "Do not feel obliged to entertain me. I only came to lend Duckworth moral support…and to keep him from doing himself an injury if Miss Winslow refuses him."

Though prudence urged her to keep her distance from the governor, Jocelyn latched onto his arm. “Do not imagine I will let you off that easily. I want to hear all about this business of Mr. Duckworth and Lily. As for the urgent discussion of wedding plans, have I not dragged you off on enough strolls this summer to admire indifferent views that you do not recognize an excuse to allow a courting couple some privacy?”

Sir Robert chuckled. “I fear I will never master your subtlety when it comes to such matters, my dear.”

“Why do we not take a stroll and admire a truly fine view?” she suggested. “After having been away for so many weeks, I was struck anew by just how splendid it is.”

And after being continuously in his company for so many weeks, a brief separation and the prospect of a longer one had made her realize the intensity of her desire for this man.

They wandered over the wide, sloping front lawn toward a tall red maple, its foliage the hue of well-aged red wine.

“I must tell you,” said Jocelyn, “how vastly relieved I am that your Mr. Duckworth has decided to declare himself at last. I was on the point of seeking your advice in the matter. What on earth has kept him silent for so long?”

Sir Robert hesitated for a moment. “Would you subject me to a tirade if I told you it was a sense of duty that prevented Duckworth from proposing to the girl?”

“Tirade, indeed!” Jocelyn swatted his arm with one hand while she clung to it with the other. “What impudence! When have I ever subjected you to a tirade?”

“On the subject of duty?” Sir Robert pretended to ponder the question. “I believe the most recent occasion was yesterday around three o’clock. I recollect it quite clearly.”

“Nonsense!” Jocelyn could scarcely speak for laughing. “That was a spirited exchange of views, nothing more. You have not heard a tirade on the subject of duty until you have been subjected to one from my father."

She must sound as tiresome and pedantic as her father—but the opposite tack. Perhaps the marquess did not *mean* to be tiresome and pedantic, either.

Jocelyn refused to dwell on that thought. "Besides, we were discussing your Mr. Duckworth. Give me an account of him and I promise no tirades. I shall listen as meek as you please."

Though Sir Robert looked dubious of her assurances, he wasted no time telling her what she wanted to know. Jocelyn had far greater difficulty than she expected holding her tongue while she listened. When at last the governor finished speaking, she was fairly bursting with questions.

"What is to be done? If you brought the young man here hoping Lily will refuse him, I fear you will be disappointed."

"Why, has Miss Winslow told you she loves him?"

Jocelyn shook her head. "Heavens no! Lily is far too reserved for that. But a woman can see the signs when another of her sex has tender feelings for a man."

Perhaps it was easier to recognize those signs in someone else than in one's self? The thought staggered Jocelyn. "I was afraid Lily might have discouraged Mr. Duckworth because she could not bring herself to desert me. She is every bit as dutiful as he…which may be their undoing, poor dears."

"Do not fret for them," Sir Robert reassured her. "I have told Duckworth if Miss Winslow will have him, they must make their home at Government House for as long as I am in office."

"And after that?"

"When I leave, there will be an appointment or two in my power to award. I have promised Duckworth the best of them. The colony needs clever young fellows like him in positions of responsibility."

Lily Winslow had become especially dear to her over the past few months. The prospect of her wedding such an admirable young man overwhelmed Jocelyn with relief.

She seized Sir Robert's hand and raised it to her lips. "That is so good of you!"

Clearly the man *was* capable of considering happiness ahead of duty. There might be hope for him yet.

He did not appear embarrassed by her outburst. Indeed, he looked quite pleased. "Do you suppose it will be possible to include one more wedding with the others next Saturday?"

Jocelyn fancied she could see her joyful smile reflected in Sir Robert's eyes. "I am certain it will."

His fingers tightened around hers. He raised them to stroke her cheek. He looked as bewildered as she by the next words that left his lips. "What about *two* more?"

Chapter Fifteen

"Two more?" Jocelyn repeated the words as if they belonged to some particularly exotic foreign language. "Two more what?"

Her question almost brought Sir Robert to his senses. He had blurted out his proposal in the heat of a moment that was rapidly going cold. But his training as a soldier would not allow him to retreat once he had committed himself, no matter how tentatively.

"Two weddings, of course." He mustered his arguments in good order and commenced to bombard her with them. "I know I am not the kind of man to inspire the passionate attachment you felt for your first husband, but I am not interested in sentiment. You have convinced me that the right sort of wife could be an invaluable asset to a man in my position."

He recalled Barnabas Power saying something to that effect when Jocelyn had first arrived in Halifax. It had taken far too long for him to see the wisdom of it.

Jocelyn did not answer right away. She looked rather dazed by his declaration, but not repelled by it. That was all the encouragement Sir Robert needed to continue. He'd won many a battle that had gotten off to a less promising start.

"I believe the past weeks have amply demonstrated how well we can work together. I am convinced if we join forces, we can do some good for the people of this colony, while maintaining a bond of mutual respect and congenial companionship. Can there be a better system for a successful marriage?"

Satisfied that he had made a compelling case for himself, he fell silent to await her reply.

But her answer was neither the acceptance he had hoped for, nor the refusal he dreaded with unexpected intensity.

"Do I understand correctly, Sir Robert? Have you just tendered me…an offer of marriage?" Her tone made it sound the most preposterous notion in the world.

Perhaps he had gotten off to a less favorable start than he'd reckoned. But he was in too deep to do anything but forge ahead and hope to salvage the situation.

"I have, ma'am." Her lack of enthusiasm made him speak with more reserve and formality than he'd intended. "And I hope you will not refuse me out of hand. You must admit, the kind of life I can offer you is nearer the one to which you were born than is your present situation."

She wrenched her hand from his grasp. "I abandoned the life to which I was born when I made my first marriage, sir. *If* I were inclined to wed again, it would not be for social advancement."

"Of course not! I mean…forgive me, that was not what I meant to suggest." Confound it! He was a miserable failure at polite conversation. What had ever made him suppose he could advance an acceptable marriage proposal?

"What *did* you mean, then?" Her gaze searched his. But what was she hoping to find?

He sucked in a great draft of air and tried to express his true feelings…even though he was not certain what they might be. "Only that I am convinced you would make a fine governor's wife. But my proposal is not motivated entirely by professional considerations. The truth is, I have enjoyed your company this summer, more than I ever thought possible. I should be very sorry to lose it."

Her expression softened in a most appealing way. "I have enjoyed your company, too. But surely that is not sufficient foundation upon which to base a marriage. Not even when coupled with your *professional considerations.*"

"Damn it all, Jocelyn! Can you not tell I find you a very attractive woman? Ever since that morning we kissed, I have not been able to stop recalling it and wishing we could do it again… often." Seeing her astonished look, he added, "I hope that does not offend you."

She dismissed his suggestion with a gurgle of merry, infectious laughter. "Some of the girls assume, because I am a widow, I must be ancient. But I am not ancient enough to be offended when an attractive gentleman confesses to finding *me* attractive. Or when a gentleman I have enjoyed kissing admits he enjoyed it, too. Come to think of it, a lady is probably *more* apt to be flattered by such declarations the older she gets."

Jocelyn found him attractive? She had enjoyed kissing him? These Sir Robert took as very encouraging signs indeed. Forgetting they were in clear view of both the house and the coach road, he whisked her into his arms and treated her to a kiss he hoped they would both enjoy as much as the last one they had shared.

For an instant, he feared his memory of their previous kiss might have become exaggerated. But when he felt her lips yield beneath his once more, it was even better than he remembered. They were so warm, soft, sweet…

And responsive. She did not accept his kiss in passive stillness but welcomed and returned it with such tender eagerness it took his breath away.

At last his lapsed discretion caught up with him. He drew back from Jocelyn just far enough to gaze deep into her eyes. "You will have me, then?"

"Have you?" Her lips, still dewy from his kiss, faltered when she tried to smile. "Now *that* sounds a very inviting prospect. But as for your offer of marriage, I fear I must decline it."

"Decline?" Sir Robert wondered if his ears were playing tricks on him. "How can that be?"

Astonished by Sir Robert's sudden proposal, Jocelyn had almost given him a different answer than the one she knew she must. Now his look of bewildered distress almost made her recant her refusal. But she could not forget the harsh lessons she'd been forced to learn in recent years.

"It can be because it must be, Robert. When my father cut me off without a farthing for marrying against his wishes, I discovered how dependent I had been upon his approval. When Ned died and I was left with almost nothing, I realized I had been dependent on his survival and his regard for me. The life I have now may not seem like much to you, but I have gained it by my own efforts and no man's whim can take it from me. My independence has cost me too much to give it up, even for all you offer."

She gave a rueful smile, hoping to coax one from him in return. "And you do have a great deal to offer a woman. I would be lying if I claimed I am not tempted. By your kiss in particular."

The governor scowled and stiffened to his most severe parade-ground posture. "Refuse me if you must, but I will thank you not to mock me, madam."

"Now you are angry." She caught his hand and gave it a beseeching squeeze. "And it will spoil everything between us until I have to leave for England."

The prospect of her departure provoked a hollow ache deep in her belly, which she did her best to ignore. "What happened to your resolve never to marry? You said it would not be fair to a woman."

"My situation has changed." Sir Robert tried to look very solemn and remote, but Jocelyn glimpsed a plea in his eyes. "England is not at war and I am no longer on active military service."

She gave a slow, regretful shake of her head. "In all your years of soldiering, have you ever known peace to last for long?"

He opened his mouth to reply, but the words seemed to stick in his throat. Jocelyn could almost hear the litany of recent conflicts marching through his thoughts. *The American Revolution, the French Revolution, the Napoleonic Wars* and the recent hostilities between England and America. Sir Robert closed his mouth again.

Jocelyn needed no more answer than that. "You are still a young man. What if war should break out again and you should be called to active service? Would the fact that you had a wife prevent you from answering that call?"

His brow bunched. "Are you saying you refuse to marry me unless I am willing to put your happiness ahead of my duty?"

It sounded so selfish when he put it like that. "I am saying I *cannot* place your duty ahead of my happiness. I wish with all my heart I could oblige you, but I cannot."

Robert stared past her, out toward the placid waters of the Bedford Basin. "It seems we are at an impasse, then. So what is to be done? Do we ignore the attraction we have both freely admitted then bid one another a cool farewell when you return to England for the winter?"

His question sparked a scandalous notion in Jocelyn's mind. Only scandalous if they were indiscreet, she reminded herself. And Sir Robert Kerr was the very soul of discretion.

Though he refused to meet her gaze, he had not detached his hand from her grasp. She ran the pad of her thumb over his palm in a suggestive caress. "We *could* do that, I suppose. Or we could…indulge our mutual attraction for the time we have left. If we both find the arrangement congenial, perhaps we could take it up again next spring when I return."

That made him look at her again. "What on earth are you proposing?"

Jocelyn ran the tip of her tongue around her lips to moisten them while casting him a tantalizing glance through her lashes. "I am saying that I cannot be your wife…but I should enjoy being your mistress. I believe I could make you enjoy it, too."

His features remained impassive, but she sensed passion and propriety waging a fierce battle within him. Though strong and hot, passion was new and rather foreign to his nature. Propriety had ruled him for many years. It held the high ground and had plenty of allies—duty, prudence, restraint—with which to flank and rout the vigorous assault of his upstart desire. Thwarted, passion seized its only available outlet in the vigor of his refusal.

"Impossible!" He wrested his hand from hers with violent force and backed several steps away as if he feared his resolve might not hold. "Do you understand what you are suggesting?"

"Better than you do, I'll wager." Though vexed by his resistance, she could not be truly angry, for she knew it did not signify an aversion to her. "Do not let an overabundance of sense make you foolish, my dear. If we both agree to a brief liaison without coercion or expectations on either side, where is the harm?"

"No." He turned and strode away from her. "I refuse to consider it." Then, in a tone sharp with desperation, he added, "Do not tempt me!"

Jocelyn hiked up her skirts and darted after him.

"Very well," she gasped. "I promise I will not raise the matter again, except to say this—if you should have a change of heart at any time between now and the day I return to England, you have only to say the word and I shall be willing."

He did not reply, but a slight hitch in his stride assured Jocelyn he had heard her.

"Now slow down and take that scowl off your face," she ordered him. "Otherwise people will wonder what is the matter. Then there could be all sorts of scandalous speculation even if we behave with perfect propriety."

To her surprise, the governor came to an abrupt halt. "You are right, of course. But imagine the gossip if we were caught in a compromising situation."

"If we were caught..." Jocelyn flashed him a sly smile. "I reckon we are clever enough to avoid that, don't you?"

His eyes narrowed. "What happened to your promise not to tempt me?"

"I said I would not raise the matter and I have kept my word. It is not fair to expect me to withhold comment when you bring up the subject. If it takes so little to tempt you, perhaps you want to accept my offer more than you are prepared to admit."

"I never denied wanting you!" Raw hunger for her blazed in his eyes and fairly crackled in the air around him.

If only she could persuade him to sate it on a banquet of forbidden delicacies!

A burst of high-pitched giggles drifted down from the upper balcony of the lodge. The sound acted on Jocelyn and Sir Robert like a bucket of cold water dumped over their heads. They started and hastily backed away from each other.

Jocelyn looked up to find the last several unwed girls from the bride ship peeking at them over the balusters.

"Were you looking for me?" she snapped. "Or were you eavesdropping for amusement?"

"We didn't mean to eavesdrop, Mrs. Finch." Louisa switched from giggles to near tears in the bat of an eye.

"And we didn't hear anything," vowed Sophia. "We were looking for you, ma'am. Mr. Duckworth said you wanted to speak to us about wedding plans."

"I wanted you to give Lily and Mr. Duckworth a little privacy." Jocelyn hoped Sophia was telling the truth about not overhearing her conversation with the governor.

Even if she were, this embarrassing intrusion cast doubt on Jocelyn's claim that she and Sir Robert were clever enough to avoid being compromised. Clearly when passions were engaged between them, cleverness could not be relied upon.

"Mr. Duckworth?" Louisa brightened up again as quickly as she had been cast down. Jocelyn did not envy her future husband.

"And Lily?" said Sophia. "You mean—?"

"I meant no more than what I said." Jocelyn treated the girls to her sternest look, though she feared its effect was likely diminished by distance. "And I will not permit any speculative comments when they return. Is that clear?"

"Yes, Mrs. Finch." The girls retired from the balcony, whispering to one another.

Jocelyn turned to resume her conversation with Sir Robert only to find he had slipped away. She muttered a curse under her breath. More than ever she longed for just one night with him. It might be the remedy she needed to purge her troublesome feelings for him.

But it did not look as though she would get the opportunity to find out.

* * *

If you should have a change of heart at any time between now and the day I return to England, you have only to say the word and I shall be willing.

Jocelyn's tantalizing offer haunted the governor for the next few days as preparations went ahead for the last bride-ship weddings, including that of George Duckworth to Miss Lily Winslow. Sir Robert was delighted for the young couple—when he was not consumed with envy of their happiness.

Over and over, he told himself it was foolish to regret Mrs. Finch's refusal of his marriage proposal. After all, he had not even meant to ask her. He'd simply been swept up in a romantic moment. What if she'd accepted him? That would have been a far greater problem, surely.

While her social and organizational skills might have been considerable assets for a governor's lady, her sense of decorum left much to be desired. She'd begun their acquaintance by challenging him to a duel in front of half the town. And lately she had offered herself as his mistress out on the lawn of Prince's Lodge, where any number of people might have overheard.

If she had agreed to marry him, her subsequent behavior would have reflected upon his reputation. How could he have trusted her not to disgrace him when she neither understood nor cared for the notion of duty? Clearly he was far better off without her.

But no amount of rational argument eased the sting of disappointment in his heart. Nor could it keep him from imagining the result if he accepted her scandalous proposition.

He tried to stay busy, forcing himself to concentrate on his work, but it was a constant struggle. Nights were the worst. The very act of undressing made him picture Jocelyn nestled in his bed, one perfect, bare breast peeping out from under the coverlet. In his fancy, her eyes held the shameless sparkle with which she'd challenged him. *You have only to say the word and I shall be willing.* The memory of it never failed to make his throat tighten and his loins ache.

He tried to delay retiring for the night until he could scarcely keep his eyes open. He tried imbibing a quantity of brandy before bedtime. Neither banished his beguiling visions. The brandy only weakened his will to resist them. On the eve of the weddings he found himself riding toward Prince's Lodge at an unholy hour, with decidedly unholy intentions. What folly might he have committed if the driving rain had not sobered him up in time?

Damn the rain! That was the trouble with Nova Scotia—the whole wretched colony was too bloody wet!

Fortunately, a brisk wind blew the rain clouds out to sea before morning. The day of the weddings dawned sunny and warm, in direct contrast to Sir Robert's temper. Dragging himself out of bed, he ordered a pot of strong coffee, which he drank while being groomed and dressed for the first marriage ceremony of the day.

Duckworth was no help at all. "Do I look all right, sir? I had a devil of a time with my cravat—all thumbs this morning."

"You look fine, I promise you." Sir Robert took another swig of coffee and glowered at himself in the looking glass. "Even if you did not, you have only to stand beside me and you will appear impeccable by contrast."

Duckworth stepped in front of the glass and began to fiddle with his neck linen. "Did you not sleep well last night, sir?"

Not last night. Not the night before. His last restful sleep had become a fast-fading memory. He was not accustomed to sleeping poorly. In his campaigning days, he had been able to doze off under artillery fire.

"Neither did I." Duckworth untied his cravat then commenced to twist and fold and tuck the long fillets of linen into their proper configuration. "I kept worrying Miss Winslow might change her mind about marrying me. You don't think she will, do you?"

"Of course not. Your bride is far too sensible a young woman to contemplate any such thing." A shame Jocelyn Finch did not share some of her charge's prudent dependability.

But then she might not stir his banked passion as she did now. One moment he dreaded the thought of seeing her again, the next he ached for even a brief glimpse of her.

When at last he spied her sitting in a pew near the front of Saint George's, looking deceptively demure, his pulse began to pound in his ears and his knees went quite weak. He managed to make it up the aisle thanks to the bride's steady arm.

He had every intention of sitting apart from Jocelyn but at the last moment his resolve failed and he slipped into the pew beside her. He tried to keep his attention fixed straight ahead, but his eyes refused to cooperate. Several times during the ceremony he found himself glancing sidelong at Jocelyn, until at last she caught him.

In the flicker of an instant their gazes locked, her bewitching lips curved upward in a little smile that mingled flirtation and triumph.

When the Duckworths retired to the vestry to sign the parish register, she turned toward him and whispered, "Please don't spoil this lovely day by being cross. I promise I will be a model of restraint and do nothing to embarrass you."

He dared not risk turning to look at her. But he acknowledged her plea with a curt nod. Her restraint was not the only one he doubted.

His wordless response did not seem to satisfy her. "If you can be civil to me for the rest of the day," she whispered, "I promise I will stay out of your way until I return to England. You need never lay eyes on me again."

Her bargain left Sir Robert with a sick, empty feeling. Could he stand to be parted from her forever—especially with so much left unresolved between them? The past three days absence from her felt like months. The only thing that had made it bearable, he realized, was his certainty of seeing her today.

He did not get a chance to speak until the newlyweds walked up the aisle together. Then, while everyone else's attention was on the bride and groom, he reached for Jocelyn's hand. "I beg your pardon. It *would* be unfortunate to end such a pleasant summer on an unpleasant note. If you can tolerate my society, I will make every effort to be more sociable. And I sincerely hope today will not be our last meeting before you depart these shores."

She shook her head. "If you do not wish it, then it will not."

"Good." Sir Robert offered her his arm to escort her from the church.

Perhaps for the remainder of Jocelyn's time in Nova Scotia they could pretend their conversation on the lawn of Prince's Lodge had never taken place. Sir Robert wondered if his powers of imagination could stretch that far.

What had possessed her to make Sir Robert Kerr such a scandalous proposition? Jocelyn had asked herself a hundred times since that afternoon. She had not received very satisfactory answers. Now, as she stood on the very spot where she'd received and rejected the governor's offer of marriage, she asked herself once again.

Night wrapped the Nova Scotia countryside in a warm embrace. A gentle breeze carried the aroma of fruit and flowers at their fleeting moment of ripe perfection. The murmur of conversation and laughter drifted through the open windows of Prince's Lodge. Her reception to celebrate today's nuptials was winding to its close.

Soon the brides and grooms would depart for wherever they intended to spend their wedding nights. As she'd done so often that summer, Jocelyn had taken each of the girls aside for a private talk about what some might have called "wifely duties." Jocelyn had avoided those odious words, referring instead to "the physical pleasures of marriage."

She longed to share those pleasures with Sir Robert—but not within a marriage. Perhaps if they had been in love, she might have taken the risk of accepting his offer. But she was not in love…at least she didn't think so. She was not inclined to examine her feelings more closely in case she should discover otherwise.

For Sir Robert had been quite frank about the practical nature of his feelings toward her. He wanted a skilled hostess, a congenial companion and willing bedmate. Sentiment was of no consideration. Was such a solitary man even capable of love?

"There you are." The governor's rich, resonant voice came winding out of the night behind her, drawing closer with each word. "I was beginning to worry."

Jocelyn turned to see his tall, spare figure, an imposing shadow against the faint light that spilled from the windows of the house. "Worry about what? That you would find me trying to quell another riot on the doorstep?"

He responded with a muted chuckle. "My concern was rather more vague in nature."

The thought touched Jocelyn just the same. "You needn't have fretted on my account. I only came out for a breath of air and to compose myself before bidding farewell to the last of my charges."

She did not mention that all her thoughts had been preoccupied with him. Tonight might be the very last time she would see him, for there was no compelling reason to bring them together in the days ahead.

"That is why I came looking for you," he said. "I overheard some of the young ladies express a desire to leave soon."

"Then I had better not delay them, had I?" She tried to sound bright and eager as she headed toward the house.

When she brushed past him, Sir Robert thrust out one strong, warm hand to graze her bare arm. "A few moments more will make no difference, surely?"

Part of her wanted any excuse to linger in the shadows with him. But another part could see no sense in prolonging contact that would only frustrate them both. "What is there to say in a few more moments that we did not discuss at length the other day? There is no point in trying to argue one another out of the way we feel. It can only create ill will between us and I should regret that more than anything."

He wrapped his arms around her from behind. "It was not *talking* I had in mind."

As he bent forward, his hair tickled Jocelyn's cheek and his lips grazed her neck, sending all manner of delicious sensations rippling through her. The moist heat of his breath whispered over her bare skin, hastening a little with every exhalation. Hers sped up to match his.

Jocelyn gave a sigh of pleasure mingled with wistful longing as she raised her hand to caress his cheek. He drizzled kisses from the base of her ear, down her neck and over her shoulder, then back up again. One hand stole slowly upward from her waist until it reached her breasts, closing over one with a gentle squeeze that made Jocelyn tremble.

"What are you trying to do, Robert?" she demanded in a husky murmur. "Taunt us both with what we cannot have? You bid me not tempt you…mmm….and I have made every effort to behave decorously…ahh…around you."

"So you have," he whispered between strewing kisses through her hair. "But I have discovered you need not say or do anything provocative in order to tempt me. You need not be within five miles—a single thought of you is temptation. Overwhelming temptation."

"Do you mean—?" Lost in the pleasure of having him fondle her breast, Jocelyn could scarcely form the words.

"Mmm." Robert nodded. "I will make my official departure shortly. Slip away as soon as your guests have gone and meet me down at the music pavilion."

Earlier in the evening when they'd danced there, Jocelyn had caught herself wishing all her guests would disappear, leaving the two of them in sole possession of the place.

Now it seemed she would get her wish.

Chapter Sixteen

"Why, Mrs. Finch," cried Lily Duckworth with a moist catch in her voice, "I thought you would be sorry to see the last of us go, but you look quite radiant."

Raising a hand to smooth Lily's fair hair, Jocelyn could feel the rosy flush of arousal glowing in her cheeks. "How can I be sorry to part from you when you have all made such happy matches? Today has been the fulfilment of everything I've worked to accomplish this past year. Can you blame me for reveling in our shared success?"

"No indeed, ma'am." Lily's new husband bowed to Jocelyn. "You have every reason to be happy and proud. I wish I could recall the toast His Excellency proposed to you on the evening after the weddings in Liverpool. I believe it would capture the spirit of my gratitude perfectly."

He turned toward the governor, who lurked on the edge of the crowd. "Do you remember what you said, sir? It was rather eloquent, as I recall. Perhaps you could repeat it now?"

Sir Robert shook his head. "If it sounded so to you, I suspect you had too much of that privateer's punch, Duckworth. The members of my council can cheerfully attest that I am never eloquent."

When his self-deprecating gibe drew good-natured laughter from the crowd, he acknowledged it with the brief flicker of a smile. But when his eyes met Jocelyn's, they smoldered with feverish desire. That look made her want to grab a broom and use it to chase all the other guests away!

Perhaps Robert read her thoughts. Or perhaps, now that he had decided to accept her offer, he was eager to commit himself before discretion made him change his mind. "Surely I have proposed enough toasts to Mrs. Finch in the past weeks that one more cannot add to her awareness of the esteem in which we hold her. After her tireless efforts this summer, I reckon we cannot give her better thanks than a good night's rest."

Moving toward her through the crowd, he caught her hand in his and bowed over it, pressing his lips to the backs of her fingers. "As a mark of my regard, ma'am, I shall be the first to depart. I hope the rest of your guests will not be tardy in following my example."

Nothing in his tone, manner or countenance betrayed the governor's true, roguish intentions. No question the man had hidden depths she was impatient to explore.

Donning his hat, Sir Robert mounted his chestnut gelding and rode off into the night. The newlyweds were quick to follow in their various traps and gigs, some only hired for the day. A few of the other guests looked as if they would have liked to prolong the celebration, but the governor's parting words shamed them into setting off for home without undue delay.

When Jocelyn had finally bid farewell to the last of her guests, she returned to the house for a moment to find Miz Ada supervising a number of girls hired to help prepare and serve refreshments. They were collecting dishes and straightening furniture.

"You did a marvelous job tonight," said Jocelyn. "Why not wait and clean up in the morning when you are fresh and rested? If you would care to help yourselves to food and punch, there is plenty left over and it will not keep."

The servant girls curtsied and thanked her, their handsome brown faces alight with smiles.

Jocelyn feigned a yawn. "It has been a long day, but I am still rather keyed up from all the excitement of the party. I believe a little stroll in the fresh air might help me sleep."

Miz Ada nodded. "Should I scald you some milk, ma'am?"

If Jocelyn had truly wanted to sleep, she might have accepted. The cook's scalded milk with a pinch of sugar and a dusting of nutmeg was a soothing and toothsome sleeping potion.

With a pretence of reluctance, she shook her head. "You have done quite enough cooking for one day. I don't imagine *you* will need a cup of scalded milk to put you to sleep."

As she slipped out of the house, Jocelyn heard the cook ordering her helpers to bring all the leftover food and punch back to the kitchens.

She had not gone more than a few steps from the house when one of the young sentries called out to her. "Anything wrong, ma'am?"

"Quite the contrary, I am only taking a little stroll to help me sleep." It was not altogether untrue. The music pavilion was quite nearby and Jocelyn had always felt deliciously drowsy after lovemaking.

"Would you like an escort, ma'am?"

"How kind of you to offer. But I only plan to take a brief turn around the garden before retiring. I shall be fine on my own. Now that all the young ladies are gone, I doubt we will be bothered by any intruders. You and the other guards are welcome to enjoy some of the food and drink left over from the party."

"That's very handsome of you to offer, ma'am. I'll tell the others. Enjoy your stroll. It's a fine night for it."

Jocelyn headed in the direction of the garden, then disappeared into the shadows and practically flew down the lane to the music pavilion. As she drew nearer to the water, she could hear the lapping of the waves as they caressed the shore. A gentle breeze whispered secret endearments to the trees.

Another noise from the beech grove at the base of the knoll made her jump and her heart hammer until she realized it was only the soft whicker of a horse. Sir Robert's chestnut gelding no doubt. Jocelyn tried to laugh off her foolish spasm of panic, but she could not.

What would happen if they were caught together?

She had little to lose. Reputation did not matter nearly so much to a woman who had no interest in society or remarriage. Her employer, Mrs. Beamish, did not give a fig for propriety, bless her charitable heart. She was not apt to dismiss Jocelyn from her position for a single romantic indiscretion. Sir Robert, on the other hand, stood to lose everything that mattered to him—his position, his reputation and his dignity.

As she hesitated, caught between yearning and apprehension, his voice whispered out of the darkness luring her toward him. "What kept you? I was beginning to fear you had changed your mind."

His shadow detached itself from that of the pavilion. By the silvery light of a slender sickle moon and a shimmering swath of stars, Jocelyn could make out his arm extended toward her. He caught her and pulled her into his embrace.

"I must be mad!" His lips blundered with tender eagerness over her face—her eyelids, her nose, her cheeks. "You drive me mad and have ever since that first moment I saw you step off that ship."

Something about his words sent a heady surge of power through Jocelyn. Tilting back her head, she let wanton laughter gurgle deep in her throat. "Do you want me to stop?"

Her own teasing question roused her earlier doubts. If Sir Robert abandoned discretion, did she care for him enough to curb their headlong flight into a sweet, shared madness?

How could he resist the seductive sheen of her white throat in the starlight?

Almost of their own will, Sir Robert's lips closed over the warm, fragrant flesh again and again. "I do not believe it is in your power to stop. This is a runaway enchantment. Who knows but it might be dangerous to rein the thing in."

"Magic? Madness? Can this be our sober, sensible governor speaking?" More laughter bubbled out of Jocelyn, fresh and sweet as spring water.

And just as necessary to him as water or air? Surely not! More like delicious, intoxicating wine that a temperate man might sample to his enjoyment on occasion, but make a habit to his peril.

"Would you have me sober and sensible?" He affected a severe tone and left off ravishing her lovely throat to stand at attention. "You are the enchantress—I am yours to command."

She rewarded his playacting with more laughter. One delicate hand roved up his dress tunic to find his cheek and caress it. "I think you must guess by now that I will have you any way I can get you, Your Excellency. But you must unbend a little, otherwise the disparity in our heights will make it difficult to kiss."

"That will never do at all, will it? Unless…?" He seized her, one arm around her back and the other beneath her bottom. Then he lifted Jocelyn until her lips were level with his.

The deep, hot kiss he administered was anything but sober and sensible. Her arms went around his neck. With one hand cupped behind his head, she pressed him closer, making him her very willing captive.

But after a few moments, he reluctantly broke from their kiss and set her on her feet again.

"This will not do, either, I'm afraid." He panted for breath as if he'd marched all the way from Fort George in full kit. "Whenever I kiss you like that, my knees threaten to buckle. It would not be very romantic if we ended up in a heap on the ground."

"Perhaps not." Jocelyn reached up to twine a lock of his hair around her finger. "Though it is flattering to think I could bring a man like you to his knees. What is to be done then?"

"I feared you would never ask." He extracted her hand from his hair, pressing a kiss to the inside of her wrist where he fancied he could feel her pulse galloping. "Follow me and you shall see. Well, not *see* perhaps…but *find out* at any rate."

Like any experienced campaigner, Sir Robert had scouted the terrain in advance, making note of any features he might later exploit to his advantage. Not that he meant to make a conquest of Jocelyn—rather a passionate alliance, or mutual surrender.

Clasping her hand in his, he led her into the unlit pavilion through its wide double doors. The interior of the circular chamber was even darker than outside with only the faintest starlight glimmering through the windows.

Sir Robert groped toward the spot he had scouted out, towing Jocelyn behind him. Earlier in the evening while dancing, he had taken little notice of the chairs arranged in groups of two and three around the perimeter of the room. Upon returning here with quite another purpose in mind, he recalled seeing at least one chaise lounge.

His foot struck something solid. He bent and ran his free hand over the object before him.

"Here we are." He tugged Jocelyn toward it.

"Where are we?" She edged forward with tiny, cautious steps. "I can scarcely see a thing. Oh!"

His hand still clasping hers, he felt Jocelyn lower herself onto the chaise. He sank to the floor beside her. "There, is that not a better trysting spot?"

"Perfect!" She reclined with a voluptuous sigh. "I vow, if I did not know better, I might fancy you a practiced seducer."

For an instant, her bewitching banter robbed the night of its magic. "But you do know better. I am anything but *practiced* in the amorous arts. I hope I will not disappoint you."

She disengaged her hand from his then ran it up his arm to hook around his neck and pull him toward her. "The only way you could possibly disappoint me is if you were to go away. Now, enough talking or we will waste the whole night with it and be no closer to...what we came here for."

The eagerness of her tone allayed his misgivings and rekindled his desire. "For a passionate enchantress, you do talk remarkably good sense."

He eased her back onto the chaise and for quite some time thereafter did not waste a single moment in talk—his lips and tongue being much more agreeably occupied.

Disappoint her? Not if he kept up as he had begun!

Jocelyn settled back onto the gently sloping arm of the chaise lounge, surrendering to the delightful depths of a late summer night and Robert Kerr's kisses. He cradled and stroked her face as he drank her in. Now and then, his large hands blundered, driven by urgent need, but always tempered with unexpected gentleness that touched her. Clearly his aim was not only to take his pleasure, but to share it with her.

The lush heat of his kisses roused her, wakening the familiar, delicious ache in her breasts and between her thighs. When at last he trailed one hand down her throat toward her bosom, she arched her body to meet it, expelling a soft sigh of anticipation.

For a time she was satisfied to have him pet her through the light fabric of her chemise and gown. But soon it was no longer enough and she yearned for the touch of his fingertips on her bare breasts. Perhaps he sensed what she wanted, or perhaps he was driven to make a more intimate acquaintance with her body. The reasons did not matter to Jocelyn, only the result.

He eased the small, gauzy sleeves of her gown off her shoulders then tugged down the low-cut bodice until her breasts tumbled free. His first touches were tentative, a mixture of uncertainty…and wonder? But her movements and soft sounds of pleasure soon emboldened him. Giving each breast its due, he nestled his warm, smooth palm over them, teasing her sensitive nipples between his thumb and forefinger.

It made Jocelyn eager to explore his bare chest with her hands and feel the thrilling friction of taut, muscular flesh rubbing against the soft fullness of her bosom.

"You must be hot in that tunic." She fumbled with the buttons.

"On fire!"

She did not begrudge the few moments his hand parted from her breasts to throw off his sash and tunic.

"And is that cravat not strangling you?" She pulled his neck linen loose and freed his shirt from where it tucked into his breeches.

When those had joined his other garments on the floor, she twined her arms around his neck and pressed herself against him, reveling in the provocative sensation. He found her lips again and kissed her as if they had been parted for months rather than minutes. Then he lowered her back onto the chaise and set out to claim with his lips the territory his hands had explored.

Her breath caught in her throat when his mouth closed

around her outthrust nipple and his tongue swiped over it. That imprisoned breath gushed out again when he reached down and slid his hand beneath the hem of her gown to caress her legs. His fingers climbed from her calves to her thighs igniting a raging fever of need within her. Accompanied by the tantalizing suction of his mouth upon her breasts, it was almost more than she could bear.

His hand crested the top of her stocking to caress the hot, bare skin above. Thank heaven he did not stop there, or he might have driven her mad with desire. Loose folds of muslin bunched over his forearm as he roved higher. Until at last he grazed the nest of fine springy hair between her legs.

The soft sigh that wafted from his mouth sent a cool tickle over her moist breast, which rippled through her whole body. He turned his head, rubbing his clean-shaven cheek against her bosom as he gave a gentle tug on her lower hair, then stroked her with the backs of his fingers. When he burrowed deeper into the sultry cleft between her thighs, she whimpered and writhed at his softest touch.

"Please," she begged in a hoarse whisper as she reached for the buttons of his breeches, "I must have you. Now!"

His answer was a velvety rasp. "I was just thinking the same thing."

He bestowed a parting kiss on her breast and anointed the tips of his fingers with the slick moisture of her arousal. When he broke contact with her to wrestle down his breeches, her body ached for his touch. In a frenzy of impatience, she sat up and reached toward him.

Her fingers brushed against his taut, straining shaft, freed at last from its tight prison of buckskin. Ignoring the almost painful urgency of her own desire for a moment, she wrapped her hand around him in an admiring caress. Just then she would have given anything for a flicker of light by which to see him.

He responded to her touch with a deep, ravenous growl. "Do not tax my restraint any further, I beg you! Not tonight."

His urgent plea roused her almost as much as his touch had, for she'd believed him a man of infinite restraint. It thrilled her to discover his strict self-control had limits after all—and that she had the power to push him beyond them.

"I suppose I can oblige you," she purred. As if her own need would have permitted otherwise! "If you will oblige me?"

"So I shall…with the greatest of pleasure."

That promise eased Jocelyn's reluctance to let go of him. But she swore to herself if the occasion should ever arise, she would truly challenge the boundary of Robert Kerr's self-control.

As he hovered over her, she hiked her skirts higher and parted her legs to receive him.

"Oh, yes!" she whispered as he mounted her, sating one need while rousing others.

She had never expected to feel this blissful sensation again. Something in her sensed that Ned would not have wanted that. Dearly as she'd loved him, she knew better than to imagine he would have denied himself as she had intended to.

Sir Robert froze, then, and a peculiar tension gripped him, unlike the tautness of escalating desire.

"What is it?" Jocelyn whispered. "Do you hear someone coming?"

She had been too deeply immersed in their foreplay to notice anything quieter than an artillery barrage.

"It's not that."

She heaved a sigh of relief that was almost a sob. "Thank heaven!" If they were discovered and he should suffer disgrace on her account, she would repent it always. "What is wrong then?"

Part of her did not want to know. At least not until they had finished taking their pleasure. But some bewildering compulsion mastered her passion and made her lift a hand to his cheek. "Tell me."

He flinched from her touch. "We must stop."

"Now you are mad!" She clenched around him. He *couldn't* do this to her! To both of them!

"Perhaps I was, but I have come to my senses, for a moment at least. I cannot take the chance of getting you with child. Why did I not think of it until now?"

"Is that all?" Jocelyn felt as if her heart had begun to beat again after an alarming lapse. "Put it from your mind. I would never have come here tonight if I'd had any fear on that account."

"You are barren?" Why did he sound so sorrowful? It would mean they could indulge their desire without consequences. Besides, she had no husband and no intention to remarry. What could her ability to conceive possibly matter?

"I believe so. I wanted desperately to have a child with Ned, but it never happened."

Turning his head into the hand with which she'd caressed his cheek, Sir Robert pressed a kiss to her palm. "I'm sorry."

What kind of talk was this for a man and woman to have in the midst of lovemaking? Jocelyn could not decide whether to laugh or cry or shriek with frustration!

"Perhaps this *is* a bad idea." She tried to pull away from him, but the movement sent a shudder of pleasure through her.

"Perhaps it is." He began to withdraw, then plunged in again, as if he could not help himself.

"We should stop while we still can," murmured Jocelyn, but her hands groped for the taut flesh of his backside. When he tried to retreat, she gripped him tight and thrust her hips up to hold him.

His lips sought hers as he buried himself deep inside her again.

"I think..." he gasped out the words between frenzied kisses, "it may be...too late."

His movements grew faster and the force of his kiss more intense.

"Mmm." Jocelyn's senses took fire again. After the brief lull, her pleasure felt even more potent. "Too...late."

They spoke no more, communicating instead in a primal language of touch, movement, instinct and urgent wordless sounds. Their kisses grew more erratic and reckless as they gasped for breath, racing together into a tempest. It smashed them into each other with increasing force until it tore them rapturously apart. Then, for a wondrous, fleeting instant, it melded the two into one.

Afterward they did not have the luxury of lingering in each other's arms, trading tender kisses and murmured endearments. While the time lasted, Jocelyn savored it almost as much as what had gone before. To her delight, she had discovered that beneath Sir Robert Kerr's facade of grave diligence lurked a lover of great passion and tenderness.

Rather than sating her desire for him, as she had hoped, their starlit tryst made her long for him more than ever.

Chapter Seventeen

In the better part of twenty years spent soldiering, Robert Kerr had undertaken a good many difficult tasks. But he had seldom done anything more difficult than parting from Jocelyn after their tryst in the music pavilion and riding back to his empty bed in Government House as if his whole life had not been irrevocably altered.

"Your Excellency?" The sonorous voice of Horace Chapman intruded on the governor's private thoughts during a Privy Council meeting. "About the matter of the supplementary funds requested by King's College?"

Sir Robert scowled, hoping his countenance had not betrayed his scandalous musings. "Give them half what they've asked for. But only on condition they enter into talks with Dalhousie about merging."

There stood that fine new building across the Grand Parade from Saint Paul's, empty for want of funds to obtain a royal charter of incorporation. Meanwhile King's was falling into decay, its administration riven by a bitter feud between the president and vice president.

"They'll never do it," muttered Barnabas Power.

"Never do what?" asked Sir Robert, less than half his thoughts given to the matter. "Merge or talk?"

"Oh, they'll talk themselves blue in the face. Not that it will avail them…or us."

Was it his imagination, or had Power become even more antagonistic toward him? "It will be a start at least. That is why I suggest giving them only half the sum they request. If they dig themselves deep enough in debt, it might make them more amenable to do what must be done, no matter how distasteful."

"You may be on to something, sir." Lewis Brenton sounded surprised to hear himself admit such a thing.

"Rubbish!" growled Chapman. "I say give the governors of King's what they ask for straightaway so they'll leave off pestering us with their endless petitions."

"Grease the squeaky wheel, you mean?" Brenton shook his head. "Do that and you'll only convince all the other wheels to squeak louder."

"You talk as if the college governors were a raft of beggars!" Chapman huffed.

A lengthy debate ensued, which Sir Robert knew would resolve nothing. He endeavored to stem the waste of time, but he might as well have been trying to hold back the powerful Fundy tides. Defeated in his efforts, he lapsed back into his own thoughts, only to find no more accord among them than among the members of the council.

A lifetime of prudence reproached him for last night's folly. How could he have put his whole career in jeopardy for the sake of an hour's passing pleasure?

But what pleasure! His pulse pounded faster just recalling it, and his flesh smoldered at the memory of Jocelyn's touch.

"May I ask, Your Excellency," demanded Chapman in a tone of outrage, "what you find so blasted amusing about this issue?"

Realizing his mouth had relaxed into a befuddled grin, Sir Robert hurriedly assumed his usual grave expression. Meanwhile, he plundered his mind for a half way believable excuse.

"Not the…er…issue itself. But Mr. Brenton's remark about the squeaky wheel." He forced a chuckle that he doubted would convince anyone.

The members of the council all stared at him as if he had taken leave of his senses. Sir Robert wondered if he had. He'd jested with Jocelyn about going mad, but it was no laughing matter. From the day the *Hestia* had first dropped anchor in Halifax Harbor, Mrs. Finch had distracted him from his duties. Lately she'd driven him to a state of distraction that might become permanent if he did not take steps to remedy it.

"I reckon we have worried the bone of this college question far longer than it merits." He exploited the council's watchful silence to get a word in. "Let us move to the next matter on our agenda. Funds to erect a lighthouse on Seal Island."

He spoke at some length and with surprising power about his visit to the island during his summer tour. To his dismay, he sensed the council members were paying no more attention to his words than he to theirs.

"The good people who chose to settle that lonely island have saved several lives that might otherwise have been lost. But they have witnessed and mourned a greater number of lives lost to the sea."

He exerted all his resolve to keep his thoughts from straying off this worthy subject to Jocelyn and his blinding infatuation with her. "Gentlemen, if they are willing to undertake this solitary and dangerous work, how can we deny them our support?"

Barnabas Power smothered a yawn. "No one here will argue it is a worthwhile project, Kerr. But the end of the war has brought lean times for the colony. Lighthouses are not to be had two-a-penny—especially off in the middle of nowhere. Where would we get laborers? Not to speak of materials."

"Three-quarters of the ships sailing around the southern tip of the colony are not even bound for Nova Scotia," added Chapman. "Most are headed for New England or New Brunswick. Why should we bear the cost of protecting *their* shipping?"

"What are you proposing?" asked Brenton, who loved to egg the others on by playing devil's advocate. "That we cede Seal Island to New Brunswick…or to the Americans?"

Chapman's jowly face turned the color of a ripe plum. As a young Loyalist, he had lost all his property, his first wife and his infant son when the family had been forced to flee their home in Pennsylvania. Thirty years later, he still harbored bitter resentment toward his former countrymen. "Not while there is breath in my body!"

He commenced to voice his objections, which were as numerous as they were vehement. Sir Robert glared at Brenton for getting him started, but he knew better than to interrupt. If Chapman decided a lighthouse on Seal Island would benefit his old enemies at Nova Scotia's expense, his influence was such that the funds might never be voted. At the very least, they could be delayed until the governor's term expired, after which the whole project would quietly die of neglect.

Sir Robert barely stifled a curse. The Seal Island lighthouse promised to save a great many lives. Whether those lives were Nova Scotian, British or American mattered little to him.

During his days as a soldier, he had never questioned the need to fight his country's enemies and often to kill them. Yet every life he'd taken weighed on his soul. Now he had the opportunity to help *save* lives and to make his colonists' lives better. He must not risk it in a fleeting quest to gratify his desires.

Once the council meeting adjourned, he returned to his study and took up his pen.

"Most esteemed lady," he wrote. It would not do to name her in case his letter fell into the wrong hands. "Allow me to express my gratitude for the great honor you have shown me in our recent dealings."

Would she be amused to read his stilted, formal description of their very passionate encounter? Would her eyes sparkle with impish delight? Would her dark curls dance when she threw back her head to laugh at his excessive propriety?

"I shall not soon forget your kindness." Nor the sweet torment of her touch! "And will always count myself fortunate in the pleasure of our acquaintance."

After a moment's careful consideration, he dipped his pen in the inkwell again and underscored the word *pleasure* with a bold stroke.

He wrote a few more tepid expressions of regard then came to the true point of his missive. "For many reasons of which you are well aware, I deem it best that we…"

That they…what? Not see one another again?

While that might be what he meant, he hated how callous it sounded—as if, having made use of her, he was ashamed of the incident and wanted nothing more to do with her.

He was racking his brain for a more gallant turn of phrase when Will Carmont strode into his study followed by Mrs. Carmont and Jocelyn Finch.

Sir Robert jumped to his feet.

"You see?" Will addressed the ladies. "I told you he would be hard at work—even with the indispensable Mr. Duckworth off on his honeymoon. Where have the happy couple gone, by the by?"

Sir Robert opened the top drawer of his desk and stuffed his letter to Jocelyn inside. One look at her, and somehow he knew he would never finish it.

* * *

What had the governor been writing that he'd put it away with such furtive haste? It had nothing to do with his official duties—of that Jocelyn was certain.

"I believe the Duckworths were going as far at the inn at Twelve Mile House, last night," he said. "Then taking the stage to Windsor today."

Had the newlyweds enjoyed such fine sport as she and the governor last night? Jocelyn tried to catch his eye to communicate her question with the secretive hint of a smile and the discreet arch of a brow.

"What brings you all here this afternoon?" He would not, or could not, look at her. "Would you care to join me for tea?"

Will Carmont shook his head. "Another day, perhaps. We are on our way home after fetching Mrs. Finch from Prince's Lodge. Now that all her young ladies are married off, there is no need for her to rattle around a place that size by herself until she returns to England."

"No, indeed." The governor sounded as if he were referring to a perfect stranger rather than a woman he had come to know on the most intimate of terms. "I beg your pardon, ma'am. I should have made some provision."

For a moment Jocelyn was tempted to resent his formality. But she could not, any more than she could resent his height or his blue eyes. The man had a severe facade he presented to the world. But he'd allowed her to see behind it, to the warmth and passion of his most private self.

"By no means, Sir Robert." She would not embarrass him by being too familiar, but fondness warmed her words. "You were kind enough to make provision for me and my charges when we first arrived in Halifax. I would not wish to be deeper in your debt."

Unless he would accept her favors as payment. Jocelyn

suppressed a grin that might betray her wicked thoughts. "The Carmonts have offered me their hospitality for the remainder of my stay in Nova Scotia."

"How long may we hope to enjoy your society before you are obliged to leave us?"

He met her gaze for only a fleeting instant. But in the depths of his eyes Jocelyn glimpsed his hunger for her—no more sated by last night's encounter than hers was for him.

"The *Hestia* should be coming for me sometime in the next fortnight. With fair winds, it could arrive as early as tomorrow."

It wasn't as though she would never see the man again. She would be back next spring with a new group of brides, assured of a warm welcome and aware of what pitfalls to avoid. Somehow, that prospect did not soothe Jocelyn as it should have.

"We've come to invite you to dine with us tonight," said Colonel Carmont, "if you have no prior engagements. A nice cozy meal—just the four of us. What do you say?"

After a moment's hesitation Sir Robert replied, "I have no other engagements. I would be pleased to dine with you. What time should I come?"

"We will expect you at seven," said Sally, who had been unusually quiet until then. "I know we can count on you to be prompt."

Jocelyn sensed unvoiced laughter beneath her friend's words. Did Sally find the governor's punctuality amusing? Or did she suspect his feelings and trust he would not be late for an engagement that might be his last with Jocelyn for some time?

"Indeed you can, ma'am." The governor gave a slight bow, clearly taking Sally's remark as a compliment. "I appreciate the invitation more than I can say."

Sally hooked her friend and her husband by the arms. "Now we must leave the governor to finish his work. And we must get Jocelyn settled in at our house. I, for one, hope we do not see that ship back in Halifax Harbor for at least a fortnight."

They bid their goodbyes and set off.

"Oh my!" Jocelyn came to a sudden stop as they headed out the back door of Government House. "I just remembered something I meant to tell Sir Robert. Go on and I will join you in a moment. It should not take long."

"But you will see him again in a few hours," said Sally. "Why not wait and tell him then?"

Jocelyn shook her head. "My memory is so dreadful these days, I fear I will forget if I delay it."

She dashed back to Sir Robert's study where she found him facing the window that looked onto Hollis Street and the harbor beyond. He started at her sudden appearance, as if she had caught him doing something improper. But when she approached, he opened his arms and gathered her into a swift, fierce embrace.

Grazing his cheek with hers, she whispered, "I hope you are not sorry for what happened between us last night."

He bent forward to kiss her. "I must admit, I do have one urgent regret."

"I feared so." She pulled back to search his expression. "Tell me."

He bent forward, pressing his brow to hers until his blue eyes filled her vision like the wide sky far out at sea. "My only regret is that it was too dark for me to see you stretched upon that chaise."

A powerful surge of relief buoyed Jocelyn and swamped her at the same time. She gave a shaky laugh. "If that is all, I hope we may find the means to remedy your regret…next time."

"Tonight?" The urgency of his tone assured her he had no other regrets. At least none of any consequence.

She nodded. "At the Carmonts? I trust Sally and the colonel to keep a confidence even if they find us out."

"Very well, then. Tonight." His kiss told her the hours until then could not pass quickly enough.

If the Carmonts suspected an amorous relationship between their guests, they gave no sign of it at dinner that night. Sir Robert could not recall when he had enjoyed dining out so much. Will Carmont doled out the wine with a very liberal hand and before long he and his friend were regaling the ladies with stories from the campaigning days. Jocelyn and Sally countered with amusing tales their first London Season.

The food served that evening was nothing out of the ordinary—Windsor beef braised in ale, some new potatoes and other early vegetables. But seasoned with banter, comradeship and delicious anticipation, it tasted better than any dinner Sir Robert had eaten in a long while.

After the meal, the four of them retired to the sitting room and spent the rest of evening in more lively conversation over several hands of whist. Sir Robert relished every moment. If only Jocelyn had accepted his proposal, he might have looked forward to many nights like this one.

He comforted himself with the hope that a few months' separation might convince her there was more between them than physical desire alone. Perhaps, this time next year, she might look upon his marriage proposal with more favor. Especially if he used the time to compose an appeal that sounded less like a dry business arrangement.

But how would he bear to be apart from her for so long?

As the hour grew late, Sir Robert began to wonder how he and Jocelyn would secure their planned rendezvous.

Then suddenly Will Carmont pushed away from the card table. "I must beg to be excused. I fear something I ate at dinner has not agreed with me. Or perhaps it mixed ill with the wine. I am not feeling at all well."

Mrs. Carmont sprang from her chair almost before he got the words out. "Poor dear! I must tend you."

"No need, Sal." The colonel headed for the door. "You must see to our guests. I beg your pardon for spoiling the end of a pleasant evening with my indisposition."

"Nonsense." Sir Robert laid down his cards. "This evening has been too pleasant for anything to spoil. I should be on my way now in any case. I hope tomorrow finds you much improved."

Before he finished speaking, Will bolted from the room and up the stairs with noisy haste.

"Oh, dear." Sally glanced from her guests to the stairs and back again. "I really must go to him, poor dear. Jocelyn, can I prevail upon you to see Sir Robert out?"

"Of course." Jocelyn waved her friend on her way. "I shall be happy to make myself useful. Now go tend to your poor, suffering husband."

"What a shame," said Sir Robert when Mrs. Carmont had rushed off after her husband, leaving Jocelyn and him alone in the sitting room. "Will Carmont used to have a stomach of cast iron. The things I have seen him eat! I hope he is not ill on account of bad food."

Jocelyn gave him a strange look as she rose from her chair and circled the table toward him.

He reached for her. "You are not feeling ill are you?"

She fell into his arms, shuddering with silent laughter.

"Jocelyn? What is it?"

She gasped for breath, struggling to curb her runaway mirth. "Will Carmont…should have gone…on the stage…rather than into the army!"

Assured that she was not ill, Sir Robert could fully enjoy the sensation of having her in his arms again. "Are you saying that indisposition of his was all a sham?"

"Perhaps not. But I did find it odd they gave me a guest room on the ground floor, claiming the upstairs ones were being repapered."

"I see." He owed Will Carmont a bottle of very fine brandy. "Then shall we take advantage of their hospitality?"

"A capital idea!" Jocelyn lunged up on her toes to plant a playful kiss high on his cheek. Then she caught his hand in hers and led him out into the entry hall.

After a thorough look around to make certain there were no servants lurking, she grabbed his hat off a peg beside the door and thrust it at him.

"Go wait for me," she whispered, "through the last door on the right."

As he stole off down the hallway, Sir Robert heard her open the front door then call out in a loud voice. "Good evening to you, sir! Do come again!"

The door swung shut with a deep, loud *thud,* which Sir Robert used to cover the furtive sounds of him slipping into her bedchamber.

Jocelyn joined him a few moments later, bearing a candle she must have taken from the sitting room. The warm, frolicsome light of its flame played over her features as she lofted a teasing glance at him. "I do not want you to have even a single regret about tonight."

For a moment he puzzled her meaning. Then he recalled saying he had been sorry not to see her naked.

With a slow shake of his head, he took the candle from her and set it on the nightstand. "I am certain I will not."

Turning back, he held out his arms to her. When she stepped into his embrace and raised her face to invite his kiss, his heart felt full to bursting.

Their second encounter was quite different from their first. As much as Robert welcomed the light by which to admire

Jocelyn's ripe, womanly beauty, it made him rather self-conscious—unable to spout the romantic fancy that had bubbled out of him the night before. Perhaps that was not such a bad thing, for tonight they were obliged to speak in the softest of whispers, if at all. And to stifle the sounds of pleasure they'd voiced with such abandon in the darkness of the prince's music pavilion.

Having blunted the sharpest edge of their desire only the night before, and with the threat of discovery far less, they were able to take their time exploring new sensations and savoring each to its fullest. True to her word, Jocelyn took mischievous delight in testing the limits of Sir Robert's self-control. She subjected him repeatedly to blissful torment with the tantalizing play of her hands and mouth until he feared he would strangle on his stifled moans of pleasure.

At last, when he writhed on the knife-edge of need, she slid on top of him, sheathing him in her sultry depths.

"Now," she whispered, "we must take it slow and gentle. The Carmonts and their servants may not be very sound sleepers."

He could only accept her terms with a convulsive nod and remind himself to keep breathing. He was her prisoner, albeit a very willing one. Trained from a young age to fight and conquer, he found surrender an amazing novelty. Yet when he recalled their wild gallop to release from the previous night, he rued the necessity for restraint.

Then Jocelyn began the slow, sinuous roll of her hips, urging him degree by blissful degree to heights of yearning he had never suspected let alone explored. Her exquisite breasts, on which he'd earlier feasted, now rubbed against his chest in a provocative counterpoint to the hot, moist grip below. Unable to accept an entirely passive role, he raised his hands to cup the smooth lobes of her bottom and fondle them.

She quivered at his touch, sending shards of pleasure skittering through him. Then a surge of ecstasy engulfed him, so powerful it jolted him again and again. He bit his lip bloody and all but burst his lungs in an effort to muffle a bellow of savage release. The force of it propelled him beyond consciousness to a place of explosive enchantment.

The week that followed taxed Colonel and Mrs. Carmont's powers of invention as they contrived one reason after another to absent themselves at the last moment each evening, leaving Jocelyn alone to see the governor on his way…or not.

At first Jocelyn found the days long, even with Sally's witty company. Then she got an idea that excited her almost as much as her anticipation of a tryst with Sir Robert that night. She dug out her little writing box, which was by now almost empty of paper.

"Whatever are you scribbling?" Sally raised her head from her needlework. "And why are you chuckling to yourself?"

"It is a report about our tour of the colony this summer." Jocelyn paused long enough to take up her penknife and trim the nib of her quill. "I mean to offer it to Mr. Wye for publication in his newspaper."

"How nice." Sally dug out her sewing scissors and clipped a thread. "You must have had a more amusing time on that tour than you told me about."

"It was very interesting and enjoyable." Jocelyn dipped her pen in the inkwell then began to write again. "But that is not why I was laughing to myself."

"Do enlighten me." Sally wet the end of a fresh thread between her lips to ease its passage through the narrow eye of her needle. "I detest being on the outside of a joke."

"It isn't a joke. More getting a little of my own back—at least I hope so. The editor of the *Gazette* has been such a thorn in Sir Robert's side. I should like to turn the tables and make his newspaper a vehicle to rouse popular support for some of the governor's projects."

Sally shook her head. "I don't follow you at all."

"Listen to this." Jocelyn set down her pen and read aloud part of what she had written. About Seal Island and how the survivor of one wreck had been found frozen to death, crouched over a pile of wood he'd tried to set on fire after crawling out of the frigid sea.

"Oh dear!" cried Sally when Jocelyn had finished. She wiped her brimming eyes. "I had no idea. Those poor people! What can be done?"

A glow of satisfaction kindled in Jocelyn's heart. Sally was a lively companion and a loyal friend, but she had never been the most tenderhearted of women. If she could be moved to tears by such an account, it boded very well indeed for Jocelyn's plan. "Sir Robert wants to have a lighthouse built, but the assembly and council are balking, pleading poverty."

"The brutes!" Sally sniffed. "I'll wager Chapman is behind it. Horrid Horace, Will calls him. I shall put a flea in Mrs. Chapman's ear the next time I see her. And I may suggest the bishop speak to him about his lack of Christian charity."

Jocelyn returned to her writing, her lips stretched in a broad grin. With luck, Sally would not be the only one calling for immediate action to address the situation on Seal Island. And an addition to the National School, so girls in Halifax could receive instruction. And the plight of the local Indian people, which was a grief to the governor.

Mr. Wye accepted Jocelyn's first article with surprising alacrity and demanded as many more as she cared to submit as quickly as she could write them. He even offered to pay her for her efforts which, after a moment's hesitation, she accepted.

After all, this might be an additional source of income

worth exploring when she returned to England. If a woman hoped to maintain her independence, she could not afford to put all her eggs in one basket.

During the course of the next week, Jocelyn wrote more articles during the day, then welcomed Sir Robert to her bed at night. And though every new encounter served to deepen their pleasure in each other, she found herself enjoying their dinner, conversation and cards with the Carmonts almost as much. And her satisfaction in helping the governor with his work.

Now that her compelling physical attraction for him had an outlet, she began to see there was far more between them. She admired his dedication to the welfare of the colony and she enjoyed his company, flattered to be allowed a glimpse of the private man behind his public facade.

She suspected he *could* love her, given time and the proper encouragement. Though still wary of losing her hard-won independence, she toyed with the notion of accepting if he proposed again before she had to leave for England. Fate seemed eager to foster the match as day after day passed with no sign of the *Hestia's* return.

Jocelyn had just dropped off her latest article at the *Gazette* printing shop on Grafton Street when Mr. Wye summoned her into his cramped little hole of an office. Was he going to beg her to remain in Halifax and continue writing for him? She had heard from many quarters that her "Summer Tour of Nova Scotia" series had been very well received, boosting the *Gazette*'s circulation.

As she took the seat Mr. Wye offered her, Jocelyn noticed the top of his desk was piled with London papers from which he reprinted much of his news. The packet ship must have arrived that morning.

Mr. Wye picked up one newspaper and shoved it under her nose. "Is there any truth to this, Mrs. Finch?"

"Truth to what?" Jocelyn scanned the page of crowded columns wondering what the editor could mean.

Then she spotted the bold, ugly headline and her heart sluiced down into the toes of her shoes.

Chapter Eighteen

"Who Chaperones The Chaperone?" Will Carmont made a face as he read the headline aloud. He and young Duckworth huddled in Sir Robert's study perusing the newspapers. "Bloody hell! Where did the *London Gazette* get such rubbish?"

Sir Robert glanced up from an editorial in *The Spectator.* "Keep reading and you'll soon discover the source."

"It's that Sykes creature!" Duckworth slapped down a copy of *The Herald* on Sir Robert's desk with violent force. "My Lily told me all about her. I'll wager you'd find more honest women in the gin dens of Barrack Street! No doubt she made up this pile of slander to revenge herself against Mrs. Finch for sending her back to England."

Will Carmont looked bilious. "What I cannot fathom is why the papers would print such stuff."

"You must admit, the story has all the elements that make for titillating reading." Sir Robert bunched the newspaper he was holding in his fist. "A lecherous colonial governor. The beautiful chaperone to a shipload of brides—who just happens to be the estranged daughter of a marquess. A near riot on the property where a royal duke once resided with his mistress.

Innocent girls being seduced by the soldiers set to guard them. What does a trifle like the truth matter compared to all that?"

"I see what you mean." Will exchanged papers with Duckworth. "The stories do not tally very well with one another do they? This one claims you demanded…er…romantic favors…from Mrs. Finch in exchange for your support. The *Gazette* says she seduced you into cooperating. Both bloody rot, of course, but I reckon it does make for more salacious reading than her winning your cooperation in a chess match."

Sir Robert gave a grim nod. "I'll wager you anything that Sykes woman caught the ear of someone in England with his own ax to grind."

"Enemies?" Will's brows shot up. "Of yours?"

"My appointment as governor was not universally popular in Whitehall." Sir Robert leaned back in his chair as he expelled a long sigh. "You must have heard the grumbling about 'Wellington's Waterloo Warriors' getting so many colonial appointments. I reckon someone seized upon this scandal to discredit the duke as much as anything."

All he'd ever wanted was to do a little good for the people of Nova Scotia and to make his old commander proud.

"Blackguards!" Will began to pace the study. "You must mount a counteroffensive. The press may reckon the truth a trifling matter, but the High Court will take a different view. There are laws against libel, written to protect innocent people from this brand of irresponsible—"

"I am not taking anyone to court, Will."

The colonel stopped in his tracks. "A strongly worded letter of denial, then, with supporting testimony from me and others who know the truth of the matter."

Sir Robert shook his head. "I cannot refute these charges. And you know why."

"Yes, but..." Will sputtered. "I mean, it's nobody's business. You must... Damn!"

Damn, indeed. Any effort to rebut the stories in these newspapers would only drag his reputation and Jocelyn's deeper into the mud. Neither of them could stand up in court and swear they had never been intimate. The true circumstances of their liaison hardly mattered.

Sir Robert recalled a pithy saying of his mother's. *It's better to stay silent and be thought a fool, laddie, than open yer mouth and prove you are.* In this case, better to stay silent and be presumed sinful than to launch a protest that would expose his scandalous secret.

The study door flew open and Jocelyn rushed in. "I came as soon as I heard—"

She started at the sight of the colonel and Mr. Duckworth.

"I beg your pardon!" She began to back out of the room. "I can see you are busy. I never would have... Only, I was so distressed by what I read in the papers."

She caught her lower lip between her teeth. The full, sweet lower lip he had suckled on last night while fondling her breasts. His body roused at the memory. Sir Robert cursed himself. Were these lies in the press really so much more shameful than the truth?

"Please don't leave on my account." Will Carmont headed for the door. "I must be going at once. A...an...an inspection...at the Grand Parade!" He caught the governor's eye. "We'll talk over the matter tonight at dinner. Sally's sure to know what to do. A good head on her pretty shoulders, that woman."

"Will."

"Eh?" The colonel paused in his hasty exit.

"Please give Mrs. Carmont my regrets." Sir Robert tried to bring some order to the pile of newspapers strewn over his desk. "As matters stand, I had better not dine with you tonight. I do not want your reputation tainted by association."

Will Carmont had barely gotten out the door when Duckworth suddenly remembered urgent duties elsewhere and hurried off. A brittle silence settled over Sir Robert's study.

Jocelyn shattered it with a quivering sigh that broke off in a choked sob. "You said I would be the ruin of you." Her face crumpled like a child's. "Can you ever forgive me?"

"Forgive?" He nearly tripped in his haste to circle his desk and fold her in his embrace. "My dear Jocelyn, don't talk such foolishness! You have no reason to reproach yourself. I am a grown man and I made my own choices. In spite of all this, I do not repent them. I can only hope you will not either."

His political reputation might end up in tatters, but society tended to forgive a man's romantic misadventures as long as they did not involve adultery. A woman's reputation was far more easily tainted. And that taint could have grievous consequences. There might still be one way to salvage Jocelyn's reputation, however.

He leaned forward and canted his head so her hair whispered against his cheek. "We must marry now." If this whole shameful business gave her reason to agree, then he could live with the humiliation. "It will be for the best. Surely you must see that?"

"No, I do not see it!" Struggling free of his embrace, Jocelyn wrapped her arms around herself, one hand rubbing against the opposite arm in a gesture of agitation…or self-comfort. "For us to wed under these circumstances would only confirm our guilt in the eyes of anyone whose opinion we value."

He did not want to heed her, but reason compelled him.

"In that case, I must resign my post." Under the circumstances, what other honorable course was open to him?

"No!" cried Jocelyn. "You must not. I could not bear to have cost you your position. Those reports are false. We became lovers long after everything with the bride ship was settled. I did not seduce you to gain your cooperation, any more than you used your power to coerce me. Like a hasty marriage, your resignation would only be taken as a sign of guilt."

"What are we to do, then?" Robert kneaded his throbbing temples. "It will only be a matter of time before Mr. Wye gets wind of this rubbish and circulates it throughout the colony."

Jocelyn flinched at his words.

He knew what that meant. "Wye already knows, doesn't he?"

She gave a rueful nod. "He was the one who broke the news to me. As for what we are to do, I confess I do not know. I only know what we *must not* do, on any account."

Had she meant to accept Sir Robert if he proposed marriage a second time? Under other circumstances perhaps. But the arrival of the London newspapers had altered circumstances beyond repair.

Jocelyn stared at the copies of the *Spectator* and the *Gazette* littering the governor's desk. They covered up official papers such as the assembly bills he must sign into law, petitions from new settlers for grants of land, the survey for a proposed system of canals to run from Halifax to the Bay of Fundy. In the same way, Jocelyn feared this scandal would overshadow all the worthwhile work Sir Robert had done for the colony. And it would be her fault.

She must find some way to salvage the situation. Whatever it took, she would do it.

She backed away from the governor, each step a wrenching effort. "Promise me you will take no hasty action in this matter. Give me a little time."

His shoulders sagged. "Time to do what, Jocelyn?"

The unfairness of the whole situation riled her temper. "I don't know! But it is not in my nature to give up without a fight."

He nodded and the grim set of his features softened. "Did I not say you would make a fine general?"

If she were a general and this her toughest battle, the tenderness she felt for him was a traitorous ally at best. She must retreat before it betrayed her. Even a word of farewell might sabotage her resolve. So she jammed her lips together, turned away from him and fled.

Only when she had reached the street did she pause to gasp for breath. When a man stepped out from the shadow of the governor's stable and walked toward her, she scarcely noticed him until he spoke.

"Mrs. J. Finch was seen departing Government House in some haste at nine minutes past four o'clock on the afternoon of Tuesday instant," said Mr. Wye. "She was unaccompanied."

For a moment Jocelyn puzzled his strange greeting. Then she realized he was quoting from a report he meant to publish in the *Gazette.* Her initial dismay evaporated in a flash of rage. Here was an enemy she could engage in open battle.

Perhaps the editor mistook her instant of stunned silence for weakness. "Do you have an explanation for your presence here, ma'am? Perhaps you have a statement you wish to make about the allegations against you and Governor Kerr?"

Jocelyn fixed the man with a haughty glare that would have done her father proud. "Naturally I came here as soon as you informed me of these vile slanders. I offered His Excellency whatever assistance I can provide in clearing his name. The London papers have printed a pack of lies spread by a malicious person of dubious character, who wished to revenge herself upon me. I deeply regret that in doing so she stooped to blacken your governor's good name, and, by association, the character of this fine colony."

The glitter in Mr. Wye's granite eyes dimmed a little. For

the first time since Jocelyn had met him, he appeared at a loss for words.

Certain that loss would be temporary, she took advantage while it lasted. "I am certain you must be offended by the tone of those reports, sir, and anxious to defend Nova Scotia against such intolerable defamation."

What could he say to that? She had summarily drafted him to her side, whether he wanted to be there or not. Whatever her opinion of the man in other respects, she could not deny his ferocious loyalty to the colony.

She left him muttering dark condemnation of "London scandal mongers" and "sensation seekers." But any satisfaction she drew from the encounter had dissipated by the time she reached the Carmonts'.

One look at Sally's face told her no explanations were necessary. She was grateful for that much at least.

"Come and sit down, my dear!" Sally pulled her toward a chair. "Will told me what happened. How awful for you both! Let me call for tea, or would you prefer something stronger?"

"Tea will be fine." Jocelyn sank onto the chair, allowing herself a momentary lapse into despair. "I need to keep all my wits about me just now. And I would not want to give the newspapers grounds for claiming I have taken to drink."

"By the way," said Sally as she rang for a servant, "a letter came for you while you were out. A boy from the *Hestia* brought it."

"The *Hestia?*" Jocelyn grimaced. "It must be from Mrs. Beamish, demanding an explanation. Or perhaps my head."

She had been so worried about how this scandal would affect the governor, she'd given no thought to how badly it might reflect upon the bride-ship scheme. In a selfish quest to satisfy her own desires, she had jeopardized the two things she cared about most. How could she ever hope to make things right?

Sally crossed to the hearth and retrieved a sealed letter from the mantel. "Would you rather wait to read it? Until you've had a nice cup of tea, perhaps? Or a good night's sleep."

"Or hell freezes?" Jocelyn held out her hand for the letter. "If I thought any of those events would make the contents more palatable, I would wait. But I am certain they will not, so I might as well get the worst over with. Hmm? The writing does not look like Mrs. Beamish's."

Yet there was something familiar about the spiky script. When Jocelyn turned the folded packet over to break the seal, she understood why. Impressed in the wax was the Breckland crest. The letter must have come from her father.

"No doubt writing to scold me for bringing further shame on the family." Perhaps she *should* wait to read it. Or perhaps she should tell Sally to toss it in the fire. Then again, could her father say any worse of her than she'd already thought about herself? Before her nerve failed, she broke the seal, unfolded the paper and began to read.

My dear daughter. The opening salutation surprised Jocelyn after what she had been expecting. No doubt her father considered it the proper form of address even if he no longer truly held her dear.

I have read with dismay some accounts in the London newspapers of your troubles abroad. This was more in keeping with the tone Jocelyn had expected. What came next was not.

Rest assured I give no credence to reports of wrongdoing on your part. If, however, this Kerr fellow has imposed upon you, send word and I will exert all my influence on your behalf with the Colonial Office to have him swiftly removed from his position.

"Jocelyn," cried Sally, "whatever is wrong?"

She tried to reply, but a sudden tightening of her throat

would not permit it. Her father's offer was quite the opposite of what she wanted. But the fact that he had offered, after all that had passed between them, moved her.

Though I deplore your present situation, I must confess my gratitude to the newspapers for informing me of your whereabouts. I regret I have some unhappy news to convey.

"There *is* something wrong." After a brief word to the serving girl, Sally rushed back to her friend's side. "Do tell me how I can help?"

A tear slid down Jocelyn's cheek, but she recovered her voice. "My brother. Do you remember him? Lord Thetford. I had rather hoped he and your sister Caroline might make a match of it. The poor fellow has been dead these two months and I knew nothing of it."

The full consequences of her decision to cut herself off from her family suddenly struck her. "His wife died three years ago, giving birth to their younger son. My father now has charge of the two little boys. He writes to ask if I might return to England to supervise their upbringing."

I am an old man, broken in spirit over the loss of my sons and the estrangement of my daughter. The latter I regret most, for it is a misfortune of my own making, one I might have prevented. Was he trying to flatter her so she would do his bidding? Impossible! The marquess had never been one to flatter or plead when he could order or demand. But he was pleading now.

I know I have no right to ask, but for the sake of your young nephews, I must.

"Will you do it?" asked Sally.

Slowly Jocelyn lowered her father's letter to her lap. A hundred conflicting thoughts raced round and round in her mind. Yet, in the eye of that tempest she discovered a center of calm certainty. Perhaps the time had come for her to embrace what she had resisted for so long. "I think it is my duty."

"Will!" Robert sprang from behind his desk and seized his friend's hand, wringing it until poor Carmont winced. "What news? I have been at my wit's end!"

"You look it." The colonel extracted his hand from Robert's grasp then flexed it gingerly. "I do not think I have ever seen you as rough as this. Not even on that miserable forced march to Corona. Have you slept at all? When did you eat last?"

Robert shook his head. "It does not matter. Tell me of Jocelyn? Is she well? Has she changed her mind and decided to marry me after all?"

Will Carmont winced harder than when Robert had shaken his hand. "I did not know you'd asked her."

"Twice."

Unable to abide his friend's pitying expression, Robert spun about and strode back to his chair, dropping onto it with a sigh. "I have been waiting for news of this scandal to break in the *Gazette,* but Wye has printed nothing. I do not understand. What is he waiting for? I have never known him to keep silent about anything that might stir up controversy and sell more papers."

"Jocelyn had a word with Mr. Wye, I gather," said Will. "Convinced him all the reports from London amounted to a defamation of Nova Scotia, as well as you and her."

For the first time since those newspapers had landed on his desk, Robert smiled. "She is a remarkable woman. I must speak with her and try to convince her—"

"No!" Will began to pace the width of the study. "That would not be wise. I'm almost certain my house is being watched. And this place, too, no doubt. Wye could be holding his fire until he feels he has proof of his own about an improper connection between you and Jocelyn. That is why she sent me with a message for you."

"Well, spit it out, man! Why did you not tell me before? What does she say?"

"She is going back to England. Sailing on the *Hestia* tomorrow morning."

He had expected as much. So why did this confirmation of what he had foreseen come as such a blow?

"Will she come back in the spring with another bride ship?" Or would the scandal make that impossible?

After a moment's hesitation, Will Carmont shook his head. "She has had bad news from home." Briefly he relayed the facts—the death of Jocelyn's brother, her two young nephews orphaned, the marquess's appeal for her help, Jocelyn's decision.

"I am sorry to be the bearer of such news," Will concluded. "Jocelyn begs you to stand firm and not dignify these accusations with a response. She is convinced this will all blow over once she leaves Nova Scotia."

Robert surged out of his chair and strode to the window, staring out toward the harbor where a ship waited to take Jocelyn away from him…forever. "I am convinced of quite the opposite."

"You *are* in love with her!" said Will. "I thought as much."

"Then you knew more than I." Why had it taken him so long to see it? Perhaps he'd been too frightened by the intensity of his feelings to own them for what they were.

"Does she love you?"

"I told you she turned me down twice when I proposed to her. I reckon that speaks for itself."

He wished his friend could say something to convince him otherwise, but Will's subdued reply disappointed him. "I suppose it does. She bade me tell you on no account to come down to the harbor tomorrow. She does not want to give Wye a scrap of ammunition to use against you."

Jocelyn *could* have come to care for him. In spite of everything that had happened, Robert knew it with a strange, unshakeable certainty. But how could he stand in the way of *her* duty after harping upon his all this time? Neither did he wish to prevent her reconciling with her father. Beneath her bitterness toward the marquess and her desire for independence, he had sensed her unspoken regret over their estrangement.

Somehow he rallied his composure enough to return to his desk and take up his pen. "Tell Mrs. Finch I shall honor her wishes. And tell her I believe she has chosen the proper course."

When he had finished scribbling a few words on the paper, he sanded it quickly to dry the ink. "Tell her I will always treasure my memories of this summer and that I wish her every possible happiness."

He folded and sealed the tiny note. Then he rose and thrust it into Will Carmont's hands. "Give her this."

In spite of what she had instructed Colonel Carmont to tell Sir Robert, Jocelyn still found herself scanning the small crowd assembled at Power's Wharf with restless anticipation. But the governor was not among them.

She stifled a contrary pang of disappointment. What had she expected, after all? For the man to do the opposite of what she'd bidden him? To show up this morning in front of witnesses to see her off? Risking the possibility that one or the other of them might lose control of their feelings in a shocking public display that would well and truly wreck his career?

"Goodbye, Sally!" Jocelyn clasped her friend to her. "It was the best of good fortune to find you here. Do not let us lose touch again, I beg you! Write to me and come to visit me at Breckland whenever you find yourself in England."

"Indeed I shall, my dear." Sally clung to her. "I wish you were coming back next spring!"

"May I write you, too, Mrs. Finch?" asked Lily Duckworth when Jocelyn turned to her.

"May?" she cried. "Why you *must!* I will expect all the news from you of my bride-ship girls. I hope there will be many happy events to announce before the year is out."

Though she dared not say it, she also hoped Lily might include the occasional scrap of news from Government House.

Miz Ada stepped forward and thrust a small basket into Jocelyn's hands. "There's a crock of preserved limes in that and a cake. It's soaked in plenty of rum, so it should keep good. You take care of yourself, now. And come back to see us when you can."

Would *that* day ever come?

"How kind of you!" Jocelyn blinked furiously. She must not start weeping or she might never stop. "I have so many fond memories of our time at Prince's Lodge. If I should see the Duke of Kent when I return to England, I will be sure to remember you to him."

She gave a start when the editor of the *Gazette* stepped forward and bowed to her.

"Mr. Wye." She bobbed a brief curtsy. "What a surprise to see you here."

"Yes…well…" He held out a packet of letters. "If you would be so good as to see these delivered to the newspapers in London. They have not been sealed, so you may read them first if you wish. I hope they may help to set the record straight about certain events."

If he had entrusted the letters to her and was willing to let her read them, they must hold messages of support for her and the governor. That came as a most welcome relief. "Thank you, sir. I promise I shall make sure they get into the proper hands."

When she had finished taking leave of her friends, Jocelyn glanced one more time around the wharf, then boarded the

Hestia and found a quiet spot on the deck from which to wave farewell to Halifax. Tucking Mr. Wye's letters into Miz Ada's basket, she set it on the deck at her feet and fished in her reticule for the note Will Carmont had brought her from Government House. She had refused to open it until the *Hestia* weighed anchor, in case it held a message that might demolish her resolve to do what she knew she must.

The first mate bellowed orders and the ship's deck swarmed with activity. Jocelyn waved to her small crowd of well-wishers on the wharf until she feared her arm would break. Once the *Hestia* had eased out into the channel and its sails were unfurled to catch the brisk west wind, she broke the seal on Sir Robert's note and read it.

"I beg your pardon," she called to a passing sailor. "Where should I look to see Point Pleasant?"

She had driven there with Sally once, but her sense of direction was so hopeless.

"That's it there, ma'am." The young fellow pointed to a spit of land on the eastern edge of town. "But you should get below. I felt a drop of rain just now and Cap'n says there's a downpour coming."

"Thank you," said Jocelyn. "I shall…in a minute."

"In a minute you could be soaked, ma'am."

Jocelyn nodded, though she had no intention of heeding his warning. Instead she gazed toward Point Pleasant, wondering why Sir Robert had instructed her to look that way.

Then she glimpsed a mounted man poised on the shore, looking out into the harbor. Could he pick her out on the ship's busy deck?

Fat drops of rain spattered on the holystoned boards of the deck as she stooped to pull the large white napkin off Miz Ada's basket. Clutching one corner of it tightly in her fist, she waved it in the wind.

For a moment there was no response from the man on shore. Then he raised his arm and waved in wide sweeping arcs.

The rain quickly gathered force, beating down upon Jocelyn. When the captain sent another member of his crew to bid her go below, she handed the man her basket to take out of the rain. "I shall be along shortly."

She continued to stare and wave at the horseman until the driving rain shrouded him from her view at last. Then the cold beads of moisture streaming down her face were joined by several warm ones.

Chapter Nineteen

To Jocelyn's surprise, a soft mist of tears rose in her eyes when she spied the towering sixteenth-century gatehouse of Breckland Manor for the first time in three years. Nothing about the old place appeared to have changed. Not that she had expected it to.

The walls of rusty-brown brick had stood for almost three hundred years, even against a roundhead assault during the Civil War. The crenellated towers with their cross-shaped arrow slots dated from the days when great houses might also have needed to be fortresses. Ten generations of DeLaceys had looked out those tall, slender windows, sat for magnificent portraits that hung in the dark, paneled galleries and eventually been laid to rest in a vault beneath the family chapel.

From her perch aboard the small gig she'd hired in the village, Jocelyn craned her neck to catch a glimpse of Ladywood, where she and her brother had often played as children. Save for a few cultivated evergreens, the trees had shed their leaves in preparation for their winter slumber. High overhead a flock of small clouds chased each other across the wide, blue Norfolk sky.

Jocelyn resisted the urge to compare its hue with a pair of beloved eyes. She'd had all the weeks of her journey to mope and pine for Sir Robert Kerr. Now she must begin a new phase of her life. Not as some living martyrdom for her past mistakes, but as a course she had freely chosen. One in which she hoped to find fulfilment and eventually, perhaps, happiness.

A young footman and an under gardener were talking together when the gig pulled into Breckland's courtyard. The pair cast curious glances Jocelyn's way.

Then, as the gig drew nearer, the footman cried, "My word! If it ain't Lady Jocelyn! It's me, ma'am—Ralph Thatcher."

"Ralph? Well, haven't you grown into a big, handsome fellow! You're just the man I need to help me unload my luggage."

"Happy to, ma'am." He helped her down from the gig then called to his friend the gardener, "Joe, go spread the word. Lady Jocelyn's come home!"

"That's *Mrs. Finch,* if you please, Ralph."

"Yes, ma'am. Of course."

It would probably take many awkward reminders before the servants became accustomed to calling her by a different name than the one by which they'd known her for so many years. *Lady Jocelyn* would be a good deal easier for them, and perhaps for her as well. But she could not let her marriage to Ned Finch go unacknowledged, as if it had never been. Or, worse yet, as if she were ashamed of it. Having fallen in love with Sir Robert Kerr had not made her care any less for Ned—though her memories of him were becoming less misty and rose tinted.

Word of Jocelyn's unexpected return spread quickly through the manor. Soon she found herself surrounded by Breckland's domestic staff, many of whom she remembered fondly. Young Ralph took it upon himself to advise the other servants of her wish to be addressed by her married name.

"Is it true you sailed all the way to Nova Scotia, ma'am?" asked one of the parlor maids. "With a shipload of brides for the settlers?"

"I did, Hannah." Jocelyn smiled at the girl, wondering if she might like a berth on a future bride ship. "It was a vastly romantic summer."

Only when an embarrassed hush greeted her words did she realize what she'd said, and guess what the servant must think.

Before she could refute the falsehoods published in the London papers, her father's voice rang out from the main entry. "My dear Jocelyn, welcome home!"

She could scarcely believe her eyes and ears. The marquess never came into the courtyard to welcome guests. But there he stood with his arms open to her.

Leaving the clutch of servants, Jocelyn advanced to greet her father. Unlike Breckland Manor, the marquess *had* changed a good deal since she'd seen him last. His dark hair had receded and acquired many threads of silver. His lean, hawkish features had become quite gaunt. His broad shoulders were bowed slightly, as if under the burdens of recent years.

She halted several steps away from him and sank into a deep formal curtsy. Part of her wanted to accept the embrace he offered, but the bitter grudge she had nursed for so long clung to her heart with stubborn strength.

"My lord, I have come in response to your letter."

A flicker of disappointment softened his stern countenance, but he rallied at once. "I felt certain you would. For the sake of poor Thetford's little sons."

"Let us go inside and discuss the matter," said Jocelyn.

She would not have the heart to abandon her young nephews, even if the marquess refused her conditions. For Robert's sake and for her own peace of mind, she hoped her father would not guess.

"Of course." The marquess ushered her toward the door. "You must be chilled from your drive. And starved, I daresay. Come into the drawing room. I will call for tea at once."

As Jocelyn stepped into the imposing entry hall, her father issued a brisk series of orders. In no time she found herself seated opposite him in the drawing room, a fine tea spread on the table between them. A frosty tension hung in the air. It put Jocelyn in mind of her first vexing interview with Sir Robert at Government House.

Once the tea had been poured and they were alone, she wasted no time stating her terms. "I am prepared to remain at Breckland and take charge of the children, my lord, but there is something I require from you in return."

"Is there something you require, Duckworth?" Sir Robert glanced up from a memorandum about the completion of a new assembly house. "Have my guests arrived for tea yet?"

For some minutes he had been aware of his aide hovering just outside the open door of his study. Twice it had looked as though Duckworth meant to enter the room. Both times he had retreated, though never going away entirely.

Now the governor's questions drew him in. Or perhaps they gave him the excuse he'd been hoping for. "No sign of Mr. and Mrs. Stone yet, sir. I shall notify you as soon as they arrive."

Mrs. Stone, the former Miss Turner, had been one of the young ladies from the bride ship. Sir Robert had taken to inviting Jocelyn's former charges and their husbands around to tea in turn with other townsfolk. He found it helped keep him in touch with the concerns of the colonists, and promoted public support for his administration. It also whiled away an hour of his day that might otherwise have been rather lonely.

"Well then, if not our guests, what has you stalking the doorway? A flaming editorial in the *Gazette?*"

Throughout the autumn, Mr. Wye had been singularly temperate in his criticism of the government. Sir Robert knew better than to suppose it could last.

"Quite the contrary, sir," said Duckworth. "Today's editorial commends the council for voting funds to erect that lighthouse on Seal Island. It singles you out for praise, sir. Something about the qualities of compassion and leadership seldom being found together in one character and how Nova Scotia has been fortunate to secure a governor who possesses both."

Sir Robert gave a wry chuckle and shook his head. "Perhaps after tea I ought to head down to the harbor and practice walking on the water."

Duckworth responded to his quip with a ready laugh. Either he was getting better at seeing a joke or Sir Robert was getting better at conveying levity. Perhaps a little of both.

"Not my guests..." Sir Robert counted off on his fingers the possible reasons for Duckworth haunting his doorway. "Not bad reports in the newspaper. How many guesses am I allowed?"

"Guesses, sir—very good." This time Duckworth's laugh sounded forced. What was wrong with the fellow today? "Ah! I believe I hear your guests now. I'll just go make certain."

When he had gone, the governor shook his head in puzzlement. Then he dipped his pen in the inkwell and jotted a note on the assembly memorandum about organizing a special levee to celebrate the official opening. After that he reread a letter he'd drafted to the Duke of Wellington.

His superiors had written recently, to him and to several prominent officials in the colony, confirming his appointment as governor and expressing their continued confidence in his administration. Certain the duke must have intervened on his behalf, Sir Robert had written to thank his old commander for his support.

He had just finished signing the letter when Duckworth returned. "It was Mr. and Mrs. Stone, sir. They're in the drawing room now, chatting with Mrs. Duckworth. Whenever you would care to join them, sir."

Sir Robert laid down his pen, then rose and headed across to the drawing room while Duckworth followed. As they passed one of the footmen, he said, "Tell Miz Ada we'll take tea whenever it is ready. I believe I smell her plum cake."

His guests and Mrs. Duckworth rose when he entered the drawing room. Was it his fancy or were both the ladies filling out their high-waisted gowns more than they had this summer?

After an exchange of bows and curtsies, they all sat down again, joined by the governor and Mr. Duckworth. Sir Robert inquired how the Stones were enjoying married life, then asked after Mr. Stone's harness-making business. By the time the tea arrived, they had settled into two parallel discussions, which continued while Mrs. Duckworth poured tea and circulated plates of cake and sandwiches.

The two ladies talked mostly of domestic matters and exchanged news about mutual friends. Meanwhile the gentlemen discussed the weather, commerce and events in the colony at large. Duckworth and Mr. Stone soon launched into a spirited debate about whether Nova Scotia and its neighbor Cape Breton should continue to be administered as separate colonies or combined into one.

Sir Robert followed their discussion with interest and some amusement until he overheard Mrs. Stone ask Lily Duckworth, "Have you had any word from Mrs. Finch about how she is getting on? I do wish we could look forward to her return in the spring with another bride ship."

"As a matter of fact," replied Mrs. Duckworth, "I've had a letter from her this very morning."

Sir Robert kept his focus on the two men, but his attention strayed to their wives. Was Jocelyn's letter the reason Duckworth had been loitering outside his study earlier?

"She writes that Mrs. Beamish was pleased with the success of the venture and is already recruiting girls for a second party to come in the spring. Mrs. Finch persuaded her to hire no less than three chaperones to accompany them. More tea?"

"Yes, please." Mrs. Stone held out her cup. "More chaperones and fewer troublemakers like Hetty and Vita would make the whole venture a good deal more pleasant for everyone. It still won't be the same without Mrs. Finch, though."

Sir Robert had to stuff a large slice of plum cake in his mouth to keep from voicing his agreement.

"Did she say how she is getting on looking after her nephews?"

"Very well by the sound of it." Mrs. Duckworth took a sip of her tea. "She writes that they are very clever, good-natured little fellows, though rather boisterous. She sounds as if she has grown fond of them already. I should think after chaperoning forty girls, the charge of two small boys must feel like a holiday for her."

Was he sorry or glad to hear that Jocelyn seemed content in her new life? Sir Robert wondered as he drank his tea and let the conversation of the two young couples swirl around him. Glad, he decided with no more than a flicker of hesitation. More than anything, he wanted her to be happy. He only wished events had unfolded differently so they could have been happy together.

As a new year dawned and winter lashed the North Atlantic coast, Sir Robert continued to honor his love for Jocelyn by following her example and forging stronger personal ties with the people he ruled.

Rather than secluding himself in Government House, he

traveled among the colonists and invited them to call upon him. He listened to their problems, their hopes for the future and their suggestions of what he could do to help them. Never had he felt a stronger conviction that he was doing his duty to the fullest.

And yet, when he retired to bed at the end of a busy day, especially a day in which Lily Duckworth had received a letter from England, his arms fairly ached with emptiness.

Then one morning, a few months later, when an unexpected south wind had blown up the coast from the Caribbean to deliver a tantalizing promise of spring, Duckworth fairly burst into Sir Robert's study.

"There is a letter for you, sir!" He handed it over with a flourish. "From England!"

Sir Robert struggled to suppress a grin. Ever since Duckworth had discovered he would soon be a father, his reactions to commonplace events had become a little extreme on occasion. "A week seldom goes by that I do not receive mail from England."

"This one's different, sir. Look at the seal. It's the same one I have seen on my wife's letters from Mrs. Finch!"

A ripple of heat coursed through Sir Robert.

"When I spied it among the post," Duckworth continued, "I thought it must be for Lily. Then I saw it was addressed to you, sir."

Sir Robert turned the letter over to confirm that it was meant for him.

"I'll just leave then, sir." Duckworth backed toward the door, grinning like a proper village idiot. "So you can read your letter in private."

Only after his aide had been gone for some minutes did Sir Robert look up from the folded packet of paper he had been turning over and over in his hands. It took him several minutes more to muster the courage to open it.

The salutation of the letter sank his hopes. The message was not from Jocelyn at all.

Dear Sir, it began after a formal address of his title and office, *I have never had the honor of your acquaintance but I have heard many reports in your favor. I hope you will not object to my communicating with you in this way.*

Sir Robert noted the closing salutation. Why on earth should the Marquess of Breckland be writing to him? It did not take long to satisfy his curiosity on that point.

As he read, his heart seemed to swell in his chest until every beat sent a faint pang through him. By the time he reached the last few words, he could scarcely make them out through the film of tears over his eyes.

"Look, Auntie!" called Nicholas Lord Thetford as he launched his toy ship across a small pond in the shadow of Ladywood. "The bride ship is sailing into Halifax Harbor."

A gentle spring breeze caught the small sails of the craft and pushed it toward the opposite shore. There Jocelyn waited, holding tightly to the hand of Lord Thetford's three-year-old brother, the Honorable Arthur DeLacey, who could not be relied upon to refrain from jumping into the pond. Young Arthur clutched a painted tin soldier in his other hand.

Bright sunshine glinted on the ripples the toy ship made as it glided through the water. It warmed the golden daffodils clustered around the edge of the pond and burnished the children's ginger curls. After the frosty twilight of winter, Jocelyn felt her heart quickening with the promise of spring.

"I expect the real bride ship will soon be arriving in Halifax." She affected a cheerful tone.

Lord Thetford thrust out his lower lip in his best five-year-old pout. "I wish you could have taken me with you when you went to London to see the bride ship sail."

"Me, too!" cried little Arthur.

Since returning to Breckland, Jocelyn had discovered those were his favorite words.

"Next year, perhaps," she said, to placate them. "This year I needed you both to keep Grandpapa company while I was gone."

She had enjoyed her brief visit to the city to help Mrs. Beamish prepare for the expedition. Warning the new chaperones about what they could expect when they reached Halifax. Entrusting them with gifts and messages for many of her friends. Letting the girls' contagious excitement and anticipation buoy her spirits.

But she had not been prepared for the wrench she felt when the ship weighed anchor and headed down the Thames without her. She'd been sorely tempted to stow away and return to the colonial town where she had left her heart.

For the sake of her nephews, she'd resisted that temptation. They had been abandoned too often in their short lives. These past months she had discovered that duty could be more than the onerous bondage she once believed. It could also be a tangible expression of love.

Lord Thetford picked up a stick he had found at the edge of Ladywood and marched around the pond to where his aunt and brother stood.

"Careful now," Jocelyn warned when he leaned over and used the stick to draw his boat toward shore. "I don't fancy fishing you out if you tumble into that cold water."

The boy ignored her words with the invincible confidence of youth, but managed to moor his boat without calamity.

"There." He checked over his shoulder. "The bride ship is docked. Come, Arthur, bring the governor down to meet it."

Arthur proudly held up his tin soldier. "That's him!"

Every night at bedtime the boys always clamored for stories of Jocelyn's adventures in Nova Scotia. Her account of the bride ship's arrival in Halifax was one of their favorites, though she had altered her version of events to be fit for young ears.

"Is it, indeed?" She laughed. "It certainly has Governor Kerr's fine military bearing, though he has far more medals."

"Medals?" Lord Thetford's small eyes widened. "What for?"

"Did I not tell you? Before he became governor, Sir Robert Kerr was a general in the Duke of Wellington's army." Somehow, talking about her lost love to the boys brought him nearer for a moment.

"I should like to meet him," her elder nephew announced.

"Me, too!" declared his younger brother.

"Someday, perhaps," Jocelyn promised them, though she knew it was not likely.

Would there be a letter from Nova Scotia today? Jocelyn hoped so. After not receiving any for over a week, she had reread Sally Carmont's last breezy missive until it was practically in tatters. One passage in particular...

He works as hard as ever, Sally had written of the governor, but in every other respect he is altered almost beyond recognition. He is so much warmer and more approachable. The interest he takes in the welfare of all your "brides" is touching—quite paternal, I declare.

In many ways Jocelyn was more content with her life than she had ever been. But those eagerly anticipated letters from Nova Scotia still made her long for Robert.

Warily she let go of young Arthur's hand. "Very well, you may take His Excellency down to meet the bride ship, but do be careful not to fall into Halifax Harbor."

The little fellow seemed to understand that he was being granted a rare opportunity to prove himself. He approached his brother with cautious steps, holding the toy governor of Nova Scotia tight in his fist.

"Well done, Arthur." Lord Thetford held out one hand to take the tin soldier. With the other, he grasped a length of thick string attached to the prow of his little boat. "Here. You may hold this while the governor greets Aunt Jocelyn and her young ladies."

The honor of mooring the ship persuaded Arthur to hand over the governor.

Thetford marched the little tin figure down a gentle slope to the lip of the pond. Then he cleared his throat in a most amusing imitation of his grandfather. "The governor's come to see this ship that has attracted so much attention. He says—"

A familiar voice took over from the boy. "Welcome to Nova Scotia, Mrs. Finch. It is an honor to have you and your young ladies grace our shores."

Dear heaven, was she dreaming? Slowly Jocelyn looked up, half-afraid her ears might be playing tricks on her. But if they were, her eyes had joined them in the ruse. There stood Sir Robert Kerr, his bearing relaxed a little from former days, but otherwise exactly as she remembered him.

She raised her hand to her lips to stifle a sob.

"No, no!" Thetford scrambled up from his crouch. "That isn't what he said at all."

"Perhaps not," replied Sir Robert in a tone as soft, warm and playful as the spring breeze. "But it is what he ought to have said. What he often wishes he'd said."

"How do you know?" demanded the boy.

"How?" echoed his brother.

"I hear you are clever lads." With unhurried steps, Sir Robert circled the pond toward them. "If you are half as clever as your Aunt Jocelyn, I think you can guess the answer to that."

Little Arthur's eyes and mouth rounded into perfect circles. He raised a plump forefinger and pointed toward the stranger. "It's him!"

"The governor, you mean?" Thetford sounded doubtful as he glanced toward his aunt. "Is he, Auntie Jocelyn?"

"It looks very like him." She spoke in a voice thick with swallowed tears, while others trickled down her cheeks unhindered. "But I cannot think what he is doing here. How will Nova Scotia manage without him?"

"Just the way it did when he was touring the colony last summer." He came to a stop a few paces away from her. "Though he likes to imagine himself indispensable, no doubt the colony runs itself quite smoothly in his absence. More so, perhaps. What cannot be accomplished by the assembly and council, with the able assistance of Mr. Duckworth and Colonel Carmont probably should not be attempted."

Out of the corner of her eye, Jocelyn spied the two little boys moving away from the edge of the pond for a closer look at their visitor.

"Were you summoned back to London?" A fearful worry gripped her. "To defend yourself against those vulgar lies? I thought that was all settled in your favor. Father promised—"

She caught herself before she said any more, but it did not matter, for Sir Robert finished her sentence. "—that he would exert his influence on my behalf in exchange for—"

Jocelyn begged his silence with a finger raised to her lips and a pointed glance at the children. She did not want her small darlings to suspect that anything but her affection for them had brought her back to Breckland.

Sir Robert appeared to understand. "—in exchange for your assistance in certain domestic matters?"

"Who told you?"

He shook his head. "That matters less than why you did not tell me."

"I was afraid you might do something foolish from motives of guilt or obligation rather than—"

The voice of the children's nurse interrupted her. "Begging your pardon, ma'am, but his lordship sent me to fetch the boys."

"I want to stay here." Thetford stamped his small foot.

"Me, too." Arthur followed his brother's example.

"We want to talk to the governor," said Thetford, perhaps thinking his demand would carry more weight if he included his brother. "I'm sure he has even better stories to tell about Nova Scotia than you, Auntie Jocelyn."

"And battles!" added Arthur with rather bloodthirsty relish for an innocent child.

Sir Robert dropped to his haunches before the boys, who had taken a position between him and their aunt. "A good officer must do his duty and follow the orders of his superiors, you know."

"Of course." Thetford gave a vigorous nod, which his brother repeated. They did not appear to guess where the governor's words might be leading.

"As head of the family, your grandfather is your superior. If he has sent for you, that is an order you must obey." Then, as if to demonstrate he understood there was more to raising children than orders and duty, he added, "If you look sharp and step lively, I promise I shall tell you all the stories you wish when I return to the house."

"How soon will that be?" asked Thetford.

Sir Robert rose to his feet. His gaze sought Jocelyn's. "That depends upon your aunt and whether she gives me the answers I require to several questions."

The nurse swooped down just then to catch both boys by their small hands. "Come along, young masters, and let the gentleman be."

As Thetford allowed himself to be led away, he turned back and called, "Tell the governor what he wants to know straight away, Auntie!"

Though she was not certain she could bear to do what the child asked, Jocelyn nodded.

"And don't forget to bring the bride ship when you come!" Lord Thetford received no reply.

Once the children and their nurse were out of earshot, Sir Robert inhaled a deep breath. "Now where were we?"

Jocelyn swallowed an enormous lump in her throat. Seeing him again so unexpectedly had shattered the fragile illusion of happiness she had worked so hard to construct.

"I was trying explain why I did not tell you my full reason for returning to England." Then, in a flash of the defiant spirit she had shown a year ago on Power's Wharf, she added, "I am not convinced I owe you an explanation."

"Perhaps you do not." One corner of Sir Robert's mouth arched upward. His eyes, blue as the vast Norfolk sky overhead, glowed with the hopeful warmth of spring sunshine. "But I am asking just the samc. You started to say you feared I might do something foolish from motives of guilt or obligation rather than something else. Might that something else be…love?"

"It might."

"The kind of love that cares nothing for propriety or duty or anything but the object of its attachment? The kind of love that will sacrifice one's next dearest aim or purpose for the welfare of one's beloved?"

Jocelyn struggled to keep her voice from breaking. "Are you saying that is what you feel for me, Robert?"

"I am saying that is what has brought me here." He closed the distance between them and took her in his arms. "I hope and believe if you search your heart you will find it is what you feel for me, as well."

"I cannot deny it." She tilted her head to hold his gaze and to accept his kiss.

When it came, it tasted just as sweet in the middle of a Norfolk heath in broad daylight as it had in the late summer darkness by the Prince's music pavilion.

At last Robert drew back just far enough to exchange a fond but wary look. "Twice I have asked for your hand and twice you have refused me. Now I must ask again and hope the third time will prove a charm. In many ways my life has never been more satisfactory than in these past months. Yet never have I been so conscious of an emptiness only you can fill. Whatever it takes for me to secure you, I will do it."

Would he truly refuse a call to arms if she bade him?

"But your duty…"

"I have a duty to you." He raised his hand and gently tapped his forefinger against the tip of her nose. "A duty to us and to our happiness—that is quite as important as any other."

But without his devotion to a higher duty, he would no longer be the man she had come to admire…desire…and adore.

Mistaking her hesitation for reluctance, he added, "If you will give your promise, I will wait as long as it takes for you to fulfil your family obligations."

"You would respect my duty but surrender your own?" She shook her head. "That I would not ask of you, Robert, nor anything else. I will be your wife the moment I am free. And I want nothing in exchange except to have you as my husband."

"Hurrah!" He seized her around the waist and plucked her off her feet as if she weighed nothing. "Hurrah! Hurrah!"

His joyous shouts filled the air, startling a small flock of birds from the treetops of Ladywood to flight.

Then he began to spin around and around with her in his arms, laughing like a man gone mad with delight. Not quite able to grasp how her life had turned on its ear in less than half an hour, Jocelyn laughed and shrieked with glee until she could scarcely breathe.

At last they collapsed onto the soft green turf in a jubilant, passionate tangle. Much to the consternation of Lord Thetford and his brother, they did not return to the house until they had exchanged one kiss for every day they'd been parted.

Epilogue

Halifax, Nova Scotia,
July 1828

"Nova Scotia." Lord Thetford seemed to savor the words as he stared out over the deck rail at the bustling garrison port of Halifax. A handsome Eton graduate, he was bound for Cambridge in the fall. "I've wanted to see this place for myself ever since I was a little fellow and Aunt Jocelyn used to tell us stories about the bride ship."

His brother, a junior cadet at the Royal Military Academy, stared up at the stout citadel standing guard over the town below. "Me, too."

Sir Robert Kerr, Member of Parliament for West Norfolk and recently appointed Minister for Colonial Affairs caught the eye of his beautiful wife and winked. Some things never changed.

In fact, Sir Robert could not have been more proud of how Jocelyn's nephews had flourished in their care. After ten years, he looked on them quite as his own sons. For a time it had appeared the boys would be all the family they would ever have. And then…

Clinging to her cousin Thetford's hand, four-year-old Edwina Kerr popped a well-sucked thumb out of her mouth and asked, "What is the *bwide ship?*"

Thetford tweaked the brim of her bonnet. "Did your mama never tell you how she came to meet your papa?"

When the little girl replied with a solemn shake of her head, Thetford cast his aunt a mischievous grin. "Shame on you, Auntie. You've neglected your duty as a teller of bedtime stories quite shamelessly."

"Oh, Ford, don't tease her." Lady Jocelyn Kerr repeated the oft-spoken plea of mothers down through the ages. "You know she is too young for those sorts of stories."

"But I haven't heard it, either," Julia Kerr piped up. "And everyone says I shall soon be a young lady." Though twice her sister's age, Julia was not much bigger. Already she bid fair to be as lovely as her mother when she grew up.

She lofted an appealing gaze at her father, which he had never been known to resist. "Will *you* tell us the story, Papa?"

Sir Robert gave his daughter's delicate hand a gentle squeeze. "I believe there may be time enough before we dock. It happened this way, you see. Ten years ago, your mama arrived in Halifax as chaperone to a ship full of young ladies who had come to marry settlers in the colony. But the letter announcing their arrival had gotten lost somehow and no one knew they were coming, until one day their ship appeared in the harbor."

Little Edwina removed her thumb from her mouth again. "Is that twue, Mama?"

Jocelyn nodded. "Indeed it is, pet."

"Naturally," continued Sir Robert, "a huge crowd gathered to see this ship that had brought so many lovely young ladies to the colony. But the governor of the colony was a gruff, cross old ogre of a fellow who thought everyone should work hard and be serious all the time and never have any amusement. He thought this bride ship, especially the beautiful chaperone, would cast a spell over everyone in the colony and make them giddy and foolish instead of minding their duties as they ought. So he marched down to the wharf and ordered the bride ship to sail away and never come back."

Edwina's blue eyes grew very round as she listened with grave attention. But her sister's elfin features took on a stormy cast and it was not long before she burst out, "What a hateful creature! I hope you fought that nasty governor and made him let Mama and the bride ship stay."

"Not…exactly." Sir Robert struggled to keep from laughing. "You see—"

His wife must have taken pity on him for she continued the tale, "You see, dearest, though the governor was rather gruff, he was *not* an ogre. In fact, he was quite handsome and he only expected people to work hard because he worked so very hard, himself, trying to make their lives better."

Julia's fine dark brows knit in a thoughtful frown as she tried to grasp the idea of someone who appeared to be the villain of the story but who still had the makings of a hero.

"I did not have anyone to fight on my behalf," continued Jocelyn. "So I challenged the governor to a duel. He showed his gallantry by insisting we settle our differences in a chess match, which he allowed me to win."

"I most certainly did not," Sir Robert protested.

"Papa!" Julia's rosebud mouth fell open. "You were the ogre?"

He gave a rueful nod. "Until the enchantment of a beautiful princess, or rather a beautiful chaperone, broke the evil spell that kept me from enjoying life."

His daughter looked quite perplexed, trying to work out how her doting papa could ever have been the way he described.

But Edwina regarded her father gravely for a moment, then shook her head. "Poor you."

Dear little soul—she could grow up to be far too much like him if he and Jocelyn were not careful.

"You needn't feel too sorry for me, missy." He seized the sturdy little figure up off the deck. Then he proceeded to bounce her in his arms and nuzzle her plump cheek until she shrieked with glee. "Like all good stories, it came out well in the end."

Very well indeed, as it happened. The marquess had refused to hear of Sir Robert and his daughter waiting to be wed. He arranged a plum appointment for his new son-in-law in the Colonial Office where Sir Robert could put his firsthand experience with colonial administration to work.

The marquess also put his London town house and Breckland Manor at the newlyweds' disposal. Several years later, when Sir Robert had been approached to stand for Parliament, the marquess has been unstinting in his support. Proud as the old man was of his grandsons, he doted even more on little Julia and Edwina, who seemed to work the same enchantment over him as their mama had over their papa.

"Gracious!" cried Julia as their ship docked at the quay. She pointed toward the crowded wharf. "Have all those people come to welcome us?"

So it seemed. As soon as the current governor had concluded a warm speech of greeting, Sir Robert and Lady Jocelyn were surrounded by old friends bowing, shaking hands and embracing. Many couples from that first bride ship were on hand with their families.

"Duckworth!" Sir Robert cried upon seeing his former aide. "Aren't you a prosperous-looking fellow! Being a magistrate must agree with you. Or perhaps it is fathering such a handsome family."

"Is that *your* secret, sir? I do believe you look younger than when we parted ten years ago."

"Liar!" Sir Robert laughed. "It is rather a trade-off, as a matter of fact. My duties in the Commons have given me a few gray hairs, but my home life keeps me feeling young."

The crowd on the wharf gradually migrated up Salter Street toward Government House. Sir Robert was surprised to find the former front entrance had been turned into an elegant fenced lawn. There another surprise awaited Jocelyn and he.

"Will Carmont, you rascal!" He ignored his friend's outstretched hand in favor of a hearty embrace. "Have you left Upper Canada undefended to go gadding off for a seaside holiday?"

"I had to drag him away from his duties," declared Sally. "But you must recall how determined I can be when I set my mind on something."

"Immediate surrender was the only option." Will pretended to cower in fear.

They whiled away the rest of that afternoon at a garden party hosted by the governor and his lady. Later the Kerrs and the Carmonts sailed out to Birch Cove where the governor had loaned them the use of Prince's Lodge for their visit. There they found Miz Ada most happily installed, anxious to prepare all Sir Robert's favorite dishes and spoil his little daughters quite shamelessly.

The summer passed in an almost unbroken round of pleasure for all concerned. There were several splendid band concerts at the Grand Parade. Lord Thetford most enjoyed a rustic party on Powers Island cooking lobster, clams and mussels in big black pots over open fires on the beach. His brother spent many happy hours haunting the Citadel and the round tower at Point Pleasant, between hunting and fishing expeditions.

Jocelyn enjoyed frequent visits with her former charges

from the bride ship, hearing how they had fared in their new homeland and admiring their growing families. Sir Robert mixed duty with pleasure, hosting meetings with the governors of all the North Atlantic colonies and hearing briefs from the councils of Nova Scotia and Cape Breton about the prospect of combining them into a single colony again. By far his most pleasant duty was a visit to Seal Island to unveil a plaque in his honor at the lighthouse there.

"Mama," Edwina asked at dinner one evening, "is evewything a party in Nova Scotia?"

So it must have seemed to her, for Jocelyn, Sally and Mrs. Duckworth were planning a grand picnic to cap off their visit, reuniting all the bride-ship families. The changeable Nova Scotia weather gave them a little anxiety, but the day of the picnic dawned sunny and warm.

That afternoon there were games and races and treats for the children, as well as boating jaunts around Birch Cove and the pond behind the lodge. Endless stories were told from that first summer, including several exaggerated versions of the Seige of Prince's Lodge. Everyone ate rather more than was good for them, but no one seemed to mind. A few future matches between various small ladies and gentlemen were proposed, only half in jest.

That evening there was dancing in the music pavilion, including a number of the country dances popular ten years before. Those gradually gave way to the waltz that had once been considered "wicked" but was now all the fashion.

"I declare," said Jocelyn as she twirled around the dance floor in her husband's arms, "it has been a marvelous day, but seeing all my girls again with their families makes me feel like an old matriarch."

Robert laughed away such nonsense. "You forget, my dear, how little older you were than most of your charges. Besides, if you are feeling your years, I believe I can suggest a perfect restorative."

"Can you? And what might that be?"

He leaned forward to whisper in her ear. "Perhaps after our guests depart and the children are all in bed, you and I can steal back down here…"

Jocelyn glanced toward an innocent-looking chaise lounge, then back at her husband. Her eyes glowed with dusky desire. "Are you suggesting a starlight tryst, dearest?"

"After all," he said, feigning his old earnest diligence, "I would not want to be remiss in performing my husbandly duty."

"Do your duty?" Jocelyn teased. "Or take your pleasure?"

She reached up to caress his cheek with the backs of her fingers, sending a fevered shiver of anticipation through him.

"My darling." He lavished her with an adoring gaze. "Surely you must know by now, you make every duty a pleasure. And every pleasure a joy."

* * * * *

Author Note

The places depicted in this book are quite real. Government House still stands, all the finer for having acquired the mellow grace of age. Sadly, Prince's Lodge is long gone, but the heart-shaped pond and the trails that were once part of its grounds remain, as well as the little music pavilion overlooking Bedford Basin.

By contrast, the characters in *The Bride Ship* are products of my imagination, though Sir Robert Kerr did draw inspiration from a number of fine gentlemen who served as lieutenant governors of Nova Scotia during the early part of the nineteenth century. For the purposes of this story, I have shortened that title to "governor."

I have also taken liberties with the chronology of a number of events and issues in Nova Scotia's colonial history for dramatic effect. The lighthouse on Seal Island, for instance, was not built until some years later. But the story of the real-life heroes and heroines who first settled the island is true.

A bride ship was dispatched from England to the west coast colony of British Columbia in 1862 by England's great

philanthropist, Angela Burdett-Coutts. I hope readers will enjoy my attempt to imagine what might have happened if one had come to Nova Scotia half a century earlier.
—Deborah Hale